WRATH OF THE NEVER QUEEN

Storm Lomax

Copyright © 2024 Storm Lomax

All rights reserved

The characters and events portrayed in this book are fictitious. Any similarity to real persons, living or dead, is coincidental and not intended by the author.

No part of this book may be reproduced, or stored in a retrieval system, or transmitted in any form or by any means, electronic, mechanical, photocopying, recording, or otherwise, without express written permission of the publisher.

ISBN-13: 9798341022355
ISBN-10: 9798341022355

Cover design by: Art Painter
Library of Congress Control Number: 2018675309
Printed in the United States of America

CONTENTS

Title Page
Copyright
Playlist
Dedication
Prologue   1
Chapter 1   9
Chapter 2   18
Chapter 3   27
Chapter 4   34
Chapter 5   43
Chapter 6   56
Chapter 7   65
Chapter 8   71
Chapter 9   85
Chapter 10   94
Chapter 11   104
Chapter 12   113
Chapter 13   124

Chapter 14	131
Chapter 15	141
Chapter 16	149
Chapter 17	160
Chapter 18	167
Chapter 19	174
Chapter 20	181
Chapter 21	199
Chapter 22	209
Chapter 23	221
Chapter 24	230
Chapter 25	243
Chapter 26	254
Chapter 27	263
Chapter 28	277
Chapter 29	285
Chapter 30	292
Chapter 31	300
Chapter 32	308
Chapter 33	316
Chapter 34	323
Chapter 35	338
Chapter 36	348
Chapter 37	355

Epilogue	365
Appendix	371
Acknowledgements	379
About The Author	381

PLAYLIST

Prologue

you should see me in a crown - Billie Eilish

Chapter 1

You Don't Own Me - Lesley Gore

Chapter 5

Castle - Halsey

Chapter 6

Far From Home (The Raven) - Sam Tinnesz

Chapter 7

Monsters - Ruelle

Chapter 12

VILLAIN - K/DA, Madison Beer, Kim Petras, League of Legends

Chapter 13

Man or a Monster - Sam Tinnesz, Zayde Wolf

Chapter 14

Rescue My Heart - Liz Longley

Chapter 16

Please, Please, Please, Let Me Get What I Want - The Smiths

Chapter 18

War of Hearts - Ruelle

Chapter 19

Running Up That Hill - Kate Bush

Chapter 20

I Want You To Love Me - Fiona Apple

Chapter 22

At Last - Etta James

Chapter 24

Falling In Love - Cigarettes After Sex

Chapter 30

Make Me Feel - Elvis Drew

Chapter 31

Hold On - Brooke Annibale

Chapter 32

Look What You Made Me Do - Taylor Swift

Chapter 36

Legends Are Made - Sam Tinnesz

Chapter 37

RAGE - Samantha Margret

To every woman who's been told they're too emotional, too hysterical, too angry.

Get angrier.

PROLOGUE

The quiet, polite town of Mossgarde holds its first execution in 150 years.

Mossgarde sits several hundred leagues south of werewolf territory and even further east of dragon country in the depths of a treacherous swamp. It is a series of connected platforms raised above the stagnant water, with homes built against the sides of the large trees. Very little sunlight penetrates the thick canopy, and so lanterns are strung between buildings, glowing purple with witch magic. There is a stillness in the air, deceptively so, as Mossgardians know. Underneath the soupy water and amongst the giant trees, there is a constant hum of life. Those who live here thrive. The First Home of Dragons turned the New Home of Witches.

Until today.

The spectacle of an execution has drawn a large crowd, not only of Mossgarde residents but of people from across the realm. Werewolves from Swordstead arrive clad in fur-lined cloaks, more suited to their own icy climate than the humidity of the swamp. An emissary sent from Coalsburgh stands with the werewolves. She is used to the dry heat of dragon country but her palms are clammy, nonetheless. She eyes the executioner's block with a furrowed brow.

The werewolves and the dragon stand amongst the citizens of Mossgarde, taut as a bow string. Because this is not a simple execution —it is a demonstration. A message. The people who crowd into the town square, barely large enough to hold them all, do not come for morbid entertainment. They have come to mourn.

Garbed in black, the people of Mossgarde gather to watch their queen as she is brought to the executioner's block with a cloth bag over her head.

She stumbles on the bridge connecting the town square to its neighbouring platform, but she is held steady by the towering guard behind her. His hands grip her wrists, bound behind her, as he steers her forward. Instead of her signature crimson gown, studded with jewels and draped with rich velvets, she wears a simple white dress. A dress for commoners. The crowd murmurs, a grim set to their faces.

The king arrives behind her, a garrison around him. He sits atop a croca—a lizard-like creature large enough for an adult to ride, able to traverse through the swamp water. The king remains several feet away from the chopping block, choosing instead to rest his croca on an elevated platform above his citizens.

"Good people!" His voice rings out across the throng of people, clear and firm. "You have gathered here on this historic day to—"

"What have you done with our queen?" someone calls from the crowd, sharp with accusation. A grumble of agreement ripples through the rest of the citizens.

The king clenches his teeth but is careful not to let his irritation show. It is a vital time, he knows, and he must play his cards carefully. His eyes flicker to the queen, his wife, as she wavers on the spot. Running his tongue along his lower lip, he calculates how long the drugs in her blood will last. How much time he has to sway the crowd to his favour. He makes his play.

"I understand it is difficult to see her like this," he says, not able to bring himself to say her name or title. "For me, it is even more difficult. To see the one I loved and trusted reduced to this. But she has committed the most heinous of crimes."

The king watches as mouths frown and foreheads wrinkle. He waits a few more moments, allowing tensions to rise, before he speaks.

"She has cursed our child."

A sharp gasp runs through the folk

of Mossgarde. Appalled whispers and shaking heads are exchanged. The werewolves and the dragon glance at each other and shift uncomfortably—the queen had arranged almost all their trade relations. The swamp may be humid and difficult to traverse, but it produced food year-round, unlike their own climates.

The king carefully arranges his face to match his peoples', casting his eyes down in sadness.

"Liar!"

The king's head snaps up. His lips curl slightly, but he catches it in time, smoothing his features out into something like offence. The Mossgardian who called out pushes her way through the crowd, pointing an accusatory finger.

"There is no curse! The queen is not capable of such an act of evil." She turns to the rest of the people. "We *know* her. She is one of us. She would not curse her own child!"

The king lets her speak, waiting patiently for her to finish. When a sea of angry and disbelieving faces look at him, he makes his next play. He raises his fingers and snaps. On cue, his guards pick up a cage and carry it through the crowd. Almost at once, the discontent falls away as the people stare, open-mouthed.

A monster sits in the cage. It presses its long, twisted snout against the metal bars, snarling and screaming in a high-pitched yowl.

Bulbous growths run along its scaly skin, and its limbs are bent awkwardly as though they have been broken and healed wrong. The monster throws its head back and screams.

The people nearest to it slap their hands over their ears, wincing at the blood-curdling noise. The woman who had called out before is now silent, horror etched across her face.

"Disgusting!" someone shouts. The rest of the crowd follows, jeering at the monster. The king watches, letting them work themselves into a frenzy before playing his final card.

"It is my son!" he bellows. A hush falls over the town square, punctuated by the wails of the monster. "This is what she has done to him. Instead of a newborn baby boy, she has given me this…this *beast*."

Horrified, the people of Mossgarde look at their prince with wide eyes. The king points to his wife.

"What mother curses their own child like this?" he asks, allowing just the right amount of sorrow to enter his voice.

The atmosphere turns. Where there had been mourning and confusion is now outrage. Angry cries to remove the queen's head echo through the swamp, spreading like fire. A few remain silent. The king notes their faces for later but otherwise enjoys his victory. The people of Mossgarde are on his side. He has done it.

And then something catches his eye.

The queen straightens, pulling her shoulders back into something resembling her usual posture. Even with her hands bound behind her, he sees her fingers flex as the strength returns to them. He is out of time.

"You heard the good people of Mossgarde," the king calls to the executioner. He ignores the screams of his son.

The executioner nods, shoving the queen roughly to her knees and positioning her covered head over the block. The taunts of the crowd reach new heights, laden with vitriol. The prince matches them, screaming and battering his deformed claws against the bars of his cage. The queen raises her head slightly, hearing him, and balls her hands into fists. The smell of blood is in the air.

The king raises his hand as the executioner raises his axe.

When the head of the queen rolls, Mossgarde cheers.

The werewolves and the dragon, unsettled, leave quickly. The king allows them, for now. He will not soon forget their silence. Turning away from the body of his wife, limp and bloody and empty of life, he raises his hand for quiet.

"There is still the matter of my son," he says. The prince, almost in response, lets out a piercing shriek, causing the people nearby to wince. "She has cursed him most cruelly but

I believe there to be a cure. The late queen confessed to me—perhaps due to a fleeting sense of guilt—the curse she inflicted can indeed be broken."

Optimistic murmurs ripple through the crowd, even as they grimace at the sight of the prince. The king presses his fingertips together, letting this information settle before continuing.

"True love," he says, smiling and spreading his hands in front of him. "True love can break the curse. And so, we must band together in this most trying time to free my son from his affliction."

At his words, the citizens throw curious glances at one another.

"I hereby announce a royal law," the king continues. "Once my son comes of age, each year thereafter, one young woman must volunteer to break the curse. This brave young woman will be fed and housed in my castle, and if she gifts true love to my son, she will even be named Queen." He pauses, sweeping his hands out in an open gesture he believes signifies his generosity. "For the very act of volunteering, her family will be paid most handsomely."

Parents hold their daughters close, even as the temptation of payment and the allure of royal status looms.

"Let us show we cannot be divided by the actions of one vindictive woman. Begin preparing your daughters now—in eighteen years' time, they will all be heroes."

The king gives a cheery wave before turning his croca away, his guards following closely behind. Even as he leaves, it is not unnoticed that the chopping block remains.

CHAPTER 1

25 Years Later

Shivani

Book clutched to my chest, I flee my house and run for sanctuary.

My feet pound the wooden bridge draped across the swamp, slapping the surface of the water. I ignore the damp splashes and press on, weaving across the network of raised buildings and bridges. I pass several startled villagers and ignore them as well. My arms are laden with the too-heavy book, and my legs tangle in the long fabric of my skirt. Reluctantly, I slow. Somewhere, I know he is either running behind me or still at the house, waiting for me to return.

My chest burns and my eyes water with angry tears, but I force them back. I do not want to give him the satisfaction.

It is early in the day, the first thin sheaths of morning light filtering through the cracks of the tree canopy. In the distance, through the purple haze of the lanterns, people filter quietly into the village square. Even from afar, I notice the glint of armour. Mornings are slow in Mossgarde and mostly consist of the king's pernicious guards collecting taxes, often in the form of food or drink. My father has not paid his due in some time and I have very little to spare after feeding us both. I swerve away from the village square and its guards.

Instead, I half-jog across the narrow, lesser-used bridges, moving towards the outskirts. The buildings here are derelict and the platforms groan underfoot. Faded posters cling to the walls by a single nail, benches with worn grooves from being used, homes sitting with no occupants. Ghosts of old Mossgarde. It is a struggle for me to imagine our small village as a bustling town with all this space being used.

Once I am far enough away from the village square, and with a quick glance over my shoulder to ensure no one has followed, I slow to a walking pace. I suck in deep breaths of air, pleasantly crisp against the usual stuffiness of Mossgarde. When I reach my destination—a secluded spot behind the back of an old shop— my body finally relaxes. There is a small breeze on the outskirts, enough to blow some of the humidity away. I swat at some lingering insects before finding a mostly intact bench to rest my book on. I take another deep inhale, slowing my heart.

A stubborn streak of sunlight forces its way through the swamp and I step into it, tipping my face up. Travelling merchants say Mossgarde is a dark, gloomy place, but I know nothing else. For now. One day soon, I too will feel the warmth of the sun drench my skin instead of the constant glow of witch magic lanterns.

For today, however, this quiet spot in Old Mossgarde remains one of two places I can reliably go when I need to leave my father behind, his voice rising and his breath stinking of ale.

My collection of lost items is tucked into the corner of the platform, hidden under a pile of damp leaves. I make my way over and pull one of them free—an old bucket, half red with rust. Grasping it by its rough rim, the handle long since gone, I place it carefully on the other side of the platform near my book. I take a few long strides away from it and suck in a deep breath.

My ophid, the long muscle running along my spine, is taut. All witches are born with an ophid. It holds our magic. Our au'mana. My ophid twitches, impatient and aching to be used.

I focus my magic, drawing it out until a purple glow emanates from my skin. I raise my hand, letting it swirl across my palm like smoke. Au'mana should smell like salt, although I have become so accustomed to it, I rarely notice anymore.

Unlike dragon magic and siren spells, au'mana draws on emotion. The stronger the feeling, the more powerful the magic. My aunt has told me of other witches who train for decades, carefully pulling on threads of emotion to fuel their au'mana so no one emotion dominates the others.

For me, however, I am often ruled by wrath.

I draw on the deep well of anger towards my father and my au-mana responds. I flex my hand, aiming it at the rusted bucket. In an instant, the bucket glows lavender and I feel it in my grip as though I am holding it in my palm. I close my eyes and use my au'mana to rip the rust away. Magic washes over me, warm like sunlight, as it cleanses the barrel. I smile, rolling my shoulders to stretch my ophid.

I cross the space between myself and the bucket, allowing myself a brief moment of satisfaction at the clean metal. But witch magic is not permanent. With one swift movement, I lean back and kick the bucket.

The enchantment breaks. The bucket rattles across the platform, landing with a clang against the front of the shop. The purple glow evaporates like steam from a teapot. Rust crawls over the surface of the metal once more, red tendrils burying into the silver until it reverts to its earlier state. I regard the scene as my ophid relaxes. My aunt's words ring clearly in my ears.

A muscle must be used to be strong.

Dragons and sirens learn their magic over several years, sometimes decades, while witches are born with an innate ability to tap into their au'mana. From the moment of my birth, I had a well of magic at my fingertips. But an ophid is like any other muscle—it can be stretched and strengthened. Or torn and injured.

When I was very young, I had tried to take on too much at once. My father, sick of all my books taking up space in our small home, had tried to rip one of them. At once, the house was enchanted and alive. Floorboards shook and the walls rattled and I threatened to collapse it on us both.

I was only stopped by a painful twinge in my back, bringing me to my knees. The pain nearly drove my anger into a blind rage, but I could not even stand. I had asked too much of my ophid and it had torn, putting me on bed rest for several months after. My aunt tutted and fussed over me, rubbing cooling creams along my spine and distracting me with stories.

"Just like your mother," she told me. "You inherited her temperament."

My father did and said nothing, but he has not touched my books since.

I tuck the rusted bucket back under the

pile of leaves, hidden from view despite me being the only visitor Old Mossgarde has. I collect my book, gathering it to my chest and holding it tight. I breathe deep one last time and savour the cool air. Tomorrow, I will return and strengthen my ophid again. Until then…

Despite the release of my magic, anger still simmers in my chest. I have been forced from my home, yet again, and cannot return yet. It will be several hours before my father drinks himself unconscious and I can slip back inside, hoping he awakes in a better mood.

"Bastard," I mutter.

I turn away from my pile of lost items and scurry towards my other sanctuary.

Mossgarde is a cluster of homes and buildings, the raised platforms allowing us to avoid the big below. I peer down at the water as I cross the bridges. A thick layer of algae and moss coats the surface, completely still. I shudder at the depths beneath and keep walking.

Near the village square, on a set of sturdy stilts, it's the library. It is stout and proud and the sight of it calms my heart. Unfortunately, I must pass the public house to reach it.

Many of the unsavoury types, my father included, linger outside the public house when the barkeep has tossed them out. There is nowhere else for them to go, after all. As a young girl, I would bow my head and try not to draw attention. I soon learned that meant nothing to them. Now, I jut out my chin and push my shoulders back and snarl and snap at whoever believes himself entitled to look upon me. My mother's daughter, indeed.

Most of them have come across me before and so turn their eyes away. But there is one who is either too inebriated or too bold to care. I feel his eyes on me.

"Where are you off to in such a hurry?" he calls. His words slur together like muck.

I meet his eyes but do not slow my pace.

"Why don't you come and join us for a bit of fun, eh?" His grin is lecherous. I do not break pace, but I change direction towards him. "That's right, we'll—"

He is cut off when I slam my book across his face. He crumples to the floor, dazed. The other men look at me.

"Good morrow, Miss Shivani." One of them inclines his head and nearly stumbles forward, catching himself just in time. The stench of ale is apparent. "What enchantment was that?"

"None," I reply, regarding the man I knocked down. He blinks rapidly, blindly grabbing at the wall of the public house to haul himself up. "Just a heavy book."

"Off to the library, then?"

"I am." I inspect my book, making sure I didn't get blood on it, and silently apologise to it for using it as a weapon. "The examiner from Frostalm is visiting in a few months."

"University?" one of the other men pipes up, his voice gruff.

"House of Learning," I correct him. "Universities are in Coalsburgh."

He rolls his eyes.

"Don't know why you bother."

"Why do you bother spending your time and money on drink when you have a wife at home to look after?" I bite out. He has the grace to look ashamed, casting his eyes downward.

"Let the girl do what she wants," the first man replies. "It's a far cry better than staying here with a king bent on slaughter."

He spits out these last words before turning away. With a sinking feeling, I realise I recognise him. His daughter was the latest in a long line of Never Queens. Women sent to break an unbreakable curse. Six months to break the curse, to gift true love to the monstrous prince, before their head is forfeit. Six months of mourning before the next is chosen. A barbaric cycle, leaving only bodies in its wake. Another reason to leave Mossgarde behind.

"My condolences," I murmur, unsure what else to say. He only grunts in response. He has already spoken out of turn, and others have been put to the chopping block for less. But perhaps he does not care anymore. Only one more week until the next Never Queen volunteers, and his daughter is forgotten.

"You should get going," the other man tells

me. He looks pointedly at the man I hit as he begins to find his bearings once more. I agree and leave quickly, a weight on my chest that had not been there before. At five-and-twenty, I am one of a rapidly dwindling pool of women in Mossgarde of marriageable age. I had never, and would never, volunteer. I can only look on as others line up and hope one of them breaks the curse, freeing the Beast of Mossgarde. At least until I am accepted into Frostalm's House of Learning and I can escape this place.

The first and only time I witnessed a maiden being put to the chopping block, Aunt Meena had gripped my hand tight. Her eyes were like steel. She whispered to me just loud enough so only I could hear.

"I wonder if the prince is cursed or the entire village."

CHAPTER 2

The library, although small, makes the most of its space. Books pile high on every surface, including most of the floor. The air is laden with the pleasant musk of paper and ink. People rarely visit anymore, and when I arrive, only my aunt sits in the corner.

She rests on a small stool, her back against the wall and her legs propped up on a low shelf. One of her legs, made of smooth, polished wood and decorated with intricate purple patterns, pokes out from beneath her skirt. She jumps when I enter but relaxes when she sees me, sagging back against the wall.

"Oh. It is only you, Shivani," she breaths, hand on her chest. "You frightened me."

"Apologies, Auntie." I smile sheepishly. "I did not mean to interrupt."

She closes her book and waves a hand dismissively.

"Nonsense. You know full well you are

welcome here anytime." Her eyes glance over me. "What is it?"

"What is what?"

"Do not play the fool with me, child," she says, standing and dusting herself down. "Not that good-for-nothing father of yours, is it?"

The question is rhetorical. It is always my good-for-nothing father. I sigh heavily and sit down, placing my book on another stack of books.

"He has gambled my savings," I say miserably. Anger bubbles beneath the surface of my skin. "The fee I need for Frostalm House of Learning…it is gone."

Aunt Meena sits back, her eyebrows knitted together.

"Oh, Shivani…" She reaches across to place a warm hand on my arm. "An absolute wastrel, that man is. A wastrel and a fiend."

Fury and sadness rise to the fore of my mind as hot, angry tears spill. My ophid thrums.

"I…I do not know what to do," I say, and my voice breaks.

Aunt Meena sits quietly with me until the tears dry, her arm around my shoulders. She smells of books and spiced tea. I inhale deeply, finding comfort in the familiarity.

"You will keep studying," she says when my breathing slows again. "You are far too smart to stay here with your rock of a father weighing you down. And…" She trails off but the unspoken words hang in the air, dangling like a noose. Mossgarde is a village that eats women. Without a job or resources, acceptance into a House of Learning far away is my only means of escape.

Frostalm is known as the Roaming City, a beacon of ingenuity and riches, a civilisation built on the largest ship in the realm. Sirens do not take kindly to the implication the ship is enchanted – it is their greatest feat of engineering, in fact. Frostalm traverses the Three Great Oceans and only truly docks once every five years, at Saltrock Bay. Otherwise, visitors and traders must wait for them to arrive near one of the larger ports and ride a small boat out. If I impress during my exams, they will pay for my travel, my boat, and even house me in the student's quarters.

"But...the fee. They will not accept me, no matter my score, if I cannot pay the entrance fee."

"Fret not." Aunt Meena smiles and tilts my chin up with one finger. "The Bazaar is in a few days and the merchants are due to arrive before then. I am sure I have some valuable texts around here."

"Your books?" I blink at her. "You cannot part with those!"

"I certainly can. Now dry your tears and let us continue with your studies." Aunt Meena's eyes have that familiar steel in them. "Or will you succumb to pity?"

I sniff and take a deep, ragged breath.

"What..." I feel another sob coming and falter, inhaling a fortifying breath. "What are we looking at today?"

Aunt Meena smiles at me and gives my shoulder an encouraging squeeze.

"Today, we are reading about dragons." She stands and rifles through a pile of books behind her.

"Dragons? But we have covered so much of them," I protest but search for some paper and ink regardless.

"Oh? Is there something else you would like to read about instead?"

"What about witches?" I grin at her. She gives me an unamused look.

"You have learned much about our kind," she replies, pulling books out and putting them back again.

I glance at her wooden leg. She puts on a limp for show—the leg is enchanted. The beautiful lavender carvings are more than simple decoration. The wood moves as if it is her own limb, as it always has done, and it always will until Aunt Meena passes away or the wood is broken.

During my early studies, I once asked her why she did not enchant her other leg as well. She had laughed and told me witches cannot enchant living things. We have a great power over the inanimate, but even plants are immune to our au'mana. After learning this, I abandoned any attempts at enchanting my father and began focussing on my collection of lost items instead.

"I stripped the rust off a bucket today," I tell her.

"A small thing for someone like you," she replies, finding a shiny book and pulling it free. "Once you are in the House of Learning, you will have many projects to work on, much larger than a bucket."

"Like a library?" I smirk. One of the reasons the library stands so sturdy is because Aunt Meena enchanted the building long ago. More accurately, she enchanted a single plank of wood in the wall, allowing the whole building to fall under her spell. *Hold fast*, she told it. And so it shall.

"Exactly right. Though I imagine Frostalm has libraries much grander than this." She smiles and pulls out a second book. "Regardless, we have done plenty on witches for now."

"Alright, well, please, no more dragons?"

"How about dragons *and* witches?" she offers, hauling the two huge books over to my table. "You will need to brush up on reading the two languages. I am certain Frostalm's linguistic exam will have questions about them."

"I can already read them both." I roll my eyes but turn to the dragon book regardless. I run my hand over the cover.

Dragons do not often write their stories

down as they prefer to tell their tales verbally or through patterns and drawings. And so the few books they have written are works of art. The paper is bound by two thick slabs of sandsnake leather and carved with large, ornate designs. One word in dragon text is embossed on the cover.

"History," I read it aloud. Aunt Meena nods approvingly before pointing to the other book.

Witch books are plentiful as we enjoy reading and passing information in written language. As our strength lies in the inanimate, even our plainest books give off an ethereal purple glow, turning them into something beautiful. The scent of au'mana, like salt, supposedly lingers around it. I sniff the air to try and catch it, but all I smell are the books themselves. A sprawling title in witch tongue is written across the cover.

"A short history on the art of enchanting building materials for the use of homes and other construction," I read.

"Very good," Aunt Meena compliments. "Many people mistake the two languages as one, but once you see the differences between them, it becomes rather obvious which is which."

"And which is witch." I beam. She rolls her eyes but the corners of her mouth tug up, betraying a smile.

"Let us open the books and begin reading," she says and I oblige, turning the cover of the dragon book first.

We read until the last of the sun filters through the trees and the moss crickets start their evening chirp. By the time I leave, my head is full and buzzing with knowledge—it is exhilarating and exhausting all at once. Moonlight seeps through the canopy in thin sheets, casting tiny silver pools across the dark wooden platforms. In the distance, the glow of the firebugs is stark against the gloom of the swamp as they dance hypnotically above the water. I fill my lungs, the air only slightly less stifling at night, and steel myself for what awaits me once I return home.

I cross the network of bridges without incident, keeping to the most well-lit paths. The public house is busy but the noise is muffled. The windows are alight, the yellow glow harsh against the purple lanterns outside. I briefly watch the silhouettes through the window, relieved to see there is no one loitering outside.

Just a few platforms away lies the deserted village square. I avert my eyes from the red-stained chopping block. When the first girl stepped up to volunteer, it was celebrated. The village square was decorated with moss garlands and delicate white flowers, and all our resources were pooled to create a huge feast. It had almost been a competition for the first girl to be allowed to volunteer. They lined up to show off their talents or their beauty or both. Everyone wanted *their* daughter to be the one who broke the curse.

But none of them did.

The king paid their families, as promised, but their daughters' heads were forfeit. An incentive, he had called it. And when no one volunteered, women were taken by force. I am told Mossgarde used to be a town, but now it is a village. A village full of angry whispers and growing dissent.

After eighteen years of greedy taxes and five years of dead women, Mossgarde refused the king's call. Daughters, wives, sisters, friends—they were all hidden and defended when the guards came for them. They wielded what they could—kitchen knives or broken table legs—and said *no*. The guards were ready to rip a woman from them, no matter the bloodshed.

And then the king had stepped out.

It was the first time I had seen him in person. Imposing was the word which came to mind. Something like rage simmered beneath the surface of him, like a pot ready to boil over. But there was something else there, too. I could see it in the slight curl of his lip, the dismissiveness in his eyes. We were not people to him but prey. Something primal in my mind warned me I was in the presence of a predator wearing the face of a man.

He took his place on the elevated platform in the village square and waited for us to pay attention.

"Good people," he called out. Flattering words but I could see the sneer beneath it, like a croca gliding under the still surface of swamp water. "I know how difficult it must be to part with your loved ones. I, too, must part with my son each time he turns into his beastly form. Cursed though he is, I love him dearly."

There was not a word that fell from his lips that I believed.

"But he is larger than when you last saw him. He was a babe then but is quickly becoming a man. Stronger. More...violent." The king's voice turned sharp and low. "If no one volunteers to break his curse, he could become rampant. I dare say he could tear through this entire village."

He waited for us to absorb this before continuing, a carefully placed pause.

"Do not forget I keep him locked in Mossgarde Castle for your safety. If he should get loose...well, it does not bear thinking about."

I shudder at the memory. The cool, strategic way the king took back control of Mossgarde. Like a hand around our neck, allowing us an inch to breathe only to remind us that he could close his fist at any time. I walk briskly away from the village square. Away from the chopping block. Despite knowing my father is at home, I suddenly do not want to be outside alone.

I cross another bridge and then another, steeling myself for home.

CHAPTER 3

Our house is built around the trunk of a towering willow tree, along with three other homes. The platform is surrounded by a curtain of delicate leaves and thin, waxy branches drooping over the connecting bridges. It should feel like we are afforded more privacy than most, but I cannot help but view it as a cage. I push my way through the branches and stride over to my front door.

Inside, the candles have been extinguished, apart from one. It burns low, casting the room in deep shadow. In one corner sits our rudimentary kitchen—a single large cauldron atop a wood burner and a bucket of cold water for dishes. The other two corners are taken up by my father and I's sleep sacks, each bundled with thin blankets. The humidity of Mossgarde means we are rarely cold, except in the very deep of winter when the village receives a week of frost.

A fine mesh stretches across our windows, like all the buildings here, except Aunt Meena's home. She told me once of a time when all the homes and shops and stalls were enchanted—to keep the insects away, to keep from sinking into the swamp, to keep the wood from rotting away. Now, the platforms creak and moan underfoot, and the water rises slowly every year. Some enchantments remain, but it has been a long time since Mossgarde was truly a home for witches.

I close the front door softly behind me and strain my eyes to search the shadows. My father's corner is deep in gloom. The blanket is piled too vaguely for me to know if he is there or not. I hold my breath and creep towards my own corner.

"You punched my friend."

My father's voice rattles through the darkness, coarse with drink. I release my breath in a sigh and continue on, not looking at him.

"No," I say, sinking to the floor and tugging my blanket over me. "I hit him with a book."

"Is that an improvement?"

"Well, I did not hurt my fist, so yes, I would say so."

He only grunts in response. As my eyes adjust to the dark, I throw a glance at his corner. I make out the outline of his form slumped against the wall. The air is thick with the stench of ale and unwashed clothes. I tuck myself tight against my corner, fighting to put as much space between us as possible. My books, stacked high against the wall, encase me in a protective semi-circle as I pull my blanket up high on my body.

"I can get the fee back," my father says suddenly.

I freeze. Our usual routine after an argument is to pretend as if nothing happened. We do not acknowledge nor apologise, especially not him, lest the argument spark anew. I say nothing and wait.

"I just…I need some time."

I make a noncommittal noise.

"The guards are cheats." He scoffs and I shoot up so quickly, my spine clicks. "They rig the dice—"

"You have lost my money to the *guards*?" I screech. "You owe money to the crown?"

"Not the crown, only his guards."

"That *is* the crown. Where do you think their coin goes? Who, pray tell, do you think they bring our taxes to every morn, along with what little food we have?" My ophid thrums, taut and tense. My hands clench into fists.

"I did not think—"

"No, you did not think at all, you loathsome sack of croca shit."

The floor rattles as my father thumps his fist off the wooden boards.

"You do not speak to me that way!" he thunders.

"That was *my money*!" I scream back.

Where he had been shrouded in shadows before, he is now alight in the purple glow of my au'mana. My books float in mid-air, the cauldron rattles violently against the floor, and my father's blanket is ripped from him. The house is awash in witch magic. I feel all of it in my grasp, each pot and pan, each nail in the floorboard.

My father falls silent, his mouth twisted in a snarl, dark eyebrows heavy over his eyes. We stare at each other, the threat of my au'mana thick around us.

He has taken everything.

I clench my teeth, tears threatening to spill. I am ready to tear this home apart. What else do I have?

My father's face drops, a glimmer of fear in his eyes.

But I have Aunt Meena.

Her soft smile, her spiced tea scent, her firm hand on my shoulder, guiding me forward. *You will study*, she told me. *And you will leave this place.*

I cry out in frustration, dropping my au'mana and plummeting us back into darkness. The books, pots and everything else fall with a symphony of heavy thuds. How can I leave if the guards arrest me for destroying our house?

With an angry groan, I turn away and curl into a ball, pulling my blanket over me. Rage simmers like hot water over my skin, my heart thumping against my ribcage. I squeeze my eyes shut. My father sits silently, neither of us saying a word.

"It is our anniversary," my father mumbles so quietly I nearly do not hear him. My ears prick but I do not open my eyes.

When I do not reply, he heaves a weary sigh and I hear the knock of wood as he tips his head back against the wall.

"Thirty years…" he rasps. The sorrow in his voice lands like a boulder on my chest, nearly quashing my anger. "I have never met a woman with so much fire in her soul. The Saints themselves placed a spark in her the day she was born, I am sure of it."

Something close to grief tugs at my heart, like a child pulling at their mother's hand.

"Auntie often says I remind her of mother," I offer quietly. "I have her temperament."

My father barks in laughter but there is no humour in it.

"You? You are nothing like her. She was… passionate."

"I have passion."

"You have poison!" he spits. I flinch at his words as if they land like physical blows. "You have been angry since the day you were born. Your wrath is the thing that killed her."

"She died from blood loss," I bite out. "You were the one who was supposed to take care of her. If you must blame anyone, blame yourself."

"Saintless bitch."

"Wretched piece of shit," I fire back.

My father scoffs and picks up a bottle. When he realises it is empty, he growls and throws it back down. Not hard enough to break it but enough to send a spike of fear through my chest.

"The Saints have cursed me with you." He jabs a finger at me.

Fear curdles into anger. I choke out a scornful noise from the back of my throat at the gall of this man.

"Oh? I am *your* curse?" Disdain curls my lip. "Is that why you have stolen my coin and prevented me from leaving? You must enjoy this so-called torture I inflict upon you merely by existing. Is that right?"

He falls silent. Ale and resentment radiate from him, so thick it makes my skin prickle. I lay down with a huff, pulling the covers over.

"Keep your foolish thoughts behind your teeth and allow me some sleep," I say finally. My heart hammers like a hummingbird and I take a long breath to steady it.

The house succumbs to quiet, punctuated only by the sounds of the swamp. I almost think he has fallen asleep but then I hear him stumble to his feet. I brace myself, waiting for him to come over but instead, the front door slams shut. Whatever my father has chosen to do under cover of darkness has nothing to do with me. I shut my eyes and dream of the day I can leave.

CHAPTER 4

The Merchant's Bazaar arrives with little enthusiasm. Aunt Meena and I start early, tendrils of orange light seeping through the tree canopy our only indication of sunrise. The Bazaar used to be held in the village square, but with the heavy presence of the chopping block ever-looming, the market has since migrated to a long, wide walkway closer to the outskirts of town. Aunt Meena and I set up a small table at one end.

"Saints," she huffs, sliding off the bag of books strapped to her back.

"You might have enchanted them to be lighter," I say glibly. My own bag glows purple and I set it lightly on the table.

"Whatever for?" Aunt Meena wheezes. "I did just fine."

"Indeed."

The last of the night's fireflies dance around us as slits of daylight break through the trees. Along the walkway, a few other merchants finish setting up their stalls—three werewolves and one siren. I help Aunt Meena stack the books, showcasing their spines or intricate leather covers, but my eye continues to wander down the rest of the stalls.

"So few," I murmur.

Aunt Meena says nothing, but the corners of her mouth tug down, and she gives a brief shake of her head.

Years ago, the Bazaar had been one of my favourite times of the month. I would eagerly await the arrival of the merchants, who travelled so far from their homes to do trade with Mossgarde. Our ability to produce food year-round drew many merchants, especially the werewolves from Swordstead and the dragons from Coalsburgh. Both of their climates are harsh and uninviting so they relied on imports from Mossgarde for a time. It takes great skill to catch our swamp fish or harvest the fruit from our towering trees. Skill that left with the witches when the king's royal law passed twenty-five years ago.

A middle-aged werewolf sets up his stall next to us, carefully arranging his wares across the table. He has shed his usual furs for a simple merchant outfit with a dark blue hood draped across his shoulders. Like most werewolves, he towers two heads above me.

I am close enough to smell the pomander

hanging around his neck. Werewolves are sensitive to smells and believe different scents begat different results. I take a subtle sniff—he wears lavender to repel swamp insects and siren musk to ward off illness. A heady combination.

"Good morrow," the werewolf grunts.

"Good morrow, Darragh." I incline my head. "A fruitful journey for you, I hope?"

Darragh gives me a flat look under thick eyebrows and continues setting up his stall.

"Ah. We shall speak no more of it, then." I indicate to our stall, the table legs creaking under the weight of the books. "Can I interest you in any of our wares today?"

"Got no use for fancy paper, Shivani." Darragh glances up. "I don't suppose you have any of that croca meat?"

"The last croca farmer left just a month past," I say with an apologetic smile. "His daughter was nearly of age."

Darragh says nothing but his shoulders tense. Sweat glazes his brow and he pulls out a small, thin cloth to mop at his face. He turns back to his stall, pulling out snowberries and sharpened knives carved from the bones of mountain bears. My eyes fix on the berries, so small and few. I think back to when Darragh used to bring bowls full of them, along with moonfruit and salted goat meat.

I cast my eyes down the walkway at the few other merchants who arrived for the Bazaar.

Two other werewolves, cloaked in merchant blue, heads down. One siren from Frostalm, her deep indigo skin dulled by the low light as she unpacks her wares.

Not many traders hail from the Roaming City— they, after all, have access to many ports and all the fish they can catch. But at least one scholar faithfully arrives at the Bazaar each month. I suppose knowledge can be found anywhere, not matter how dire. The gaps between merchants grow with each passing month. I turn back to Aunt Meena's stall and move the books around to make them look as appealing as possible. With the dragon texts displayed proudly at the front, I stand back with my fists on my hips. With any luck, the display will catch the eye of the siren merchant.

Coalsburgh may refuse to trade with us, but Frostalm is where the coin is and no good scholar can pass up a valuable book. Mossgarde sits close to the Glass Sea, the calmest of the Three Great Oceans, so Frostalm would send traders via their smaller boats to the Bazaar often. Their merchants made up most of the Bazaar. Or they used to, at least.

"Very good, Shivani," Aunt Meena murmurs, nodding at my display.

Her gaze fixes on the full purse hanging from the siren merchant's hip. She raises her voice and says, "After all, these are *very rare dragon books*."

The siren glances up with red eyes, intrigued. I turn to begin arranging some of the books at the back but walk into something solid.

"Oof!" I bounce back, arms windmilling, when an arm darts out to catch me. I look up to see another werewolf grinning down at me.

"Steady," he says, pulling me back to my feet. He does not wear merchant blue but instead a red hooded cloak. The colour of Swordstead warriors.

"Eoin," I say, letting him help me up. "My thanks."

"Wouldn't be the first time you've fallen for me." Eoin winks and laughs.

"We both know that is your ego skirting past reality."

He clutches his chest in mock offence.

"You wound me. Here, it seems a quiet morning. Very little chance of a scuffle or, dare I say, a kerfuffle. Let's take a turn around town, shall we?"

I exchange a look with Aunt Meena but she only shrugs, a small smile on her lips.

"Fine," I say.

Eoin turns to Darragh, "Mind if I take a break?"

Darragh waves him off without looking up, focussed on arranging his wares. Eoin shrugs off the heavy sack on his shoulder before offering his arm to me, bowing low in exaggeration. I sigh but take it with the ghost of a smile.

We make our way through the market at a leisurely pace, passing yet more empty stalls. Eoin's pomander is more subtle than Darragh's, but this close, I can catch the scent, dark and honeyed. The bark of a sugar tree found only in the Whispering Mountains.

"How goes your travels?" I ask.

"Business could be better but nothing a smile and a bit of charm can't fix." Bravado drips from his words, coating the doubt underneath.

"What of the famine?"

"Ah, now, that's a heavy word to use." He shrugs. "We'll get by. Werewolves always do."

I twist my lips and look up at him.

"You can be honest with me, Eoin," I say. "We are friends."

He stops short, pulling me into the gap between two crooked houses.

"More than that, I'd say." He grins wolfishly, canines flashing. "Friends don't often take a tumble in the storage shed, do they?"

Eoin's eyes glitter a dark amber, his arms wrapping around my waist. My eyes trace over his features, strong and handsome. As I always do when he visits, I wait for the feelings to follow. The attraction is there, certainly, but feelings...

I gently pull away from his arms, putting space between us. His grin flickers once, like a candle flame threatening to go out. But he withdraws, putting both hands up, and takes a step back.

"Fair enough," is all he says.

Behind him, I spot the glimmer of armour and my heart stutters. The guards will be collecting their tax from the Bazaar merchants.

"Come," I say to Eoin. "Follow me."

We hurry back the way we came, away from the approaching guards before they can spot us. I lead us over the crisscross of bridges, deeper into Old Mossgarde. Not for the first time, I wish I could keep going. Just keep running further and further from the guards and the king. Further still until I reach the Roaming City of Frostalm and I am finally safe.

Instead, we stop at my small sanctuary on the outskirts of Mossgarde. Slightly out of breath, I sit on the wooden platform and slot my legs through the fence, letting them dangle over the swamp. Eoin sits cross-legged next to me, his legs too large to fit through the gaps of the rails.

"Friends," he says after a lengthy silence. He rolls the word around in his mouth as though tasting it for the first time. "You don't find many of those on the road."

"You have found one here," I say truthfully with a smile. He smiles back, his boastful grin gone.

"Then I am a lucky man indeed."

Our affinity may be bereft of the romantic pull I had hoped for, but Eoin's companionship is still valuable to me. He is a good man with a curious soul, and I am often enraptured by his tales from across the realm. From the honeylemon trees that hang over the clay homes of Coalsburgh to the steam and metal of Frostalm, I drink in each detail of lands so different to mine. He has even visited the quaint village of Caldercruix, the Old Home of Witches, where many still remain. I think of them often, content under thatched rooves in a mild climate. I wonder what would have been if my mother and aunt had not chosen to settle in Mossgarde all those years ago.

We bask in a companionable silence, broken only by the sounds of the swamp. Firebugs hover over the surface of the water as the platform creaks under us. The thick treetops rustle overhead.

"For our kinship, you can be honest with me," Eoin says softly. "What's your plan here, Shivani?"

"What can you mean?"

He waves a large hand in the direction of town, eyebrows raised.

"Are you to run from the guards forever? Hide out here in abandoned homes?"

My ears and cheeks warm and I look at him sharply.

"Of course not," I say, nettled. "I am leaving."

"Leaving?"

"Mossgarde. The king. The curse." I turn

my head away. "The whole damned place."

Eoin is quiet for a moment and then, "Your aunt?"

I squeeze my teeth together, jaw tense.

"If she chooses to stay, I will leave without her." My voice shakes and the thick swamp air sticks in my throat.

Eoin sits back, hands splayed behind him and gives a low whistle. Shame trickles through me, wrapping like a fist around my heart. I grab the bars of the fence, resting my forehead against them with a sigh.

"I do not want to leave her. But what else can I do?"

A pause.

"In Swordstead, the mountain is full of burrows," he replies quietly. When I look back at him, his face is tipped up to the canopy, eyes closed. "Big families of long-ears are common. Snow hares, you call them here. Anyway, when my father first showed me how to hunt them, he taught me to be real quiet. Because if they see you—this big, ugly predator—then boom. They'll scatter. No hesitation, all instinct. And the ones that ran first, the ones that didn't look back, those were the ones that survived."

I stare at him, my hands gripped tight on the bars.

"You'll find no judgment with me, Shivani." Eoin opens his eyes, dark and clear. "If running means survival, then you fucking run."

CHAPTER 5

Eoin bids me farewell at the edge of Old Mossgarde with an affectionate kiss on my forehead but no more.

"I hope to see you in Frostalm next season," I tell him as he slings a weighty pack onto his back.

"And I, you. I'll mind and visit the House of Learning." He flashes me his usual easy grin before placing two fingers over his heart. "The wind at your back and fire in your chest."

"Soft snow underfoot and a safe home awaiting you," I reply, finishing his werewolf farewell and repeating his gesture.

I wait until he passes through the deepening gloom of the swamp before making my way back into town.

The swamp has gone quiet, the rhythmic chirp and buzz of the day all but silenced. Nevertheless, hairs rise along the back of my neck and my heart picks up speed. My au'mana hums. I am not alone.

The harsh clink of armour cuts through the quiet. I glance over my shoulder. Three guards stand on an adjacent platform, watching me. Their eyes glint in the purple haze of the ever-lit lamps.

As soon as we lock eyes, I know I am in danger.

I think of the snow hare. I think of the hunters.

I turn and flee.

"Stop!" one of them calls after me, but their voice is drowned out by the blood rushing past my ears.

I take off at a sprint, feet hammering against the bridge. I barely make it to the platform on the other side before something hard slams into me.

I yelp and topple to the side, catching myself on the platform fence. It creaks loudly, threatening to snap. My shoulder throbs where I landed on it. The guard who tackled me scrambles to his feet and pins me down.

"Stay right there!" he orders.

In response, I open my mouth wide and scream. It is incoherent and wild, pulled from the depths of me. I writhe beneath him and he grunts with the effort of keeping me contained.

"I have nothing!" I shriek when he does not let me up. "I have nothing to give!"

"You have been—stop it!" He leans his

weight further onto me, trapping me beneath him. "You have been volunteered. The king is expecting your presence."

I stop breathing. Something hard forms in the pit of my stomach, heavy as lead. I feel like I am sinking through the platform.

The blood-stained chopping block.

The steel of the axe.

"No," I whisper, eyes wide. "No!"

I shriek and throw all my strength against the guard, kicking upwards.

"Saints!" he yelps as I fling him off me. The other guards step back in surprise, and I seize the opportunity, clambering to my feet. I push off the ground to flee again.

Another guard makes to grab me and, on instinct, I swing a closed fist at his head. He somewhat manages to pull back in time but not quite—my knuckles land hard on the side of his helmet. Pain explodes along my hand as I connect with the metal. It dulls quickly, adrenaline coursing through my veins. The guard crumples to the ground, a solid dent in his helmet.

Hard hands grab my shoulders from behind and hold me in place.

"Stop fighting it, girl," one of them growls in my ear. "The king gets what he wants."

I squeeze my eyes shut, memories invading my mind. Another head rolling. Another woman dead.

A burst of fear makes me jerk out of the guard's hands, but they hold fast, their grip digging into my skin. Physically helpless, my ophid kicks in.

Au'mana washes through me and seeps into the wood and metal around us. The platform beneath our feet begins to rattle dangerously, the stilts creaking. The planks holding us above the swamp splinter and crack.

"Quick!" someone shouts. "Before she drowns us!"

One of the guards presses a wet cloth against my face. The smell is foul, and I press my lips together, twisting my head away. The scent forces its way up my nose and I breathe it in unwillingly.

I expect to feel something but when he pulls the cloth away, my head remains clear. The only difference is the platform has stilled. There is a large crack in the wood, starting at my feet.

"Shackle her," a guard commands. I reach for my au'mana again but when I try, it is as though my ophid sleeps. Where it is normally taut and strong, it is sluggish. I try again to rouse it but nothing happens.

They have drugged me and blocked my magic.

"But I have not volunteered." My voice is hoarse and defeated. Exhaustion sweeps over me like a wave, overwhelming. I stare at the crack in the wood. The guard I punched clambers unsteadily to his feet and glares at me.

"No. But your father has volunteered you."

I stand there limply as ice-cold handcuffs are bolted around my wrists. I want to feel something—anger or sadness—but I cannot bring myself to feel anything.

I try once more to reach my magic and tears spring to my eyes when I cannot. I struggle against the handcuffs and the guards hands but the fight has left me. My father, after all this time, has finally put the last nail in my coffin. Worse…I have let him.

I close my eyes and let them lead me away.

❈ ❈ ❈

Mossgarde Castle towers over the village, ever-present and ominous. It was built on the highest raised platform and crafted from scarlet brick rather than the dark wood of the rest of Mossgarde. The construction itself had claimed many lives, breeding bleak rumours. Mossgardians whisper that the brick had originally been white but it was stained with the blood of those forced to build it. Others said the castle was red specifically so no one could see how blood-stained it really was. I do not give much regard to rumours but still, I tried to stay as far away from the castle as possible. The whispers may not be true, but the annual beheadings are real and the memories will stay with me forever.

I try to wash them away as I stand before the castle, its overbearing height looming over me. I have a moment of panic and think of fleeing again but the guards are prepared now. They eye me warily and have shackled my ankles and wrists. The one standing behind me gives me a sharp prod in the back, nudging me forward. My ophid protests.

The castle is impossible to climb without the ladder, which they only lower when necessary. Or, perhaps, with au'mana to manipulate the stilts. My lip curls, thinking of the foul drug they used to take my magic away.

One of the guards calls out, mimicking a bird cry, and a few moments later, the ladder appears. When it arrives before us, I turn to look at the guard behind me.

"I cannot climb with my ankles shackled," I tell him.

"You should have thought of that before you clocked me," he replies.

The platform looms above me and I am overly aware of the solid wood beneath my feet. I chew my lip.

"What if I fall?" I ask.

The guard's eyes slide over to meet mine.

"Then you fall. Now move."

I grind my teeth together and turn to the ladder. Shuffling close, I raise my leg to test the limit of my shackles. It will be difficult but I can do it. I reach forward and grip the wooden bar, hauling myself up.

The guards wait at the bottom in case I do fall and accidentally take one of them with me. They watch me struggle upwards in tentative steps. It is not long before the muscles in my arms ache, and each time I glance down, nausea bubbles in my stomach at the height. I press my forehead against the wood and try to steady my breathing.

"Not so strong without your witchcraft," a guard taunts me from below. I press my lips into a thin line, my spite overtaking my weariness, and pull myself up.

And then I smell it.

There is something foul in the air, lingering in the thick humidity. I wrinkle my nose in disgust and turn my head to find the source. When I do, my head snaps forward again. I always had a morbid curiosity about what happened to the heads of the maidens before me. Their bodies went to their families, but the guards always took their heads. Now I know.

The top half of the stilts are lined with spikes. Several heads are skewered there at various degrees of decay. My eyes water, both with the smell of rot and the indignity the king has inflicted upon them, even in death. My hands start to shake and I force myself to breathe through the stench and keep climbing before I slip. I will not become one of the dead holding up the king in his castle.

I make it to the top of the ladder, my legs and arms burning. A guard hauls me over the lip of the wall and grips my elbow to keep me on my feet. I sway on the spot, sucking in air before two other guards join us. Without letting me recover, they drag me to the doors of the castle.

This high up, the top of the castle penetrates the canopy of trees. Even as I am hauled away, I blink in awe at the night sky. The stars glitter against the deep black of the heavens. I am almost ashamed that I have lived for nearly two decades and never seen an open sky. Shame is quickly replaced with indignation, knowing the king has kept even the sky to himself.

I am led through the large front doors and into the throne room. Respite from the smell of the heads outside is extinguished once we step inside.

The throne room is grand, tall and wide, with thick columns supporting the high ceiling. The brick on the inside is white—making me reconsider the earlier rumours—with ornate carvings accented with gold. It is the cleanest, whitest place I have ever seen. My ragged boots squeak off the polished floor as they march me forward.

The king sits on his throne, elevated several steps above us. Grey streaks his flaxen hair, and the ghost of a thin scar sits across one cheekbone. His features are fine despite his older years but I know it is a veneer. A comely veil to cover the rot inside.

When I am finally presented to him, he barely glances at me. Boredom etched across his face, he flicks his wrist.

"Bring in the prisoner," another guard barks at the king's order. His uniform is different from the rest—white and crisp, whereas the others are muted pewter. At his command, a door leading further into the castle opens.

Out steps my father, shackled like me.

I nearly gasp when I see him and bite my tongue to keep my breath contained. He stumbles forward, led by two other guards. One of his eyes is swollen and a violent shade of purple. When he moves, he has a limp. I stare at him, but he does not meet my eye.

"Speak then," the king says, reclining his throne with a detached gaze.

My father looks at the floor. The only sound in the room is the gentle clinking of his shackles as he shifts.

"M-My king...I offer you—"

"Speak up, for Saint's sake!" the king bellows. One of the guards nudges my father roughly in the back. I nearly wince but remember he does not have an ophid.

"My king, I offer you this as a volunteer," he says, clearer now, although he still does not look up.

"And what exactly is 'this?'" the king replies and gestures in my direction. My numb shock fades as if waking up from a dream. The world rushes in around me. My stomach drops.

"My only daughter, of age and clean, my king," my father clarifies, mumbling. I gape at him.

"Hm," the king grunts before turning his eyes to me. "It appears your father has got himself into a fine mess. Only a desperate man comes to his king for a loan, but a desperate man he was."

I close my eyes briefly. I know my father gambles, but this...

"Come closer, girl," the king continues, beckoning me.

I want to do the absolute opposite, but I am pushed on by the guard behind me. I stumble forward a few steps, coming to a halt at the base of his platform. The king peers down at me.

"How old are you?" he queries, sizing me up. His gaze is lecherous. I curl my lip and say nothing in response, chin up in definiance.

"She is four-and-twenty," my father answers for me. I am unsurprised he does not remember my age. "Unspoiled," he adds, and I want to bash his head against the ground. My ophid is brimming full of au'mana, feeding off my quiet fury, but the drugs keep it out of my reach.

"Let me see her teeth," the king orders, and a guard immediately steps forward to push my lips apart. This stranger's hands groping my face is enough to send me careening over the edge.

Before he can react and I can think, I open my jaw and clamp my teeth over his finger. He screams and yanks his hand back, but I do not release him. I bite harder until my teeth sink into his flesh. Until I feel bone. Until I taste blood.

Hard fingers dig into my shoulders and pull me back as the guard clutches his wounded hand. I grin at him, showing him his blood between my teeth.

"Touch me once more, and I will rip your throat out," I snarl.

The king laughs and claps.

"Saints, I have another beast under my roof!" He chuckles.

I ignore him and turn my murderous gaze onto my father. He had been watching the events unfold, but now his eyes snap back to the floor. Like a dog who knows he has done wrong.

"I always knew you were a coward." I spit blood at his feet. "But this is despicable, even for you."

"You are just another mouth to feed, Shivani," he mumbles, eyes averted. "You are unmarried with no prospects, for Saint's sake. At least here, you may have a chance to break this curse and make us both rich."

"How dare you!" I roar. I try to throw myself at him, picturing my hands around his neck, but the guards hold me firmly. "You stole my money! *Mine*! And now you are trading my life for coin!"

"It is done." He shrugs. "There is no point in a struggle."

White hot rage blurs the corners of my vision.

"If the drink does not kill you," I hiss. "Then I will."

He stares at the ground.

"Do you hear me? I will escape from here, and *I will kill you!*" Several more guards pile in to hold me back as I thrash like a feral croca.

"I think we will enjoy housing you for the next six months, girl." The king rubs his hands together, cheeks red with amusement. "Perhaps you will break this curse of his! And I do enjoy seeing a fiery young woman learn her place."

His eyes glint, and my hands ball into fists. I want to leap forward and tear his face off with my teeth. I want to rip the smug smile from his face. But I can do nothing.

"Get her cleaned up. I want her presentable when she is introduced to my son."

The door my father came through opens again and several women pour into the room. They begin to usher me away as I quake with rage. Their faces are kind, but their grip is firm, and I am swiftly removed. I glance back at my father, his shoulders hunched and his eyes closed.

"Bastard!" I scream.

The king's laugh follows me into the castle as the doors slam shut.

CHAPTER 6

Month One

I am in a gilded cage, beautiful and stifling.

The bedchamber the guards led me to is larger than my entire house. The floor is decked with thick, plush carpet I sink into as soon as I am thrown inside. I stumble over the soft flooring before collecting myself and rounding on the guards. They close the door quickly behind them, leaving me to thump my fists uselessly against the wood.

In my house, I regularly had to fix the door as it fell apart each time it rained. But here, the door is so strong it is as though I am pounding against rock.

"Let me go!" I yell. The door absorbs the sound of my fists, rendering my attempts impotent. I resist the rising panic in my chest and flood it with all my fury instead.

I spin around, scanning the room. An

imposing four-poster bed stands against one wall, as ornate and golden as the rest of the castle. There are several clothes drawers tucked into the far corner and a vanity table overloaded with perfumes and make-up. Bile rises in the back of my throat as I think of all the dead women who likely sat there, trying their best to claim the prince's heart. And I am next. I am a Never Queen.

No.

I press my fists into my eyes until I see stars. There will be something in here which can help me. There must be.

There is a door on the right-hand wall. Breathless, I scamper over to it and twist the handle. As I swing through, I see an oversized clawfoot bathtub standing innocently in the middle of the tiled room. The walls are lined with various colourful bottles and interspersed with sponges. A washroom, nothing more. Squeezing my teeth together, I slam the door shut and review the rest of the bedchambers.

A large window spans the adjacent wall. Heavy curtains are drawn across it, dimming the room. I swipe them to the side and peer through the glass. From where my bedchamber is, the window is directly adjacent to where the canopy of trees hangs over one side of the castle. It has pushed through the brick over time, worming its way through until the branches hang several feet away from the castle walls. I start thinking of ways I can grab onto the branch from my window, but when I press my forehead against the glass, I can see the sheer drop from my chambers to the grounds below. I slam my palm against the frame in frustration.

"Miss Shivani?" a small, polite voice interrupts me.

I whirl around to a group of handmaids hovering in the open doorway. My eyes dart between them, calculating my chances of barging through. The glint of steel further into the corridor changes my mind—there will be guards waiting to skewer me as soon as I try to escape.

"My apologies, miss, we are here by order of the king," the handmaid in front tells me with a soft smile and a small curtsy. "You are due for your first meeting with the prince tonight and we are to help you."

Her eyes flicker to the vanity table. They start to step inside but I pick up a handheld looking glass and smash it against the bedframe. It explodes into a thousand shards as the handmaids shriek. I scoop up one and hold it in front of me like a knife.

"No one touch me!" I growl.

They flee. All but one. She hovers at the doorway, a notch between her brows.

"You are bleeding, miss," she says.

I glance down at my hand. Dark crimson drips like syrup from my palm.

"That is not your concern." I wave my shard of glass at her. "Get away from me. You will not take me anywhere."

She looks at me with round eyes but makes no movement. Behind her, a guard appears, scowling.

"Is she causing trouble?" he grumbles.

"No!" The handmaid shakes her head firmly. "She is cooperating."

I bristle.

"I am *not*—"

"You may go." She ignores me and continues speaking to the guard. "She will be presentable for the prince. I assure you."

I am ready to smash something else in this room but the handmaid's eyes scream at me. She gives the tiniest, imperceptible shake of her head. I drop the glass shard.

"I am *cooperating*," I bite out.

The guard gives me a disdainful look but turns away. To my dismay, I realise he is guarding my room. The handmaid signals for the rest of the maids to come back and closes the door behind them. My shoulders sag as my chances for escape within the next few hours quickly dwindle into nothing.

✷ ✷ ✷

My evening is spent with the handmaids as they clean, scrub and lather sweet-smelling cream on me. I fight the urge to cover myself in front of them, unused to being bathed by anyone except myself. My hair, which had been damp and ratty from my fight with the guards, is thoroughly washed until it gleams. Rough sponges are used to remove the grime and sweat from my skin. I sit and seethe through it all.

As I sit at the vanity table, I keep my eyes averted from my reflection. I do not want to think of myself in the same position as the Never Queens before me. Instead, my eyes constantly move around the room to see if there is anything I can use later.

"It is no use being so tense," one of the handmaids tells me while scrubbing the dirt from under my nails.

"I am quite unsure how else I should feel when I have been sentenced to death," I snap, but she does not blink at my tone.

"You may break the curse yet, miss," she replies, putting my hands down once she is satisfied my fingernails are clean.

"If you believe anyone can break the curse, you are a fool." I snatch my hand back and fold my arms. The handmaid smiles sadly.

"Perhaps," she says eventually, her voice even. She moves to stand behind me and begins to gently rub scented oil through my dark hair. The adrenaline and anger from earlier putter out, slowly replaced with exhaustion. There is something soothing about the handmaid's voice and slow, methodical movements. I fight hard not to relax into her hands.

"What is your name?" I ask. Partly to gather information and partly to keep myself alert.

"Inez, miss."

I glance at her in the mirror of the vanity table. She is older, with fine lines around her mouth and the beginnings of grey streaked through her copper hair. When she smiles, the corners of her eyes crinkle. Her fingers massage my scalp, and I lean into it despite myself.

"How long have you worked here?" I probe.

"All my life, miss. My mother worked here and when I was born, the work was passed to me."

I sit in silent horror at this but Inez speaks so casually, I am lost for words. The king's reputation for cruelty is known throughout the country, but to keep people locked up in his castle through generations of families…No one in Mossgarde knows what happens in the castle. No one but me knows there are people trapped in here. I suppress a shiver.

Inez and the other handmaids work my hair into a thick braid and drape it over my shoulder. Jewelled pins are pressed into the grooves of my braid, sparkling against my obsidian hair. They paint gold powder across my eyelids and lips, stark against my dark skin.

Like everything else here, they have made me so beautiful it turns my stomach.

They dress me in a long gown with soft shoes on my feet—shoes I cannot easily run in, I note. A sheer shawl is draped over my shoulders, and several bangles line my wrists. They remind me of the shackles the guards put on me.

The gown is unusual. Long sleeves, a low neckline and a corseted middle, tight and stifling. Mossgarde royal fashion dictates thin fabrics, draped and layered delicately to remain as breathable as possible in the stuffy air. This dress, however, is not so concerned with practicality and instead serves only to emphasise my curves. It is entirely unwelcome.

Inez looks at me with something like pride when they deem me ready.

"You are a pretty sight, miss," she says. Her accent is strange, so like a Mossgardian but not quite. "The guards will collect you when it is time for dinner."

With another polite curtsy, Inez and the rest of the maids exit the bedchamber, and I am left alone.

I tug at my gown and squirm at the uncomfortable way it pinches at my arms and waist. My irritation rises but not quite enough to overpower my weariness. I have not even eaten today. I sit on the large bed, breathing in deeply to hold the tears at bay.

I am a snow hare, trapped and helpless, at

the mercy of her hunters.

Closing my eyes, my ophid thrums, desperate to be released. The rest of my back aches, compensating for the tightness of the muscle. I reach up to stretch it.

My ophid is less sluggish now. More alive. Hopeful, I reach out to my au'mana. It hums to me, hovering just past where I can go. I raise my hands in front of me and try to conjure the swirling purple smoke.

Nothing appears.

"Argh!" I yell, my eyes snapping open in frustration.

I have no magic, no allies, no help. Aunt Meena is likely sitting alone in the library, wondering why I have not returned from my walk with Eoin.

The image of her waiting for me to arrive, only for me to never show up again, is enough to make me scream. I imagine my head on the chopping block. I imagine Aunt Meena's heart snapping in half.

I fall to my knees and unleash the rage built up inside me, curling my fingers into fists and throwing back my head to shriek. My father has stolen my future from me. He has stolen everything. I fall to the side and curl into a ball, thinking of all I could have been. The things I will never see and the people I will never meet.

I lie on the thick carpet, my ophid crippled and everything I have worked for snatched away.

I wait for the tears to come.

And then I see it.

A scratch on the foot of the bed, too small to see from standing. Eyebrows furrowed, I wriggle closer to read it.

Morraine.

My eyes widen. The name is a shard of ice in my heart, sharp and cold. It is a flash of red hair and chestnut brown eyes, a tired smile and a loud laugh.

I knew her.

Past tense.

By the time the guards arrive to bring me to dinner, my nerves have hardened, and my mind is set. They will not break me.

I will break them.

CHAPTER 7

They lead me to the dining room like a lamb to slaughter.

As I do when I walk past the leering men outside the public house, I keep my chin up and shoulders back. I track the route and create a mental map. The guards march behind me to deter me from running again. I notice the same guard I had punched before and give him a sweet smile. He scowls in return. The dent in his helmet remains.

The dining room itself is an enormous affair, befitting the ego of the king. The ceiling is high and the room is cavernous. Candles line the walls and hang from the beams running across the ceiling. Due to the sheer size of the room, they only cast a dim glow.

Despite its size, the place is bare except for a large portrait of the king looming on the far wall and a long, lonely table in the middle of the room. It is laden with all varieties of food—

more than I have seen in one place before. There are fruits and vegetables which look familiar and it takes me a moment to realise I have only seen pictures of them in books. Snowberries and moonfruit. Food only grown in Swordstead. I stifle a reaction, not wanting the king to think I am impressed or curious about how he has acquired foreign food without official trade. None of the werewolf merchants who visit Mossgarde bring food. It is too sparse for them to spare.

Despite the ridiculous length of the table, only two people sit at it. The king sits at the head, and another man—I assume the prince—sits a few seats down. I am struck by the fact they are not sitting together, but it is quickly forgotten—the smell of the food overwhelms me. A heady mixture of salt and herbs, freshly cooked meat. Nothing like the food I have survived on since I was young. My empty stomach growls loudly, but only the king looks up when I arrive.

"Splendid." He grins. He holds a leg of meat on the bone, and his plate is brimming with food. "Sit her next to her new master."

Nausea swirls at his words. Even during my father and I's nastiest arguments, he never spoke to me like this. Like a *pet*.

But I cannot deny the food. My stomach pangs painfully, reminding me of my hunger. I flex my fingers to stop them from curling into fists and decide the food is worth more than the fight.

A guard pulls out a chair next to the prince and I sit down stiffly. I cast my eyes sideways at him but he does not acknowledge my presence, continuing with his meal as if nothing has happened. My blood boils.

"Girl." The king tears a piece of croca meat from the bone with his teeth and speaks while chewing. "Eat."

He gestures at the food. I exhale slowly, desperate to resist everything this vile man offers me. But my stomach cramps in protest, and the rumbles are loud enough for both men to hear. I need to survive so I can escape, and that requires food. Reluctantly, I begin filling my plate.

To my dismay, the food is as delicious as it looks. I fight hard to eat with dignity by chewing small mouthfuls instead of wolfing it down like my stomach demands. The king watches me carefully, but I pretend I do not notice him. I continue with my slow, polite forkfuls. My back remains ramrod straight, and my eyes stay on my plate. I do not want to make myself sick with more food than I have ever eaten. I do not want to give the king ammo against me by eating like a beast at his table.

"How wonderful," he comments once I have had my fill and pushed the plate away. Neither he nor the prince spoke at all while we ate. "I do hope you enjoyed yourself. You will need your strength when my son has his way with you. He does so enjoy breaking a woman's spirit."

The aftertaste of the food, which had been so pleasant before, turns sour in my mouth. I press my lips together in a thin line.

"And he will need his strength," I say earnestly. "When I knock seven shades of shit out of him for daring to touch me."

The king falls silent. The smile slips off his face and his eyes narrow.

"This attitude of yours was amusing at first, but I suggest you learn how to hold your tongue around your betters."

I open my mouth to argue back, but I am interrupted by the prince.

"Forgive me, my king," he says. I start, almost forgetting he was there. "But as Miss Shivani is now my property for the next six months, I will have her suitably punished."

His tone is bored, as though punishing his *property* is nothing more than a chore.

"I can punish her my own damn self," the king growls, slamming his fist on the table hard enough to knock over a goblet. A servant immediately rushes out of the shadows to mop up the spilt wine.

"She is mine now, is she not?" the prince replies. His voice is even but his eyes are lowered and do not meet his father's. "I will need to learn myself. Breaking spirits, as you say."

It is subtle, but I hear the low undercurrent of sarcasm in his voice. My eyebrows furrow.

"Hm," the king grunts and sits back. "Very well."

"You are most gracious, my king."

The prince stands up, his chair scraping behind him, and bows low.

"Miss Shivani," he addresses me coldly and still refuses to look at me as though I am beneath him. "Come with me."

His hand shoots out and grabs me by the upper arm, yanking me up. I squeak in surprise. His iron grip is painful and now we are standing, I realise how much broader and taller he is than me. Dread floods my body.

"Quiet," he orders before dragging me away from the table. The servants part for us as he marches me to the door. I recognise Inez among them. She breaks away from the group and scurries after us.

"Get your hands off me!" I claw at the prince's hand but he squeezes hard enough to leave bruises. He pulls me through the corridor until we reach the door to my bedchambers. Terror seizes me and I lash out with my whole body, desperately trying to free myself from his grip like a wild animal caught in a trap. I sink my teeth into his forearm but the prince pays me no mind.

He opens the door easily with one hand

and flings me into the room. I spin, teeth bared and ready to fight. The prince stands in the doorway and, for the first time, his eyes meet mine. He opens his mouth to say something but I do not give him a chance.

"If you touch me, I will kill you," I snarl.

He closes his mouth and regards me for a moment. I stare back, eyes wild and chest heaving. Blood trickles down his arm from where I bit him and I can taste the tang of blood on my tongue.

"Yes," he replies eventually, his voice calm. "I believe you would."

I remain tense and ready to pounce as soon as he makes any movement towards me. But he does not. Instead, he dips his head.

"Goodnight, Miss Shivani," he says and then he is gone.

CHAPTER 8

My food is laced with drugs.

Every day, my ophid grows more and more lethargic. Sleep eludes me. I lay awake each night, taut with fear of an attack from the prince or the king. Or that my ophid will wither away from underuse. The magic I usually feel so strongly thrumming beneath the surface of my skin has gone nearly silent. I weep for hours, unable to do anything about it. It is not only a strength I have lost but a connection. To my aunt and my mother and my identity. It has been ripped from me. I am a witch with no witchcraft.

Crocas can outrun any other animal in the swamp, including people. Their legs are short compared to their scaly bodies, more suited to swimming in the thick swamp water. But on land, they are deceptively quick, patiently waiting for their moment to strike. In order to tame them, the croca shepherds clip a muscle at the back of their legs. Not deep enough to cripple them completely, but enough that they cannot run.

I wonder if any of them feel as I do now.
Clipped.

The maids continue to visit each morning, although they rarely speak to me. Inez brings breakfast trays filled with soft, fresh bread, salted butter, and mounds of cooked eggs. Hot tea is routinely brought throughout the day, served in delicate ceramic mugs and accompanied by bowls filled with sugar cubes. I eye them warily and yearn for the spiced cinnamon tea Aunt Meena used to make for me whenever I was stressed over my studies.

My heart aches, and hot tears bubble to the surface whenever I think of her. I dream of her library and the warm glow of her au'mana and the smell of the books. I miss drawing with her, scraping together materials to make paint, and creating art she would proudly display on the walls of her home.

I miss her, but I refuse to grieve for her. Grieving means she is lost to me, but I will get her back.

I draw my knees up to my chest and bury my face in my arms, refusing to eat the food the maids bring to me. I hope I can outlast the hunger until the drugs wear off and my au'mana returns to me. Maybe then I have a chance at escape.

After a few days, I begin to feel dizzy when I stand and my stomach cramps painfully. I attempt to get out of bed but my legs buckle beneath me, and I crumble to the floor like a piece of flimsy paper. Inez catches me before I hit the ground, her arms strong but her grip soft, and she places me back into bed.

"Please, Miss Shivani," she begs me. "You are killing yourself."

I rub my tired eyes. My limbs are as heavy as lead, and I struggle to find the energy to fight anymore. Inez glances at the rest of the maids as they peer at me with curious eyes and shoos them away. Once we are alone, she sits on the stool beside my bed.

"I know you do not trust the food," she whispers, sitting me upright against the pillows. "But it does not come from the king. I can promise you that."

"It is laced," I croak back, insistent. Tears spill down my face, but I do not have the energy to brush them away. "My ophid is…it does not work. Something is dulling it. It must be the food."

Inez picks at her nails, looking at me with worry in her eyes.

"I am sorry, miss. I do not know the intricacies of witchcraft," she says before clasping my hand. "But the food is not being tampered with. Please, just…just eat."

I eye the tray of breakfast food.

"How will you fight when you have no energy?" Inez nudges the tray closer to me with an encouraging smile. I search her eyes carefully. There is no malice there. Despite myself, I give a small smile back and take a bite of the bread roll.

As I start and end each day with a full stomach, I find my old energy returning. But my au'mana remains frustratingly out of reach. I inspect each meal thoroughly, turning over each bit of food and holding it in my mouth for discrepancies in taste before I swallow. But I am either being incredibly well deceived, or Inez is right, and the food is not spiked. Both possibilities send my mind whirring as I try to understand what is blocking my magic from me. If I can just figure it out, I can break through this castle and find my freedom again.

Regardless, I find myself sleeping better as I recover. Several days cycle on, and the threat of a sudden attack in my bedchamber wanes in my mind. I am still caged, but I am fed and—for the next six months—safe. I picture an hourglass over my head, the grains of sand trickling slowly through until my six months is up. I can escape before then. I can return to my Aunt.

But something else gnaws at me, which I had not considered. The isolation.

I am not allowed outside of my bedchambers, and it is not long before I begin to feel the first stirrings of a mad mind. I am restless. Confined. Inez is the only person I see who speaks to me. The others do not even make eye contact. Perhaps out of fear of the king. Perhaps because it is not worth getting to know a condemned woman.

My sleep becomes fitful again. I am reduced to thinking out loud during the long hours between Inez's visits. There are not even books in the room. I scour every inch of my chambers, Morraine's name scratched into my mind like the wood of the bed.

The next time Inez visits, she finds me pacing back and forth, muttering to myself.

"Miss?" She places the lunch tray down slowly as though dealing with an erratic animal. "Are you quite alright?"

"No, Inez, I am not," I say. I stop pacing to turn and look at her. I am rife with agitation and unable to stay still. Instead, I hop from one foot to the other. "I need to leave this room. I am…" I begin to pace again. "I am losing my mind."

Inez fidgets with her apron.

"Well…the king is not here…"

I brighten at her words.

"He is not?"

"His Highness left on a political trip of some sort. To Swordstead."

I am reminded of the fruits I saw during my first and only dinner with the king. I wonder what this means for Mossgarde. Worse, will this trip strengthen the king's position? I push this to the side for the moment and force myself to focus on the now.

"So, I am free to move about the castle?" I ask Inez.

"The guards will report on your movements." She shakes her head. "They will tell the king you have left your chambers."

"This is ridiculous. How am I to break the curse if I cannot even leave my room?" I huff, but the king's absence has emboldened me. I tap my finger off my chin, thinking. "Let me help you."

"Help me, miss?" Inez blinks at me.

"Allow me to come with you and help you with your tasks for the day," I explain. "I am sure you have many and…and I would be glad to be of help. It would mean I can leave this wretched room, and all the guards will see is a common girl doing servant work."

I watch the thoughts churning in Inez's mind as she casts her eyes downwards.

"Surely not all the maidens in the room were forced to remain here?"

"Well, no. They were not. But they also did not bite the prince." Inez sighs. "Very well. Perhaps you can help the kitchen staff with preparing dinner for this evening."

"I would be happy to!" I exclaim, elated at the chance of leaving these four walls. The more I learn about the layout of the castle, the more chance I have for escape.

I follow Inez out of my chambers. A guard is posted in the hall outside, standing to attention. He gives us a sharp look.

"She will be assisting us in the kitchen today," Inez tells him with a firmness I have not heard from her before. "So she may better serve the prince during her time here."

The guard gives us a long look but eventually nods. We scurry away.

The kitchen is one floor down, at the end of a set of narrow steps. Inez explains the servants rarely use these pathways as the castle is riddled with tunnels that make getting around much more efficient.

The kitchen is large, and I am surprised to see it is actually one of several kitchens, each joined and in charge of a different meal. It is full of staff, and they buzz around like the insects above the swamp water—organised but swift. I shrink back, slightly overwhelmed.

"Come." Inez pulls me gently by the arm. "Meet some of the staff."

She takes me to an adjacent room where the sweet smell of sugar hangs in the air. Chefs are lined across the counter, working in tandem. In one section, they create delicate-looking pastries. In another, others move fast to transform sugared fruit into decorative pieces. I stand in awe of them.

"This is Vanya," Inez introduces a tall, imposing woman with powdered sugar on her cheek. She regards me warily.

"It is so nice to meet you." I incline my

head. "My name is Shivani, I…"

I glance at Inez for reassurance and she smiles encouragingly.

"I would like to help today if I can," I finish, my voice wavering.

"Have you any kitchen experience?" Vanya asks. She frowns deeply, looking unimpressed.

"Uh…" I step forward as another chef comes barrelling behind me with a large casket of something thick and pink. "I have helped my aunt cook."

Truthfully, we have not cooked together in many years. When I was young, food was plentiful in Mossgarde and Aunt Meena taught me recipes from her birth town, Caldercruix. But now, most people survived on whatever they could find, oftentimes the fruit from low-hanging trees or edible reeds. I think of the food I have eaten so far in the castle and wince.

"But I have not had much experience in cooking the kind of food served here," I clarify before swallowing hard at the sight of Vanya's face.

"Is our food not good enough?" she thunders.

"N-Not at all," I stammer, wishing desperately that I could fall into a hole in the ground. Most who know me would not describe me as a timid person, but Vanya makes me feel as though I am being scolded by my mother.

"Vanya," Inez gently interrupts. "Shivani is a Never…"

Her eyes flicker to me briefly.

"She was volunteered here. For the curse," she finishes eventually. Vanya's face immediately softens.

"She is not the werewolf noble?"

I look between the two of them, confused.

"What werewolf noble?" I ask.

"No, she is from Mossgarde," Inez continues, looking as confused me. "Her father… put her forward."

"I see," Vanya says quietly. The pity is unbearable and shame burns my cheeks. "And you wish to…assist us?"

"Yes. Please. I cannot stay in my chambers any longer." The truth slips out of me, either through the heat of the kitchen or the relentless gaze of Vanya. She stares at me a moment longer before raising her hands. She claps once, sharply. The rest of the kitchen staff stop immediately.

"Eliza! William!" Vanya barks. Two young servants rush over. "Miss Shivani will be assisting us today. Please show her where to clean up."

Without another glance, Vanya turns back to her task. Her fingers nimbly arrange small pastries with snowberries buried inside. I let Eliza and Willian lead me to a large sink where we can wash our hands with chilly water and plain soap.

"My apologies, but I do not have much experience," I admit to them as we wash the suds off our fingers. "The food my Aunt taught me to cook is quite different to here."

"Do not fret, miss," Eliza tells me. Her smile is bright and earnest. There is a small gap between her front teeth, endearing me immediately. There is a sudden thickness in my throat at knowing she has spent her whole life in this castle. "Vanya will teach you well. She may look mean, but...well, you will see."

We meet Vanya at the pastry station, where she assigns us our tasks. I am set to kneading and rolling the dough into layers so thin you can almost see through them. I tear the dough the first several times and wipe the sweat from my brow irritably, but Eliza is right—Vanya is surprisingly patient with me. Soon, I roll the dough with ease and pass it on to the next station.

Vanya does not speak much as we work. Her face remains pinched with concentration and I enjoy the quiet between us. The kitchen is alive with more people than I have seen in weeks. The time goes by quickly until dinner is served to the prince in the king's absence.

Servants cart away lines of food the staff worked throughout the day to produce, moving in organised waves until the kitchen is empty. Only then do we sit to eat ourselves.

Vanya dishes out small plates of the

dinner we made. We dine on slow-cooked croca and roasted lard potatoes, perching on stools and balancing our plates on our laps. I look around at everyone laughing and eating and trading gossip. I find myself on the brink of tears but keep them at bay. I turn to Vanya instead.

"Thank you for allowing me in here today," I tell her. "It has been a welcome distraction indeed."

"I am glad of it," she replies simply.

"We have enjoyed your company, miss," Eliza pipes up, her cheeks full of potatoes.

"As I have enjoyed yours. It is...well, I always preferred the company of books to people, but I suppose we all need some connection. And I..." To my horror, my voice begins to break. My vision blurs with tears.

"It is alright, miss." Eliza pats the back of my hand. "You have a heavy burden on your head."

"Exactly," William chimes in. "The curse is monstrous. But if anyone can break it, it will be you. I am sure of it."

At the edge of my vision, I catch Vanya rolling her eyes but I say nothing. I smile at William and his young optimism.

"Thank you."

"I am curious, though, Miss Shivani." We turn to look at Vanya as she mops up the last of her gravy. "What food *can* you cook?"

I laugh and eye her mischievously.

"Would you like me to show you?" I ask.

She seems taken aback for a moment, her lips parting before giving me a small smile.

"Absolutely."

I search the vast cupboards for any familiar ingredients and settle on a few spices as well as a bag of lentils. Vanya watches me curiously as I work, keen-eyed. I can see her absorbing everything. She stands next to me at the counter with her own set of identical ingredients and copies my movements.

"There is a tale my Aunt used to tell me when we would cook together," I say, grinding the lentils using a smooth rock. "It is said that witches used to brew potions with magical properties."

Vanya nods eagerly.

"I have heard this," she says. "Potions with strange ingredients."

I smile coyly and wag a finger.

"Ah! But it is only a rumour," I correct her and begin chopping garlic into small chunks. Vanya follows me closely, although her eyebrows raise at this new information.

"It is not true?"

"A complete falsehood," I confirm. "It is sirens who are able to create liquid magic. Brewed and stewed in large pots before they carefully ladle it into glass bottles."

Vanya chops her garlic expertly, her knife gliding through the root. Her eyes are on the chopping board, but her face is turned slightly towards me, enraptured.

"One day, a witch came across one of these glass bottles. It was half-buried in the sand at an isolated beach with no footprints. When she picked it up, she saw it was empty. But there was something…distinct about it. A ringing in her ears, soft and sweet. And then she heard a voice from the sea."

Vanya stops chopping to listen.

"It calls out to her. A greeting, the witch thinks, but she cannot quite hear. Slowly… curiously…she walks over to the water. There, amongst the gentle waves of the sea, a head bobs above the surface. Almost like a human, but not quite. Green-skinned and scaly. The witch is at the edge of the land, and the water is lapping at her ankles. She holds the empty bottle in her hand, and she can still hear the ringing in her ears. So beautiful. So tempting. The person in the water smiles at her and says—"

"Miss Shivani!"

We are broken from our conversation by Inez rushing into the kitchen. Vanya jumps out of her skin and nearly drops her knife.

"Inez!" I put a hand to my thumping heart.

"My apologies." She gives a hurried curtsy. "The guards are due their kitchen inspection. You will need to return to your chambers immediately. The more of them we lie to, the more likely they are to inform the king."

My mouth dries at the mention of the king. I nod numbly.

"You are right," I say. I incline my head to Vanya, who has straightened back to her usual self. "I will send Inez a note with the recipe. I hope to see you again soon."

"As do I, Miss Shivani," she replies, but there is a grave set to her mouth, which makes me feel as though she does not believe she will.

CHAPTER 9

Month Two

Morraine echoes in my mind relentlessly. She had worked at the public house two years ago, serving patrons. We often crossed paths late at night. Me, on my way home from studying and her, leaving a long shift. We exchanged nothing for than polite nods and an occasional 'goodnight.' We were not friends, nor even acquaintances, but I knew her still. I recognised her laugh when it rang through the open windows. I can picture her weary smile at the end of the night.

Morraine's father had passed nearly ten years ago, leaving her with an elderly mother and two younger siblings. More hungry mouths than her wage could feed. She may break the curse, or she may not—her family would be cared for either way.

And now, all that remains is a small

scratch in a prison high above the trees. The bedchamber has been cleaned, sanitised of any remnants of the maidens before me. Except one inch that Morraine claimed for herself.

I spend two full days scouring every crevice of my chambers, looking for any other signs of the Never Queens before I find something. Etched under the drawer of the vanity table are the words *break the magic.*

Lying on my back, looking up at the message, I run a finger across the text. It is difficult to tell with words etched into metal and wood, but the handwriting seems different. Another Never Queen, perhaps. I stare at the word *magic*. Why not curse?

A knock at the door interrupts me. I scramble up, closing the vanity table just as Inez enters.

"My sincere apologies, Miss Shivani," she says quietly. The tone of her voice warns me she is not being overly polite, but she is genuinely sorry for something. A sense of dread creeps over me as she hands me a letter on a silver tray. I pick it up with shaking hands and read it as she looks on wordlessly. Fear blooms in my chest.

"This is for tonight?" I ask, but I already know the answer. Inez lowers her eyes and nods. "But I thought the king was in Swordstead?"

"A storm in the north pulled him back, miss." Her voice is hushed, as though speaking at a funeral. "He arrived last night and will set out again once the storm has passed."

I take a moment to absorb this before I tear the paper into tiny chunks. They flutter onto the carpet, silent.

"Leave, please," I tell her softly. "I do not wish for dinner. I need to be alone."

When the king comes for me, is left unspoken but known between us. How many of the Never Queens have received a similar letter?

"Yes, miss." Inez inclines her head but her eyebrows are knitted together in concern. As she leaves, my decision is solidified. I know what I must do.

Not long after I had started eating again and regained some clarity, I searched my chambers for anything I might use for escape. Now, I commit my list of escape items to memory and rush to the wardrobe. A bundle of clothes sit tucked into the back where I first left them. I quickly pull off my impractical gown and take thick boots and dark riding trousers from the wardrobe. I twist my long hair into a braid, pulling it away from my face. Without dinner arriving, I sit by the window and wait for the sun to set. My leg shakes, and I pick at my nails while I watch it dip below the treeline. Once the sky turns a deep navy blue, I know it is time for me to go.

I blow out the candle next to my bed, plunging my chambers into darkness. I open the window fully, pulling it back as far as it will go so I can see the wide windowsill sitting beneath it outside. The sill leads around the castle as a ledge and, as far as I can judge, it has a point where there is a gap of only a few feet between it and the nearest tree. The tree itself has not yet been trimmed, so the branches extend over the castle walls. After watching the guards for several weeks, I have noticed they patrol infrequently and with little care. I assume they are unconcerned that anyone can scale the stilts to reach the castle grounds. But it works in my favour.

I have spent every night in this room staring at both the tree and the ledge. My mind had flopped indecisively between whether either of them would support my weight or not. Especially the branches of the tree, which I will need to leap onto. Initially, I had dismissed the plan as too dangerous. But now, after the summon from the king to visit his chambers tonight…No. This is the only plan I have. I cannot leave through my door, so I will need to leave through the window.

I glance one last time at the torn paper on the carpet. My chest constricts. I turn away, swinging the window open and climbing out. Cautiously, I test the strength of the ledge by placing one foot on it and pressing down. When it does not immediately crumble, I pull the rest of my body through and clamber upright, facing inside. I grip the window tightly. With a rush,

I realise...I am *out*. I breathe in fresh air for the first time in weeks, filling my lungs with the sweet scent of the trees. Adrenaline pumps through my body and roars in my ears. The chill of the evening air nips at the exposed skin on my neck and hands, but I can barely feel it.

Slowly, I begin to slide each foot across the ledge. My fingers grip the small grooves in the wall in front of me. I press myself as closely as possible against the brick until it digs into my chest and scrapes across my thighs as I move. I hear the clink of the guard's armour some distance away. A thrill erupts in my chest at defying them without them even seeing me.

My body thrums with fear and elation. The muscles in my back twist—no, just one muscle. My ophid is responding to me. I inhale sharply and squeeze myself against the brick. Au'mana rushes through my body, up to the tips of my fingers and warms me from the inside. Tears spring up in the corners of my eyes.

My witchcraft has returned to me.

Caught up in the joy, I close my eyes and reach out to it. As I do, my balance skews. My foot slips. My eyes snap open as I steady myself, but a piece of the ledge falls from underfoot.

"Fuck!" I exhale quietly. I regain my balance quickly, pulling myself up and staying stock still. I press my forehead against the wall and take deep, slow breaths. The crumbling brick from the ledge skitters down, making an avalanche of noise against the silence of the night.

I do not move, waiting for one of the guards to notice me. My adrenaline fights against my fear of either falling to my death or of being caught, and I clench my teeth to stop them from chattering.

After several minutes, when I am almost certain I am safe from the watchful gaze of the guards, I summon the courage to continue across the ledge. I desperately want to reach out to my au'mana, but I cannot focus on both my magic and keeping my balance at the same time. Reluctantly, I push it to the back of my mind. I reassure myself that once I am safely on the tree, I will feel my au'mana again. I move at a much slower pace and test each step before fully committing.

I can do this, I think to myself, only half-believing it. *Just a few more steps.*

I reach the end of the ledge and carefully turn so I face outwards. The first thing I notice is the sheer drop to the ground below, and my body seizes up. Solid red brick lines the platform the castle is built upon. I quickly avert my eyes upwards.

"Saints..." I mutter. I slowly inhale through my nose to steady the roil within me and focus on the pinprick stars. I stand flat against the wall for a while longer until the tremor leaves my limbs, and I am brave enough to lower my eyes.

I catch sight of the tree. It feels much further away than it had from my window. Doubt pricks at the corners of my mind, threatening to invade. The branches are thinner than I had thought. Visions of falling through the tree plague me. My imagination goes into overdrive, showing me snap every branch as I plummet to my death.

I fight against a wave of panic, but it is like swimming against the current. My head whips from side to side as I assess my options. I cannot go any further from my chambers as the ledge has ended. If I turn and make my way back to my room, I resign myself to the king tonight. That is *not* something I am willing to do. I glance down. I am too high from the grounds to somehow dangle myself off the ledge and drop down. At the very least, I would break my legs, rendering me helpless while I waited for the guards to find me. The king would either follow through on his plans for me tonight or spike my head for trying to flee.

It must be the tree. I rationalise it in my desperate brain. Even if the branch breaks, it will slow my fall at least. I spy a slightly thicker branch which may be able to hold me. I turn my body slightly, aiming for that one. I can only hope the noise of the break will not alert the guards, and I can climb to the safety of the swamp unnoticed.

With no other option, I prepare myself. I bend my knees an inch and tense every muscle in my legs like a coiled spring. *It is either jump or...*I close my eyes briefly and think about the summons from the king. About what he expects from me tonight. I shake my head. No, this is the only way. I lick my lips nervously and get ready to leap.

"What in Saint's name?"

I yelp at the sudden voice from below me, already half off the ledge. I try to pull back, but it is too late, and the momentum carries me through. I spin as I fall, desperately grabbing for the ledge as the earth falls away from my feet. I hook a few fingers just in time and slam against the wall, knocking the wind from my lungs.

"Miss Shivani! What are you doing up there?" the voice calls up at me in a hushed tone laced with shock.

I dangle against the wall, my fingertips the only thing holding me up. I try to pull myself up, but my fingers are numb from the cold, and I do not have enough grip. One of my fingers slips.

I cry out, my shoulder straining. On instinct, I reach out for my au'mana, but it is pent-up and directionless. The purple glow creeps out, emanating from my body. I draw it back before I am spotted by another guard. I desperately kick my legs to try and find a foothold, but there is only air.

"No!" I gasp as panic floods my brain. My

fingers lose their grip, sliding helplessly towards the edge.

I am going to die. This is it.

I squeeze my eyes shut, tears brimming and send a prayer to Aunt Meena. The hard ledge slips out from under my fingertips.

My stomach lurches. The cold air whips past me. I have only a moment to understand I am hurtling towards the end of my life.

CHAPTER 10

"Oof!"

I land hard, but not as hard as expected. I automatically curl up into a defensive ball and find myself pressing into something firm and warm.

"Miss Shivani?"

I open one cautious eye. The prince stares down at me closely. His eyebrows are somewhere up near his hairline. The night sky is above him, pitch black except for the stars scattered across it like splattered paint.

"Am I dead?" I whisper.

The prince cocks his head.

"No…" He frowns. "You fell."

He lowers me to the ground. I realise he has caught me and had been holding me up in his arms. The information churns slowly, like treacle, in my mind. I open my mouth but find myself unable to speak. I shiver, ice cold. My body jerks erratically, and my teeth chatter.

"I-I…" I try to say something, but my

mind is empty, like a plug has been pulled and all my thoughts have drained away.

"You are in shock," he tells me, but I am not quite able to understand what he means. He sounds far away even though I know he is right next to me. I stare past his head, my mouth open. "Miss Shivani?"

"Huh?"

"We need to get you inside before a guard sees you." He wraps something thick and warm around my shoulders. I nod numbly before the words sink in.

"No!" I cry, and he claps a large hand over my mouth. I try to twist my face away, but his other arm wraps around my upper back, and he pulls me towards him, holding me tight. His eyes are wide and bore into me as he shakes his head. *Quiet*, his eyes scream.

A guard walks nearby, whistling loudly. He is mere meters away, but we are hidden in the deep shadow of the tree. The guard sighs heavily, looking bored. The prince's eyes dart to the side as we listen and stay completely still. After a moment, the guard passes. The prince releases me with a long exhale.

"We need to get inside now," he tells me firmly, but before he can move me, I burst into tears.

I press my hand to my mouth to stifle the noise, but my tears flow freely. I sink to my knees.

"Miss Shivani." The prince knees in front

of me, alarmed. I remove my hand and suck in deep breaths, trying to steady my voice.

"The-the king, he w-wants to...he s-summoned me..." I force the words out in a low whisper. My body heaves with sobs, and I feel as though I may pass out. I blink rapidly to try and clear the spots in my vision.

The prince grabs my hands and levels his eyes with mine. He breathes in deeply through his nose. Instinctively, I match him. When he breathes out in one steady exhale through his mouth, I do the same. My heart begins to slow, and my vision clears. We breathe in tandem, never breaking eye contact until I can speak clearly again.

"The king summoned me to his chambers tonight." I swallow the lump in my throat and look away.

The prince does not respond, his face plain but for the flutter of a muscle in his jaw.

"His letter said if you would not step up, he would do so instead," I finish. Another sob threatens to break in my chest, but I hold it back. "I cannot go back there. I cannot do it. I would rather die."

The prince glances up at the ledge where I had been hanging from.

"Yes," is all he says and then he is quiet for a moment.

I shiver in the cool air and pull the blanket closer around my shoulders. Briefly, I wonder what he is doing out here, but the thought is cut off when he stands abruptly. He offers a hand. I refuse it and remain on the ground. He does not withdraw.

"I am afraid I cannot help free you," the prince says. There is sincere regret in his voice, which surprises me. "But I can prevent my father from…"

He does not seem capable of saying the words. His lips are drawn into a thin line.

"If you stay in my chambers occasionally, he will believe the illusion. That I have…taken you," he tells me. He looks slightly sick. "He will not touch you."

"How do you know this?"

The prince gives a wry smile.

"Because he will not touch another man's property," he replies before looking away. "And I have done it before."

White-hot anger threatens to spark, but my body is too weary to fan the flames.

"The Never Queens?"

He nods grimly.

"And what exactly do you mean by 'stay in your chambers?'"

"Sleep there," he says, his voice even.

"In your bed?"

"No. There is an adjoining room with your own bed."

I regard the prince as he towers above me. His hand is still stuck out in front of him, offering to help me up. I glance up at the window to my chambers. I know this is my only choice but I do not know whether I trust the prince. Evil comes in many forms, and not all of them are obvious. After a moment of contemplation, I reach up and take his hand. His grip is firm as he hauls me to my feet.

"We must make haste," he says, looking pointedly at where the guard had been patrolling. "We have tarried long enough."

We head away from the castle walls and back to my prison.

The prince bobs and weaves through different routes, avoiding the guards. I try to pay attention and store the information for later, but exhaustion crawls up my body, slowing me. My limbs are sluggish and heavy. I blink several times in an attempt to clear my mind—all I earn is a worried glance from the prince.

He leads us to an unremarkable wall tucked into a back corner of the castle grounds. I watch him spread his hands and run them across the brick before pressing on one of them.

Click.

The wall comes alive, a door appearing in the brick and swinging open. My eyebrows shoot up, and I take a half-step back.

"How?" I whisper.

The prince looks back at me and jerks his head towards the door.

"We can avoid most of the guards this

way," he says before heading in. After a moment of hesitation, I follow him.

The secret corridor is dim, lined only with a few low-burning torches. The walls are dusty, and I suppress a sneeze as I step inside. The silhouette of the prince as he walks in front of me is outlined in orange by the torches. He presses on silently.

As we reach the end, he pushes open the door with caution.

After a peek through, he gestures at me to follow. He closes the door behind us—which I realise is disguised as a large portrait of the king—and I see we are outside his bedchambers.

"Quickly," he whispers.

"Halt!"

We freeze as a guard comes charging down the corridor. He gives a slight bow to the prince before turning to me.

"You were meant to be in your chambers." He scowls. "The king has summoned you. I know the maid delivered the note."

He makes to grab me but the prince's hand shoots out and grabs his arm first.

"Miss Shivani is busy with me tonight," the prince speaks, voice low. He throws the guard's arm back at him. "You may tell the king that."

The guard glances between us before giving a proper bow.

"Yes, Your Highness," he says, looking

contrite, before darting away. I do not breathe even as the sound of his armour fades away.

The prince swiftly opens the door, and we hurry inside, slamming it behind us. He begins to say something, but I am distracted by the luxury of his chambers.

It is almost a self-contained home by itself. There are a few doors leading off into what I assume to be washrooms. One of them is open to reveal a large closet lined with various royal clothing. A twinkling chandelier hangs in the centre of an ornately carved ceiling. One wall is dominated entirely by a large, red-brick hearth. It is still lit, ensuring the room is thoroughly heated. The glow of the fire bathes over me and sets me somewhat at ease. I may not have had any of the other comforts the castle offers me, but sitting in front of a warm hearth is a familiar thing.

"Miss Shivani?" the prince's voice eventually penetrates my thoughts. I blink and turn to him.

"Pardon?"

"I was saying I shall have the maids fetch you hot tea with sugar. And some brandy from my stores. I have found it helps during..." He stutters to a halt and coughs uncomfortably. "Stressful times."

I press my back against the door, eyeing him warily.

"You do not appear to agree with your

father," I say. He cocks an eyebrow, waiting for me to continue. "So why did you act such a bastard at our dinner?"

His eyes grow large before his face breaks into a wide grin. It is as though I see his real face then. A break in the clouds when the sun shines through. He lets out a bark of laughter.

"My apologies," he says. "I did not trust you at first."

I squint at him, incredulous.

"*You* did not trust *me*?" I screech and spread my hands. "What could I possibly have done when I have not even *met* you before?"

"The king has spies," he says plainly. He clasps his hands behind his back, and his face turns sombre once again. My hands drop to my sides, a short, humourless laugh escaping my throat at the absurdity.

"You believed me a spy. Me. Do I truly look like a spy?"

"If spies were obvious, they would not make very good spies, would they?" the prince snaps, his veneer fracturing for a second before he composes himself again.

"Very well, I will concede to that," I reply. He tilts his chin up, appeased. "So, your heartless, haughty attitude was an illusion? For the king?"

He bristles at my description but ignores it.

"Yes."

"And now you do not think I am a spy?"

"No."

I wait for him to elaborate, but he does not, his jaw clenched tight.

"Are you going to tell the king? About..." I gesture vaguely outside. His face softens.

"No. I will not tell my father a word."

A silence falls between us. I am not quite sure I believe him yet, but I desperately want to. I need an ally. And if he is correct and our plan works, I will remain safe from the king. For now.

"I think it has been a long night," he says, breaking the silence. "I have lavender tonic in my drawer if you require a sleep aid. But I understand if you would rather stay of sound mind."

He gestures to one of the doors.

"The adjoining room is through there. I will have the maids bring your night clothes." He pauses. "The door locks from the inside."

My shoulders sag with relief at this peace of mind. I incline my head gratefully at the prince.

"My thanks," I say and hurriedly make my way over.

"Goodnight, Miss Shivani," he says as I close the door. I pause a moment before responding.

"Goodnight, Your Highness."

I quietly close the door and lock it firmly. I am still awake when the maids bring me hot tea and a neat pile of night clothes. Once changed, I sit on the large bed and sip at the scalding liquid. Every so often, I glance at the lock on the door. It is solid and metal, sliding into place with a loud *thunk*. It would be difficult indeed to break.

For the first night in weeks, I sleep soundly.

CHAPTER 11

I wake to the sun filtering through an open window and the birds singing sweetly to each other outside. I groggily open my eyes, my head foggy with sleep. My cheek presses against a warm pillow. A blanket is drawn high up to my neck. I am in a warm cocoon of my own making. But the room is not familiar.

I bolt upright. I blink several times and rub the sleep away. Scanning the room, I see it is mostly bare except for a solitary wardrobe and the bed I am lying on. In fragments, the night before returns to me. I am in the room adjacent to the prince's chambers. My empty teacup and a mound of last night's clothes remain untouched on the floor. The lock is secure. I sink back against the pillows with a sigh.

I wonder if the prince truly meant what he said last night or if it was a cruel way to drag out my punishment. Did he really intend to keep such a secret from his father? I think of my own father and the secrets I keep from him. Sometimes to make my life easier but, more often, because I do not trust him with even an ounce of information.

Slowly, I creep out of bed and press my ear to the door. There is silence on the other side, except for the tell-tale crackle of the hearth. I stand there a moment, chewing the inside of my cheek, before I take a breath and turn the handle.

"Good morrow, Miss Shivani," the prince greets me from one of the large sofas in front of the hearth. He closes his book and places it on a side table.

He is not wearing his formal attire, instead wearing a loose white shirt and slim black trousers. The intimacy of seeing him in clothes he casually wears when no one else is around makes an unfamiliar heat crawl up my neck. My mind forces me to take note of his chestnut hair, tousled from sleep. I clear my throat awkwardly.

"Good morrow, Your Highness," I reply with a small curtsy. I linger in the doorway, hesitant.

"Please, join me for breakfast." He gestures at the empty seats. I oblige and walk stiffly over before perching on the edge of a plush armchair.

The table in front of the hearth is full of breakfast foods—fresh bread, unsalted butter, a cluster of pond apples and blue grapes. I politely pluck a single grape.

"Are you rested?" he asks, taking a sip of coffee. The aroma is strong but pleasant. I inhale deeply. He must notice my expression because he leans forward to pour me a cup.

"I am, Your Highness," I reply truthfully. The prince smiles, and his eyes meet mine. For the first time, I notice the colour of them. A clear grey, the colour of a stormy sky. Something thrums between us, and I catch my breath.

"Miss Shivani..." he says. His voice is low, and his eyes do not leave mine. He opens his mouth to continue but there is a knock at the door.

Our eye contact breaks, and the connection between us is severed. I blink, as if waking from a daydream. How odd.

"Come in," the prince calls. He sits back and upright as his royal posture returns. A guard steps in and bows briefly to the prince.

"The king requests Miss Shivani's presence for dinner this evening," he tells us. The prince's face is a mask. Except for the muscle bouncing at his jaw, which I am quickly coming to realise is his tell.

"Miss Shivani belongs to me," he grinds out. It is a sentence which would have angered me before but now it is a part of our plan. I nod agreeably.

"The king requests her presence," the guard repeats firmly. When the prince does not reply, he inclines his head and leaves.

I sit back heavily against the chair.

"What are we to do?"

The prince leans forward, his elbows propped on his knees, and runs his hands through his hair. I try to ignore the way it sticks up and begs for me to reach across and smooth it out for him. Saints, what has come over me? I quickly shoo the intrusive thought away.

"My apologies," he sighs. "I do not believe my father will bring you to harm. But he enjoys showing his power. He will likely taunt you and…other such things. But he will not touch you."

I nod slowly and think of Morraine.

"This has happened before."

"Not often, but yes. He will want to see you cowed himself, especially if I have snatched you away from him at the last moment."

The prince's face is smoothed into something neutral, verging on disdain. The way he speaks turns my stomach. I hope his contempt is for the king, not me.

"Very well." I stand, taking a fortifying breath. "I will survive through one dinner."

The prince stands as well, and we look at each other for a moment.

"Miss Shivani—"

"Thank you for your hospitality, Your Highness," I cut him off, curtsying. The prince may be my ally for now, but I would be a fool to put all my trust in one man. At any moment, he could reveal his true intentions. I do my best to ignore the way he looks at me. "I will return three nights a week, as per our agreement. I hope this is acceptable."

The prince closes his mouth and gives a curt nod.

"It is acceptable."

"My thanks." I hurry out of his chambers, feeling his eyes on me but not looking back.

* * *

I spend the day with Inez in my chambers, playing cards and drinking tea. We sit at the window and bask in the sun. I am unused to so much sunlight on my skin from the thick canopy of trees over Mossgarde. But when I turn my face to the warmth, so close to how my au'mana feels, it comforts me.

When I tell Inez I did not see the king last night, her eyes widen and she presses a hand to her chest in relief. I explain the prince came for me instead.

"Oh," she replies, blinking. "The prince requested you?"

"Yes," I lie, omitting the incident of my attempted escape.

"I did not receive a note to deliver," she muses and my heart skips.

"Um, yes, he came for me personally."

I turn away to stop my face from betraying me, and thankfully, Inez does not probe any further.

"Well, at least you avoided the king," she continues after taking a sip of her tea. "Hopefully, this storm passes soon."

She glances up, and her eyebrows furrow at the look on my face.

"What is it?"

"The king has requested me for dinner this evening."

Inez purses her lips and plays another card.

"Hm. He is likely displeased the prince claimed you at the last moment."

"What do you think he will do?" I ask. My pulse quickens despite Inez's casual tone. The prince seemed so sure the king would not come near me if he believed I was 'marked' by another man. I am not so sure.

"Nothing, miss," Inez replies with a reassuring smile. I chew at my bottom lip, unconvinced, and place a card on top of hers. "I would not like to speak out of turn of course—"

"I think we have both said enough traitorous things this morning alone."

"Still. My guess is he is using you to bait the prince into a reaction. He enjoys torturing the boy."

Inez tuts and shakes her head. With only the two of us in the room, she has become much freer with her thoughts, much to my delight.

"My advice, miss, is to keep your head down and not rise to the king's antagonising," she continues. "He thrives off the reaction he can pull from others. It is his favourite pastime. To act like a cat playing with its food."

I contemplate this quietly and draw a card from the deck.

* * *

When the sun starts to lower, Inez ushers me into the washroom so she can bathe and dress me. She works efficiently—after an hour, I am clean, creamed, and garbed in a deep red dress which skims the floor.

This gown is different from the rest. It is deceptively comfortable. There are tight, stretchy trousers hugging my legs under the skirt. Instead of the usual rigid corset bones, it is lined with a strange material mimicking the restrictive look but instead moves flexibly with my body. It lacks the long sleeves of the other gowns. Instead, the neckline reaches up high, leaving my shoulders bare. Jewels speckle the fabric in a scale-like pattern, shimmering in the light. I look at myself in the floor-length mirror, slowly turning.

"You do look beautiful," Inez compliments. She adjusts the pins holding up my hair. "This was one of the queen's favourite dresses."

"She had good taste." I smooth my hand over the garnet bodice. It is hard on the outside despite being soft on the inside.

"That she did." Inez moves to begin fussing over the few loose dark curls draped down the sides of my face. "She made it herself, in fact. Oh, a master seamstress she was. She used to say it was the dress she donned for war."

"War with whom?"

Inez looks at me pointedly in the mirror.

"Her husband, miss."

I slide my gaze back to the dress, viewing it in a new light. I feel the skirt and notice several pockets within the bunched fabric. They are big enough to hold knives. I wonder what assaults the hard bodice can withstand while protecting the wearer. The queen made this with a purpose.

"What was she like?" I enquire.

"Well..." Inez frowns, hesitation in her voice. "She—"

"The king is ready for you," a guard calls through the chamber door, followed by a loud thump against the wood. Inez takes a step back from me.

"You are ready, miss." She looks at me, admiring her handwork. "As you ever will be, anyway."

"Thank you, Inez." I turn to hug her fiercely. I wrap my arms around her and squeeze.

"Oh!" she gasps before laughing and squeezing me back. "You are most welcome, miss.

"Now!" The guard thumps harder. Inez jumps off me before spinning me around to face the door.

"Time for you to be off. Good luck."

I square my shoulders and, for the first time in my life, I pray to the Saints.

CHAPTER 12

The dining hall is darker than I remember it. Or maybe it is my mind, which is gloomy as I enter the room with my captor.

The king sits at the head of the table, but the prince is nowhere to be seen. I was hoping he would have been here for support or to present a united front. The sight of his empty chair makes my stomach sink. I glance around the room, but it is empty except for the servants waiting in the shadows. One of them I recognise from the kitchens, and they give me a subtle smile.

"How lovely of you to join me," the king bellows, grinning. He talks as though I have a choice in the matter and not as though he has taken all my choices from me. He has only said one thing to me and already my temper rises. I grind my teeth together, trying hard to focus on what Inez told me. *Do not rise to his antagonising*. With difficulty, I pinch the corners of my skirts and curtsy. I can play the cowed commoner for one evening.

"Thank you for the invitation, Your Highness," I say, keeping the venom out of my voice as much as possible. It seems to work—he gestures to the seat next to him. A servant darts out to pull the chair back for me. I incline my head in thanks to them, and their eyebrows shoot up as if shocked I had even looked at them. A flare of anger rises at their treatment, but I force it back down again. I uncurl my fists.

As soon as I am seated, I realise how uncomfortably close I am to the king. I find myself missing the prince's presence. He, at least, was able to act as a buffer between us. The king eyes me curiously.

"A fine dress," he comments. There is an unkind familiarity in his eyes like he has been reminded of something unpleasant. I shift uncomfortably under his gaze.

"Thank you, my king," I reply quietly. I wonder if wearing the dress of his late wife, whom he executed for cursing their son, was truly the best choice. Before I have time to defend myself, he moves on.

"So." He sits forward and picks up the gleaming cutlery. His knife is unsettlingly large. "How are you settling into our humble abode?"

I try to push the escape attempt out of my mind.

"Very well, Your Highness," I reply and

pick up my own knife and fork. He looks at me expectantly, and I realise I need to elaborate. "The, uh…facilities are very…magnificent."

"Indeed?" He chuckles at my obvious struggle with social niceties. "And my son? How are you finding him?"

He stabs his fork into a piece of meat as he speaks. I frown. How much does he know? His face gives nothing away.

"I…do not know him all that well, Your Highness," I reply hesitantly. "He only called on me last night."

"Is that right?" the king says evenly.

His expression is mild, but something simmers below the surface. Something I have seen in my father's face many times. Something I know well. A mixture of entitled rage and disdain. I choose to say nothing. I keep my eyes fixed on my plate, head slightly bowed.

"He took long enough to bed you, did he not?"

Silence.

"I suppose he has done well, as you appear to have learned your place after only one night with him." He laughs as though he has told an incredible joke. I press my lips together and desperately douse my anger.

"This meal is lovely, my king." I try to change the topic, taking an enthusiastic bite of my roasted rosemary sparrow. "Thank you again for the invitation."

"His mother was a bitch, do you know."

I choke on my sparrow, the meat lodging in my throat.

"I suppose the blame is on me for marrying for love instead of title," the king continues as though he does not notice my spluttering. "She was beautiful, of course. No doubt about it. But Saints! She was hard work."

He takes a large swig of his wine as I dislodge the sparrow and frantically blink away the tears springing to my eyes.

"I…" I cough, my throat burning. "I have not heard much of the queen, I admit."

The king snorts.

"A queen she was not." He raises his hand and snaps his fingers. The sound cracks through the room. At once, a servant appears with a jug of wine and refills his goblet. "In title, yes, due to me. But in every other way, she never stopped being a commoner."

I am vaguely aware of this. Aunt Meena never spoke of it, but I heard others in the village speak in hushed tones. It was a great tale of love that happened before I was born—the young, handsome king decided to forgo the many available heiresses in favour of a common girl in Mossgarde. At the time, it had been a great morale boost for the townsfolk. People believed perhaps any one of them would have a chance at riches and comfort someday.

The wedding itself was a grand affair

which some of the older members of Mossgarde still spoke about, albeit quietly and in private.

"That was the last time I used my heart to make a decision." The king chews, open-mouthed, and regards me. "What do you know of the curse?"

I shift uncomfortably in my seat.

"True love will break it, Your Highness."

"No, not that. The curse itself. What that *bitch*," he thumps a meaty fist off the table, rattling the plates and making me flinch, "did to my only heir."

He looks at me expectantly, lip curled. His eyes are ablaze.

"She cursed him out of spite, Your Highness," I recall what I have heard in the village and fight hard to keep the tremor out of my voice. He is even closer to me now, leaning forward with his hand still curled in a tight fist. I am painfully aware of how easily he could overpower me.

"Spite, yes!" He spits on the ground in disgust. "She was not just a commoner but a *monster*. Vindictive. What kind of mother curses her own son?"

He fires out each word with a terrifying poison that makes me want to recoil. I tremble with the effort of remaining composed and upright. Despite the tension in each muscle of my body, readying me to fight or flee, I refuse to cower. The role I had intended to play has evaporated under the heat of his anger.

Hold your tongue, Shivani.

I remain perfectly still, each muscle frozen in place. Eventually, the king sits back and uncurls his fist. He takes another messy drink of his wine. It leaks down the side of his mouth and leaves a blood-red trail from the corner of his lips into his fair beard.

"This is where you come in." The king flashes me an unsettling smile. I lower my eyes. "You and all the other volunteers."

Goosebumps spring up along the back of my neck and I can hear the blood rushing in my ears.

"To break the curse?" My voice wavers despite my best efforts.

The king gives a humourless laugh.

"Truth be told, I do not believe this curse can be broken."

The floor falls away from beneath me. The dress, which had been so comfortable before, becomes stifling.

"But..." My mind struggles to formulate the words. "You told us true love could break it. You said so on the day the queen died."

"Well, yes. Spirits were very low that day, you understand. Part of being a king is knowing what little white lies are necessary to keep the peace."

I gape at him.

"But why ask for volunteers? Why keep us

here?"

He looks at me as though I am stupid.

"She came from you. A commoner. I need to keep this village in check somehow and what could be a more *delicious* punishment than ensuring the rest of you common girls are pruned?"

The air leaves my lungs. I try to breathe but my vision tunnels, darkening at the edges. His words ring in my head like a high-pitched squeal.

"But…" I trail off, my mouth opening and closing.

I have been a naïve fool. The curse is unbreakable. We have been sent here to die, every one of us. I think of how my chambers are devoid of anything I could use to escape, even the shoddy ledge outside the window. Strategically placed to eliminate any chance of leaving. I think of the bloody chopping block in the village centre.

Nausea overcomes me, and I stand abruptly. The king looks up at me, curious but not alarmed.

"This is a death sentence," I croak. I place my hands flat on the table to steady myself. My legs are weak.

"Speak up, girl," the king replies with irritation. The sickness in my stomach curdles into rage.

"You…you…" I squeeze my eyes shut and

push back against the violent wrath hammering in my mind. My ophid is blazing and I desperately want to reach out to it. To raze this whole castle to the ground and the king with it.

"Go on." He sits back and raises his eyebrows, a smug smile on his face. "Spit it out."

I manage to pry my fingers open from where they had been balled into fists. They shake, but I stand firm. The guards ready themselves, and I know I have only one course of action.

"I will break it," I say.

"What?"

"I will break the curse."

Silence lays, thick as marsh water. The king throws back his head and laughs.

"You are most welcome to try! After all, each one before you has tried and now their pretty heads decorate the foundations of my castle."

I think about picking up my dinner plate and launching it at his face. I have bitten my tongue so often now my mouth tastes of blood. When I smile, it is murderous.

"I have four months. True love may not break it, but something will."

Aunt Meena taught me everything I know about the world and all the people who inhabit it. There is a limit on all magic. I can find the limit on whatever magic afflicts the prince.

"I admire your optimism," the king

replies, although his tone indicates the opposite. He gestures to the guards. "Let us see how you feel once you see this curse in person."

I swallow hard. The guards seize me, grabbing my upper arms.

"Wait—"

"Enjoy your night, Never Queen."

The guards drag me from the dining room. I struggle against them, but they hold firm, marching me down a set of narrow spiral stairs.

We reach a cold section of the castle. The rug fades into a tattered end, leaving bare brick, and the air is foul. The stairs fall into darkness with only a few lit torches on the wall. It is only when we are forced to descend them in single file that the guards let go of me.

I wrap my arms around myself to try and rub away the goosebumps springing up along my skin. I shiver against the cold. But also against the uneasy feeling I am being brought somewhere I am not meant to be.

We descend the steps slowly in the semi-darkness, unspeaking. The only thing breaking the silence is the occasional animalistic scream. It sounds both far away and far too close. It bounces off the walls, echoing around us. Despite the cold, sweat trickles down my back. There is a hard, metallic tang in my mouth from where I bit my tongue.

When we arrive at the bottom of the spiral staircase, the guards stop short. He holds up his torch, and I peek out from behind him. The dread slowly growing in my stomach transforms into fully-fledged terror.

The dungeon is lighter than the stairs, lined with several large torches. They cast an eerie orange glow across the room. More noticeable than that is the huge domed cage in the middle.

It takes up almost the entirety of the dungeon. It is made of thick, ugly metal bars running out from the brick floor and curving up to meet at a point. But it is what is inside the cage that turns my blood cold.

Its size is breathtaking, hunched over in its cage and nearly as wide. Dull scales coat its skin, interspersed with large bulbous boils, red and painful. It wields thick, sharp claws instead of hands, but the knuckles are twisted and knotted as though broken. A thick tail lined with spikes swirls behind it menacingly. Its face is warped unnaturally, as though it has been crudely carved from wet clay. Angry yellow eyes glower at us from behind the bars.

I try to take a step back, but I bump into the guard behind me.

"We shall see you in the morning, miss." He grins at me.

"No, please. Please do not leave me here."
Panic rises in my chest.

"Order of the king, miss." The other guard shrugs, and they both leave, slamming the door behind them.

    With a shuddering breath, I turn and face the Beast of Mossgarde.

CHAPTER 13

The beast screams and throws its body against the bars, slamming violently against the metal before bouncing back. It accompanies each body slam with a roar that goes straight through my body and freezes it in place.

Angry. Feral. *Hungry*. My breath quickens.

"What curse is this?" I whisper to myself, eyes fixed on the beast.

As I do so, it throws its head back and roars. Even that sounds twisted, like the screech of metal against metal.

I try opening the door but no matter how hard I pull, it is locked. I suppose it was built to keep the beast at bay, so I would have little chance of breaking through. Resigned, I find the least damp section of the brick floor and sit down. I draw my knees up to my chest and wait for the prince to turn back. I pray the bars hold.

The air is sour, and the beast's screams

are punctuated by a dripping dampness on the walls. I squint at the creature through the cage and notice marks on its back. It looks like a large tattoo with swirling black ink, but there is something else in the pattern.

A word in dragon text blazes between its shoulder blades.

I try to get a better glimpse of it, but the beast twists and turns in anger, thumping against the cage. I shiver and wrap my arms around my knees. Absently, I roll my tongue around my mouth to rid it of the metallic taste.

"What a horrid place to be," I say softly, half thinking out loud and half speaking to the animal in the cage.

It must hear me. Its head swivels to turn a blazing yellow glare onto me. For the first time, it ceases its relentless banging on the bars. But its mouth is still twisted into a snarl, teeth bared. I cock my head to the side, wondering if it can understand me.

"I thought my cage was bad, but I believe yours may be worse," I tell it, looking around. "And you were cursed at birth, so..." I chew the inside of my cheek, eyebrows furrowed. "How much of your life have you spent here?"

The beast gives a half-hearted roar. It bangs a twisted fist against the cage before slumping down, its back against the bars. Its thick tail flops to the side. The only thing I can hear is its ragged breathing, but I see the glow of its eyes staring at me.

We sit in silence for several minutes. I try to ignore the chill nipping at me and still the quiver in my hands. I am satisfied the bars will hold despite the brute strength of the beast. Eventually, in the silence, my eyelids grow heavy.

It has not made a noise in quite some time and the eerie light of its eyes is extinguished. If I could not see the silhouette of its hulking form laying slumped in the cage, I might think it is not even there. Is it asleep? *Does* it sleep?

I shift uncomfortably on the ground, my arms wrapped tight around my knees. I am struck by how much more nervous I was to sit across from the king than I am in the presence of this beast. At some point during the long night, I fall into a shallow sleep.

※ ※ ※

I awaken suddenly to a wet snapping. My head shoots up from where I had been resting it on my knees, and I squint blearily at the cage.

Snap.

This time it is followed by a strangled cry, distinctly human. I hastily get to my feet and inch closer to the cage. The orange glow of the torches bathes the beast in light, but...it is not a beast anymore. It is something between animal and man.

There is another painful snap and the

prince falls to his knees, hunched over. The bones in his back move and rearrange themselves as he cries out. His scales split to make way for the bloody human skin underneath. His inky black tattoo emerges underneath, and I realise the word in dragon text is hidden amongst the design. The large boils between his scales burst painfully. His face twists and contorts into something more human.

I rush to the bars of the cage, wrapping my hands around them.

"Your Highness?" I call. My voice is laced with worry. I have never seen such painful magic inflicted on another person before.

The prince does not, or cannot, reply. Instead, he sobs violently, his whole body shaking with the force of it. He curls into a ball on the ground.

"Move, please, miss."

I am startled back by a sudden voice behind me only to see several of the guards have reappeared. One of them jangles a set of heavy-looking keys. A burst of fury erupts in my chest.

"You!" I point at them. "You abandoned him! How could you leave him alone like this?"

The one with the keys shrugs.

"His condition is more beast than man," he replies evenly. "It does not make a difference."

"Does not make a...?" I stare at him, mouth open. "You heartless piece of swamp scum. You are the beast here!"

"Take it up with the king." The guard sneers before pushing past me. I resist the urge to punch the back of his head and let him open the cage.

The prince has not moved from where he is curled up in a tight ball. Two guards march over and haul him to his feet. He cries out in pain, but they ignore it.

"Careful!" I yell at them.

"Listen, miss," another guard rounds on me. "This is a regular occurrence around here, so do not get all high and mighty with us. The prince is fine, as he always has been."

"I did not realise she was so close to the prince," another guard pipes up, smirking. "One night with him, and she falls at his feet."

"Do not be absurd," I snap back. "Only a man bankrupt of empathy would confuse basic compassion for friendship."

He opens his mouth to retort, but the other guard waves his hand.

"Leave it," he says, and his tone is final. They drag the prince away.

I take a moment to douse my anger before I say something which will land me in further trouble. The last thing I want is to attract more attention from the king. I scurry after them.

The guards ignore me the entire way, including when they place him back in his bed. For my part, I ignore them back and quietly seethe. By the time the prince is laying in his chambers and the guards are gone, he has regained consciousness.

"Miss Shivani," he greets me. His voice is strained and weak.

"Your Highness," I reply and take a seat at his bedside. "How are you feeling?"

The question sounds foolish as soon as it leaves my mouth. The prince responds with a pointed look and a raised eyebrow.

"Fantastic," he replies. His tone is so dry I burst out laughing. His face cracks into a wide smile, but when he laughs, he winces in pain. I clap a hand over my mouth to stifle the laugher.

"Apologies." I lower my eyes and wipe the smile from my face. "This is no time to laugh."

"It is always a good time to laugh. Saints, you more than anyone should have more of it." The prince clutches at his blanket with tight fists but the corners of his mouth curl up in an attempt at a smile.

I sit back and sigh.

"As you do, I am starting to realise." I run a hand through my hair, catching my fingers on some of the delicate pins.

"Yes, well... Anyway, please make yourself at home. There are books over..." He groans suddenly, holding his ribs.

"Your Highness?" I half-stand.

"It is alright," he gasps. "Would you... lavender tonic...?"

He nods at a drawer near the hearth.

"Of course." I rush to the drawer and retrieve the pain relief for him.

He raises his hand to take it, but seeing the quiver in his arm and the pain twisting his features, I wave his hand away.

"Here." I bring the bottle to his lips and gently tip it. A thin trickle of the fragrant fluid escapes into his mouth. He accepts it gratefully.

"My thanks," he murmurs. To my surprise, a tear rolls down his cheek. It cleaves a trail in the blood still caked onto his skin. It is followed by another and then several more. My shoulders sag as I watch the prince stare vacantly at the ceiling, his breathing ragged with pain and tears flowing freely. My heart aches. Without thinking, I reach for his hand and grasp it tight.

His eyes flicker to mine, a dark grey in the dim light. Something tugs at me, something I do not understand.

We sit quietly as the lavender tonic takes over, and he drifts off to sleep. I watch his features smooth, and his chest rise and fall gently. I look at our hands, fingers intertwined. Despite the rest of his body relaxing into a deep slumber, his fingers do not lose their grip on mine.

CHAPTER 14

I rouse from a deep sleep with a groan, eyes bleary. I try to make sense of my surroundings, but everything is tilted sideways. My neck aches, and I realise I am slumped onto the prince's bed. My head rests on the top of his covers while the rest of me sits on the stool.

I gasp and bolt upright.

"Saints!" the prince yelps.

"Shit!" I yelp in response, equally startled. I wince and groan at the twinge in my neck from sleeping in such an awkward position. The prince regards me, half-sitting against his many pillows with a book in his hands.

"You gave me a fright." He shakes his head. "You were sleeping quite peacefully until you decided to awaken with such…" He eyes me, frowning in annoyance. "Vigour."

I rub my neck, my face scrunched while my brain catches up. *I am in the prince's chambers*,

I think to myself. I stayed with him while he recovered and...I glance at him sheepishly.

"I must have fallen asleep."

He raises an eyebrow but says nothing. I remember the expression on his face last night—the mixture of hurt and helplessness twisting his features. I remember the cloudy grey of his eyes, open and vulnerable. I search for any traces of it left but his disposition has returned to his usual aloofness. I sigh and stretch to rid myself of the ache in my neck.

I am still wearing the queen's crimson dress. Despite being more comfortable than other gowns, I doubt it was intended to be worn for this long. The bodice presses into my back and cramps my ophid, forcing me to twist to the side and stretch it. I catch the prince glancing at the dress before fixing his eyes back on his book.

"Why did you not wake me?" I ask, looking pointedly at the book he read while I slept unawares next to him.

"You seemed content," he replies, still reading. He licks a finger and turns the page. "Why? Do you have somewhere to be?"

I look at him so sharply he flinches.

"If that is supposed to be a particularly callous joke about my imprisonment, you can tend to yourself next time," I snap. The venom in my voice surprises even me, but I am too angry and tired to care. A deep crimson blooms across the prince's cheeks.

"N-No," he stammers, his decorum evaporated. "My apologies, Miss Shivani. I did not think before I spoke. I did not…"

He closes his book and places it on his lap, sighing.

"I would not make light of your situation, I assure you. I only…I only wish to know if you are willing to stay a while longer."

The prince looks at me earnestly, the cracks in his stoic mask showing. My irritation subsides. I study his face to search for signs of the simmering rage his father holds beneath the surface. But I can see none. Not even a trace of the beast I witnessed last night remains. *That does not mean it is not there*, I warn myself.

"Yes," I tell him, sitting back. "I can stay. On the condition you answer a question for me, completely honestly."

I do not know where my boldness comes from, but I know my dinner with the king last night has only served as a reminder, it does not matter how much I try to please and appease him or the prince. I will be executed at the end of six months, regardless. I lock eyes with the prince, determined.

"That would depend on the question," he replies, and I roll my eyes.

"Fine. Do you know how to break the curse?"

The prince slumps back, frowning.

"True love."

I quietly note the tinge of bitterness in his voice. He glances behind me, through his window, but when I twist to look, there is nothing there. I turn back to face him but his eyes fix on a distant spot and his jaw is set. Is he lying?

"No," I say firmly. "The *real* way to break the curse."

"That is the *real* way. What are you talking about?"

I lean forward, my elbows on his bed, and look him hard in the eyes.

"Do not lie to me," I tell him quietly, and his face scrunches in confusion.

"Have you gone mad? What in Saint's name am I supposed to be lying about?"

I sit back as we stare at each other. There is a beat of silence as I search his face. He does not look away. He is telling the truth.

"You truly do not know," I say finally, and we both hear the pity in my voice. The prince narrows his eyes. "The king...lied. About the curse. Or about how to break it, at least."

The prince scoffs.

"A poor joke."

"Your Highness..."

He grips his book so hard his hands begin to shake. Gently, I explain everything the king told me. He sits and listens with quiet fury.

"So, all those women died for nothing," he eventually says. "They had no chance of breaking my curse."

I do not know what to say, so I stay quiet.

"And..." his voice breaks slightly. "I will be a monster forever."

"No, no." I shake my head and grasp his hand. "You are not a monster. And we will break this curse."

He averts his eyes and gives a slight shake of his head, disbelieving.

"We will," I insist. "Before I was...before I came here, I studied many kinds of magic."

This catches his attention. He locks eyes with me again and sits up straighter.

"You did?"

I try to tell him about Frostalm and my application to the House of Learning but the words stick in my throat. I cough and blink away tears.

"Yes," I croak. "And I know all curses can be broken."

The prince's eyes light up, and I find myself smiling back. Optimism washes through me, sparking fires of renewed determination.

The prince is not well enough to leave his bed, but we break fast together regardless. The maids bring us breakfast trays, and we share the meal while I stay by his bedside.

"I have read many books on curses," I tell him, smothering butter across another slice of bread. "But I have never seen anything like your transformation."

"It is alright." He gives me a sad smile. "You can say monster. Transformation does not do it justice, I have heard."

"But you were truly not a monster. You were something else. It was...well, it had scales and a long jaw. You looked in pain."

The prince leans forward, intrigued.

"I must admit, I have no clue what I look like during these times. I only remember snippets. The only descriptions I have heard are..."

He presses his lips into a thin line, looking stricken. I think of the king and how a man such as that would describe what I saw.

"Unflattering?" I attempt a half-smile.

"You could say that," the prince replies with a strained smile of his own and sits back.

His eyes are cast downward, and his hands are clenched tightly. I swallow, my chest aching for him. His chestnut hair falls forward over his forehead, and I notice a light smattering of freckles across his nose and cheeks. For some reason, this makes my heart start to race.

"Do you paint, Your Highness?" I ask softly. The prince looks up at me. His expression is neutral except for the smallest downward tug of the corner of his lips.

"I am afraid not, Miss Shivani."

"When I am feeling melancholy, my favourite thing to do is paint," I tell him. "I did not have access to many paints, but sometimes my aunt and I were able to scrape enough ingredients together to make our own. I would paint, paint, paint until I ran out. It made me feel better. Calmer."

The prince watches me, the firelight dancing in his eyes. My palms go slick.

"Do you have something similar, perhaps?" I ask. A tremor enters my voice that I fight to steady.

"Yes," he says softly. "Gardening."

"Is it…farming of some kind?" I struggle to picture what he means by gardening.

He laughs, a delightful sound bursting from his chest. I am so startled I laugh back.

"My apologies." He grins. It transforms his face in a way I cannot look away from. "I should not have laughed. That was rude of me. Gardening is planting flowers or herbs and such."

"So you can use it for food?"

"Yes, but also for pleasure."

I cock my head, not understanding.

"There is nothing quite like planting a seed and nurturing it, watching it grow, seeing it bloom." As he talks, his eyes glaze over. There is love in his face.

"It sounds wonderful, Your Highness." I smile at him, a warmth in my chest that comes not from the hearth.

The prince looks at me then, and it is not a gaze I have ever known before. It is intense. So intense, my heart is a fist pounding against my ribs, and my breath catches in my throat. I do not know what to say, so I say nothing. All the while, his eyes linger on mine, glinting like folded steel.

"Thank you for staying with me last night." The prince raises his hand as if to place it over mine but hesitates and draws back. "I would urge you to stay in my chambers for the next few days. At least until my father finds something else to draw his attention."

"Oh." I look around. "Yes, you might be right."

"I do not have any paints, unfortunately, but you are welcome to any books you find."

I twist my neck to look at the collection of books lining one of his walls. They are colour-coordinated. A great sorrow wells up as I find myself missing Aunt Meena's messy library.

"I am sorry," the prince says quietly. I blink at him. "You must miss your home."

"Yes." The sadness leaks into my voice.

The prince catches his lower lip between his teeth. He clears his throat.

"You mentioned a House of Learning," he prompts gently. "And that you studied magic?"

Grateful for the change of topic, I nod eagerly.

"Yes, and History. Although I was considering Linguistics also."

"History and Linguistics." He sounds impressed. "I suppose the two would be closely related."

I blink at him.

"Are they?"

"Of course." The prince shrugs. "If you only read one language's history, you only read one side. And history rarely has one side."

I give him a side-long look, silently impressed myself.

"Quite right," I agree. "History should be viewed critically, I believe. Whoever wrote it or said it will have their own biases."

The prince's cheek curves in a smile.

"It has been a long time since I had such a lengthy conversation with anyone," he tells me. His ears tinge pink at the tips. This time, when he reaches forward, he does not falter. He lays a large hand on top of mine. The air thrums around us. "I—"

"Excuse me, Your Highness."

We are interrupted by a knock at the door. One of the guards steps inside. The prince immediately looks away, and the spell is broken. I am left flustered, though I am unsure why.

"Yes?" the prince addresses the guard.

"The king has summoned you." The guard glances at me but says nothing else.

"Right," the prince replies and his posture becomes rigid. "Please excuse me, Miss Shivani."

I look at him, but he averts his eyes from mine. His expression is even, and the inch of warmth in his disposition dissolves so quickly, I wonder if it had ever been there. As I stand to move to the adjoining room, the prince calls after me one last time.

"Please do not wear my mother's dress again."

CHAPTER 15

I spend a week playing the role of subservient common girl, ferrying myself to and from the prince's chambers every few nights and enduring degrading comments from whatever guards I pass that evening. I grind my teeth together and avert my eyes. I do my part painfully. And, as the prince said, the king does not call for me again. But it is not enough. I need my freedom back.

At night, I lay awake and wonder. The prince, on the night he caught me outside my window, took us back through a secret tunnel built into the walls. I chew the inside of my cheek, staring at the ceiling. The window in my bedchamber has proven an ineffective way of getting outside these walls. But the tunnel is hidden and seemingly even the guards are unaware of it. If I can use it to leave the castle, I can do what I originally intended—scale the overgrown tree down to Mossgarde.

The tunnel was joined to the portrait outside the prince's chambers, so I waited until the next time I was due to stay there. I try to keep my nerves contained, but the prince must sense something.

"Miss Shivani," he says from his armchair, looking up from a book. He always maintains a respectful distance and usually does not speak much. The sound of his voice startles me.

"Yes, Your Highness?"

"Are you well?"

I press my lips together and nod. He cocks an eyebrow but says nothing more, turning back to his book.

After turning in for the night, I quietly change into the stash of clothes I had taken some days earlier. Comfortable leggings and a loose cotton shirt with flat-bottomed boots. I wait patiently until the moon is high in the sky, and I am certain the prince is asleep.

With effort, I steady the tremor in my hands and softly open my door. The prince's room is quiet except for the gentle crackle of the hearth. Through the orange glow, I see the silhouette of the prince as he lays in his bed. His back is to me, the covers drawn up over his shoulders. I watch him for a moment to be sure he is sleeping. He does not move, and I can hear soft snoring under the sound of the fire. I exhale slowly, quietly, and steal out of my room.

My boots are heavy, so I move with care,

planting each step carefully and freezing at the slightest creak of the floor. When I reach his door, my heart is thunderous, but the prince remains asleep and unaware. Silently, I leave.

The portrait is mere metres away so, with a quick glance down the hall to check I am alone, I pull it open to reveal the passageway. I step inside quickly and close the door behind me, plunging me in near darkness.

I take a moment to allow my eyes to adjust. There are infrequent torches on the walls, burning low, and all I can hear is the sound of my own ragged breathing. I breathe deep, despite the dampness in the air, before making my way through the passageway. I take slow, shaky steps, my nerves fraught. At any moment, I expect the prince to burst into the passageway behind me, ready to drag me back into my cage. Part of me does not believe that is true, but the other part does not want to trust the son of my captor.

I push the thoughts away. They are not helpful or improving my mood. The damp presses in around me, chilling my bones, and I curse myself for not bringing a thicker jacket. *No matter*, I think. *Mossgarde will be plenty warm, even at night, when I make it back there.*

I reach the end of the tunnel and press my hands against the door. I know it is disguised on the other side but still, I am reluctant to open it. Despite the gloom, I feel safer in the tunnel, knowing I am somewhere the guards do not know about. But I have no choice. To turn back is to resign myself to the king and his chopping block. Steeling myself, I push the door open.

"What in Saint's name?"

I stifle a cry at the sudden voice, locking eyes with three guards. They stare at me, eyes wide and swords half-raised, a few feet outside the passageway door. They must have been patrolling the area right as I opened the tunnel.

No.

Without thinking, I bolt. Bursting between them, I make it several feet before I am caught. Rough hands yank me back and throw me into the passageway. I land hard on my side, something snapping painfully against the rock. I shriek, clutching my ribs, and desperately scramble back.

"Don't let her escape!" one of them yells. I try to stand, but the pain is blinding. A guard hauls me up, his fingers dipping into the flesh of my upper arm.

"What the fuck is this?" he says, looking around the passageway.

"Get her to the king," another one pipes up.

"No," I gasp, but they ignore me. My face contorts as a wave of agony courses through me, and I struggle to breathe.

"Shut it."

"Not...not the king," I insist, wheezing. "Take me back...to the prince."

"I said shut it."

My ophid thrums with indignation, and I curl my lip at him. A vile insult rises at the back of my throat.

"That is enough."

The guards turn to look behind me but I do not need to look to know who spoke. They exchange glances before straightening, and the guard who grabbed me releases my arm. I curl into a painful ball, clutching my side.

"She was attempting—"

"I know what she was attempting," the prince interrupts. His voice could cut glass. Saints, not only have I been caught, but I have also made an enemy of one of my only allies.

The guards take a step back as the prince's arms slide underneath my knees and back. With little effort, he picks me up from the floor of the passageway. I try to look up at his face but spots explode in my vision.

"I will deal with her. Return to your stations at once."

"But—"

"*At once.*"

The guards fall silent as the prince turns back into the passageway and follows the tunnel back to his chambers. I want to say something —an apology, a thank you, anything—but every breath I draw is like broken glass in my chest. Instead, I wheeze painfully and clutch the thin fabric of his nightshirt.

When we reach his chambers, the prince

lays me gently on his bed. I try to draw in a slow breath, but I'm stifled by the pain in my side. Tears start to fall.

"I will need to see the wound," he says. His voice is gentle, a far cry from the sharpness before. "May I?"

He gestures at my shirt, his face plain except for the telltale muscle in his jaw. After a moment's hesitation, I give a small nod and take my hand away from my side.

The prince delicately peels my shirt up, revealing one side of my torso. He is careful not to expose any more of me than he needs to, which I should not be grateful for but am. I look down. Black and red blooms across my ribs, where my skin is bruised. The prince inhales sharply, his brow puckered.

"My apologies," he says before gently pressing on the bruise. White-hot pain burns like fire in my torso. I squeeze my teeth together to keep from crying out.

"The bone," he says, pulling back. "I believe it is broken. It is painful indeed, but it will heal by itself."

"How...long?" I gasp, blinking away tears.

"A few weeks, I would think."

I groan and close my eyes. I have precious little time already, and now, I will have even less.

The prince pulls my shirt back down, covering me again, before turning to his nightstand. I watch him as he searches for the lavender tonic.

"My...how the...tables turn..." I wheeze in between short breaths. The prince frowns, uncorking the bottle.

"This is no time for joking," he says firmly. "You could have—"

He cuts himself off, pinching the bridge of his nose and squeezing his eyes shut. Silence falls over us.

"I am sorry," I say softly, my voice barely above a whisper.

"No." He waves a hand. "I cannot and will not be angry at you for attempting to leave. Do not be sorry."

The prince takes a deep breath, steadying himself, and gently tips the lavender topic past my lips. It is sickly sweet, but the effects are immediate—the sharp edge of pain in my ribs dulls to an ache. I relax into the bed.

"I knew what you were planning to do," the prince confesses. "I followed you."

Through the haze of the lavender tonic, I squint at him.

"Why did you not stop me?" I ask. My voice is slightly slurred, my tongue heavy in my mouth.

"Why would I? You deserve to leave this place. All of you have." The jaw in his muscle flutters again. "I just wanted to make sure you left safely."

My eyelids droop as a deep sleep beckons

me. The worries and fears plaguing me seem so distant now. Absently, I reach for the prince's hand. I feel his fingers interwoven with mine, warm and solid.

He says something, but I am already falling into the depths of a dreamless sleep.

CHAPTER 16

Month Three

The end of the summer months is signalled by the Firebug Festival. Each year, the firebugs buzzing around the humid swamps of Mossgarde migrate to warmer climates. I have fond memories of Aunt Meena holding my hand tight as she took me to the village centre when I was young. She made sure to wrap a thin scarf around my neck to keep the first nip in the air out. We, and the rest of the village, gathered to watch the glow of the firebugs as they started their long journey.

"Does the king allow you to watch the firebugs?" I ask Vanya as I roll dough in the castle kitchens. It is the first time she has allowed me to partake in kitchen tasks since my injury. I find myself enjoying the rhythmic back and forth as I knead, able to ignore the twinge in my ribs.

"He does," Vanya replies simply. I am

unable to take my eyes off my dough in case I roll it too thin but surprise shoots my eyebrows up.

"Really?"

"Half of us," she concedes. "The other half must work through it."

"Oh." My shoulders sag. "Well, that is a shame. They are beautiful, indeed."

Memories of Aunt Meena flood my mind, spiking a pain through my chest. I pause, hands shaking, and move the conversation on.

"H-have you ever seen them?" I ask.

"No." If Vanya notices the tremor in my voice, she does not comment. "I work instead."

"Every time? Why?"

Vanya gives me a side-long look.

"If I do not work, the work does not get done." She glares at other staff, who immediately scurry away.

"That is untrue!" Eliza pipes up from the sugar station. "That time you had a fever and you were in bed for *days*. We worked okay then."

"Enough talk." Vanya waves us off. "Keep rolling."

Eliza and I share a smirk but keep quiet. I feel like I am a young girl in the presence of Aunt Meena in one of her sterner moods.

I stay until dessert is served to the king, and we have our own smaller share afterwards. Once the pond apple pie is eaten, I say my goodbyes and make my way back to my chambers. My mood darkens.

The prince has not often spoken to me since the night I fractured my rib. I stayed in his chambers for a few days after, out of the way of the king. Inez checked my bruises, fussing over me and ensuring the correct dose of lavender tonic. But the prince stayed in the adjoining room, rarely acknowledging me.

I continue to visit his chambers every few days as we had agreed but his room is always vacant. I only hear him return after I have gone to bed and locked the door. Each morning I awake, he has awoken earlier and disappeared.

Inez had brought me news from the other servants—the prince told the king I was rightfully horrified by his transformation and I had been scared into submission. The thought brings bile to the back of my throat. But I know it is necessary to deceive the king. There has been no word on my second escape attempt.

Despite this, the longer the prince ignores me, the more I am uncertain of his intentions. The image of the warm, passionate prince I had spoken to is rapidly fading. Instead, it is replaced by the cool, aloof man I am acquainted with.

But when I return to my chambers, there is a note on the bed. I pick it up, curious. The paper is thick and stamped with royal ink. Sweat breaks out on my palms at the thought of another note from the king but I relax when I realise it is signed by the prince.

Be ready at sundown.

If it was a note from anyone else, it would be ominous. *Perhaps it still is*, I think to myself. After all, he has not spoken to me since that evening. I chew my bottom lip, contemplating, before deciding on the benefit of the doubt. I consider calling for Inez to help me get ready but there is a chance she will be one of the servants permitted to view the firebugs. I do not want to disturb her evening, in that case, so I dress myself.

The corseted dresses are too difficult, and I spend several frustrating minutes trying to fasten them before giving up. Instead, I pull on a loose-fitting dress, my hair poured loose over my shoulders. I have seen the prince in far worse states so I do not think he will mind. And if he does, it shows more of his character than mine.

As the sun dips below the trees, I hear a knock at my door.

"Enter."

The prince steps in, donning a deep blue tunic threaded with gold. He is clean-shaven, and his hair is combed. My stomach flutters, which I internally scold myself for—he has been ignoring me. He does not deserve my frivolous affections.

"Miss Shivani," he greets me and inclines his head. "You look lovely."

"Yes." I sniff, even though I do not agree. He must sense my irritation because he has the grace to look contrite.

"I apologise for—"

"You have nothing to apologise for, Your Highness," I interrupt him. "We are not friends. You do not owe me your time, and nor do I owe you mine."

The prince swallows.

"Nevertheless," he continues, "I would like to show my thanks for your help when I was…in a poor condition. Especially now you are mostly recovered."

He stretches out his hand. I look at it hesitantly, chewing my lip. How was he aware my rib was nearly healed?

"Not as friends," he continues. "But as allies?"

His eyes are earnest, and my resolve quickly crumbles.

"Very well. As allies, then."

I put my hand in his before sliding it up to rest in the crook of his elbow. He smiles so widely, the corners of his eyes crinkle. *Damn him.* I find myself smiling back.

The prince leads us to a wall lined with shelves. Various vases and books sit innocently on the wood, and I throw a curious glance at him. He reaches behind one of the shelves, and a moment later, I hear a click. Another hidden door. The prince squeezes his fingers between the gap and pulls, revealing the passageway.

"How many secret tunnels are there?" I ask as I follow him inside. I make sure to close it tight behind us.

"I could tell you how many I know of," he replies, grabbing a torch and leading the way. "But I am quite certain there are others I have not discovered."

"How *did* you discover them?"

"There is little else to do other than explore, and I have had a lifetime to do so."

I fall silent, a twinge of sadness in my chest. For as much as I am trapped in this castle, I have only tasted a drop compared to the prince.

The passageway is steep, made almost entirely of rough-hewn steps. There is no other light except for the low orange glow of the prince's torch, and I stumble several times.

"Here," the prince says after my third near-fall. "Hold out your hand."

He reaches behind himself to hold my hand and guide me up the steps. It is slower but safer. My cheeks warm as my hand clasps his but I remind myself it is only to stop me from falling.

"We have arrived," the prince announces when we reach the end. I respond by wheezing, my rib protesting with a dull ache.

As we step out from the passageway, a cool breeze brushes over me, and I realise we are outside. I blink and look around.

We are high, somewhere near the top of the castle, where a room used to be, but most of the walls and ceiling have crumbled away. There is enough brick left to shelter us from the elements but the great hole in the corner of the room allows us a wide view of the evening sky. Flickering torches light up the small area, and when I cross over to the wall, I can see down to the grounds below. It is full of servants, the tops of their heads moving around as they find a good viewing spot for the firebugs.

"What…?" I trail off, unsure of what I want to ask.

"The firebugs," the prince clarifies. "I thought you would like to see them."

"But…why?" I squint up at him, brows furrowed.

The prince cocks his head.

"The people of Mossgarde watch the migration, do they not?"

"Well, yes."

"I had hoped this would…" He hesitates and gives me a sad smile. "Be a comfort to you."

I turn to look out over the wall. We are high enough that I can see over the treetops and into the distance. Where the swamp of Mossgarde ends, and the fields begin. Ice-peaked mountains line the horizon, one standing taller than the others. The mountain housing the city of Swordstead. Somewhere in one of the Three Great Oceans, Frostalm cuts through the sea. The House of Learning. My freedom.

I look at the servants bustling below us, and I know somewhere even further below, deep in the centre of Mossgarde, my Aunt Meena sits and waits for the firebugs without me.

A great sob explodes from my chest. I clap my hand over my mouth, but it is too late. I crumple to the ground as tears stream freely down my cheeks. My body heaves with each violent sob as though it is being ripped out of me.

"Miss Shivani?"

I turn my face away from the prince, squeezing my eyes shut. Shame burns my cheeks, but he does not say anything more. I feel his presence as he sits near me but allows me my space. I wrap my arms around my knees and cry and cry and cry.

My tears eventually dry, the pain ebbing away but never quite gone. I take a shuddering breath and wipe my face with my sleeve.

"Here," the prince says softly and offers me a cup of hot tea. I stare at it, startled.

"W-Where did you get this?" I ask, my voice hoarse.

He nods at a wicker basket sitting between us.

"I prepared it for tonight."

"Which means the servants prepared it."

He looks affronted.

"*I* prepared it. Myself. You are not the only one who visits the kitchens."

I look at him for a long moment and accept the tea. It is soothingly warm. I take a sip, and it eases my throat, raw from crying. I glance at the basket and spy a long container there, likely where the tea is stored.

"It is still hot." I cock an eyebrow at the prince. He picks up the container and pours himself a cup.

"A gift from Swordstead," he explains. "There is a structure within which keeps whatever is inside warm for much longer than you would expect."

"Extraordinary," I murmur, running a finger across the container. It must have been a royal gift—I have never seen such an item in the merchant wares. Inadvertently, I think of Frostalm and all the new and wonderful things I would have learned there. A lump forms in my throat again. I take a large gulp of tea to ease it.

The prince opens the rest of the wicker basket to reveal an assortment of treats. Delighted, I pick out a small snowberry cake.

"What happened here?" I ask after taking a bite.

The prince frowns and looks at the gaping hole in the side of the room. A light wind whistles past the brick.

"I am…not quite sure. Dragons, perhaps?"

"Dragons?"

The prince spreads his hands and shrugs.

"They are the only things I can think of who can come this high."

I chew on my cake thoughtfully. Below us, the chatter of staff floats up like leaves on a breeze.

"Dragons did live here," I say. "Originally. The First Home of Dragons turned the New Home of Witches. I have not found any texts about why they moved."

"Perhaps we moved them." The prince's voice is quiet. I look out over the treetops.

"Yes. Perhaps we did."

The sun slips below the horizon, and the sky fades to a deep blue. The first stars start to wink overhead.

"I have never seen so much of the sky before," I say, keeping my eyes on the stars. When the prince gives me a quizzical look, I continue, "The tree canopy is too dense. The only way to see the sky is to leave Mossgarde."

Or to be imprisoned in the castle, I think with a bitter irony. It took losing my freedom to gain the sky.

"You are welcome here any time."

I smile, stomach fluttering. The prince looks down at me and smiles back. We are standing close enough for our arms to brush off each other. Even though there are several layers of fabric, it is enough to send goosebumps along my arms. And then, out of the corner of my eye, the first firebug appears.

It ascends slowly, just a glowing orange dot against the trees. The sky deepens into black, and a hush falls over us both. We watch the firebug dance up and up until it soars well above the treetops.

It is followed by a few more. And then more. Before long, firebugs ascend in their thousands. They fill the night sky, drifting upwards and towards the horizon with purpose. They move nearly in tandem. It is as though they are not individual firebugs but one giant creature swirling like fluid. My breath catches in my throat, and I clench my hands over the wall.

In Mossgarde, once the firebugs cleared the tree canopy, they were no longer visible. But here, the prince and I watch until they disappear into the distance. Even after they have gone, I find my gaze stitched to the horizon, searching for them still.

"Thank you," I eventually say. My voice is thick.

"It was my pleasure."

When I look up at the prince, his chestnut hair flutters in the breeze. His eyes are soft, and they catch my gaze. My pulse quickens. Whatever feelings I tried to bury have come back twice over. And I have no hope of stopping them.

CHAPTER 17

Inez wakes me one morning as usual, but she has a sly smile playing on her face as she does.

"What?" I ask groggily, sitting up in bed.

"I bring news."

The smell of croca bacon and butter fills my nostrils as she places the breakfast tray on my lap.

"Bad news?" I ask warily. When she shakes her head, I exhale deeply and reach for the bread rolls. "Then what?"

"I will need to show you, miss," she replies with barely concealed glee. I cautiously agree. I am only slightly reassured by Inez's sunny attitude which means it is unlikely to be anything torturous.

She walks me through the castle halls. We pass by the guards pressed against the walls, unmoving and upright. I feel a pinch of sympathy for them to be expected to fulfil this strict role even outside of the king's gaze.

Nerves eat away at me despite knowing I should be elated at a rare escape from mine or the prince's chambers. Even my visits to the kitchen have become less frequent as the guards started to question my presence there. I realise, with disgust at myself, I have become so accustomed to my cage that even stepping outside of it feels wrong. With effort, I straighten my back and stride with purpose next to Inez.

She leads me only a minute or so away from my chambers, although it feels like miles, until we reach a door I do not recognise. I eye it curiously.

"Where are we, Inez?" I ask.

"A thanks from the prince," she replies, beaming, before turning the handle and throwing open the door.

I step in, and my mouth drops.

The room is slightly bigger than my chambers, but the far wall is made entirely of glass, allowing sunlight to flood into the room. Huge bookcases line the left wall. But instead of books, the shelves are filled with hundreds of paint tubes and tubs of turpentine. Large bundles of brushes are bound together and made up of various sizes and thicknesses. On the right wall, blank canvasses are stacked against each other. In the middle, an easel sits patiently.

"What…" I breathe. "What is this?"

"It is yours, miss," Inez replies. "To use

as and when you please. The guards have been informed that you are allowed to and from your chambers and this room. They will not stop you."

"It..." My hand flies to my mouth as I choke back a sob. "It is mine?"

"A thanks from the prince," she repeats with a wide smile. "For tending to him during his recovery and for accompanying him to the Firebug Festival. Oh! There is a lock on the door so you may enjoy your privacy."

I open my mouth to speak, but my mind has gone blank. I am overcome. I want to cry and laugh and curl up all at once. Inez takes notice and steps back outside.

"I will give you a moment," she says before closing the door gently behind her. It is only after she has left that the tears begin to flow.

Eoin once told me about the deserts of Coalsburgh. It is hard for me to imagine somewhere so bare and dry, so different from the swamp. The heat, I understand, but Eoin likened it to living in a kiln. The air lacks moisture, unlike the thick heat of the swamp. The dragons in the desert live off water from hardy plants that grow there, relying mostly on imported trade. But, he told me, if you are brave enough to traverse the sands outside of the city, you may come across an oasis. It is a small spot in a barren land, bursting with life. Green plants, fruit, even water. Crystal clear, a shade of blue not found anywhere else in the world. A true sanctuary.

The art room quickly becomes my oasis. For the next week, I spend more time in my art room than I do in my chambers. I take my meals there and paint late into the night until Inez comes in to drag me to my bed. The ache in my heart still hurts. But, for the first time since I was blocked from my au'mana, I feel connected to Aunt Meena again.

As I slide paint-dipped brushes across the canvas, I think of her often. Her toothy smile whenever I would give her a new painting or her fists on her hips as she stood back to check if it was hanging squint on the wall. Her enchanted leg and enchanted library. Her skill in witchcraft, which she passed down to me. Her very presence would calm me as she sat in the corner of the library while I hunched over scraps of paper, studying or painting. For her, for Morraine and the rest of the Never Queens, I will not resign myself to this castle and its cruel king. My rib is healed, and my determination renews. I cannot afford another mistake. I cannot afford to lose more time. I must be careful.

The large windows in the art room give me a wider view outside and this side of the castle allows for the sun to flow in during the entire day. After being confined to a single room with only one window, I am dazzled by so much sunlight. Often, I will sit next to the glass wall and watch the outside world. I can see far below where the guards patrol the grounds.

I recall my conversation with the prince and his love of gardening. I inspect the grounds more closely but it is made entirely of red brick —there are no gardens nor flowers. I absently wonder where the prince tends to his gardens.

Inez and I make a routine of eating lunch together in my art room. We sit in the sun and play cards over our sandwiches. It is so comfortable, I pinch myself every night before bed and force my mind to remember the bloody block of wood in the centre of Mossgarde. I remind myself it awaits my head.

"Do all the staff live together?" I ask Inez one day as we watch the birds fly outside.

"I suppose," she answers. "The servants' quarters are more like a series of rooms all connected."

I try to picture it.

"Do you have your own bed, at least?"

Inez laughs and shakes her head. Sunlight spills through the large windows, bathing her in gold.

"Those of us who work during the day use the beds at night, and those of us who work at night use them during the day."

My mouth drops, appalled.

"You do not even have your own bed? And what in Saint's name would you need to work at night for?"

"The castle requires much maintenance. And... the king can demand many things at any time." She shrugs.

"At night?" I scratch my head. Inez casts her eyes downwards, her shoulders hunching. Her food sits half-eaten on the table between us, forgotten.

"Yes," she says quietly. "He has favourite handmaids who he likes to summon. For... entertainment."

My breathing quickens, and my hands curl into fists. I remember the note he sent me, summoning him.

"He is a tyrant," I whisper, rage turning my voice to gravel. "Despicable."

Inez clasps her hands on her lap and takes a deep breath, eyes watery.

"It is not only the women. He enjoys humiliating the men as well. The only ones who are immune are the guards, and even then..." Inez's nostrils flare. "When they are in training, they must go through a loyalty test."

"What is that?"

"I do not know." She shakes her head, a deep line between her eyebrows. "Once they become a guard, they do not speak of it."

The weight of this sits on my shoulders like lead. Half of my sandwich is in my hand but I put it back on the plate, my appetite gone.

"You do not deserve this," I say. "None of you do."

Inez does not respond. Her eyes are fixed on the horizon. Silently, I make her a promise.

It is not only my freedom I must take but everyone's.

CHAPTER 18

There are no books in my chambers or my art room for me to research the prince's curse. I ask Vanya and Inez and even Eliza but they have only hand-written fiction, passed between them. I recall the books in the prince's chambers and so make my way there one evening.

I use the secret passageway to avoid the guards and knock on his door. No response. When I knock again and hear nothing, I decide to try the door. It opens easily, and I peek my head around.

The prince's chambers are empty.

I linger in the doorway, reluctant to make him think I am invading his privacy. After a few moments of dithering, I decide it is worth it. I need to understand this curse if I am to leave unscathed.

I close the door softly behind me and hurry over to the bookshelves.

The books are arranged by colour, so I am forced to tilt my head at an awkward angle to read each title individually. Still, it is more organised than Aunt Meena's haphazard stacks, so I make do. I pass over several books about horticulture and gardening, their jackets free of dust and clearly recently used. Instead, I gravitate towards the dustier books, blowing gently on the spines so I can read the titles.

Tales for the Young, one of them says in dragon text. I frown. As far as I am aware, no dragons reside in Mossgarde anymore. They used to, many hundreds of years ago, leaving behind only faint remnants. The books in dragon text my aunt have are rare finds. To see one buried under a layer of dust in the prince's bedchambers is strange indeed.

I delicately run a finger along the spine and make to pull it free, but the door slams open behind me. I snap up and spin, hand on my chest.

The prince is held up by two guards as they drag him into the room.

"Your Highness," I breathe out, heart still thumping.

"Miss Shivani." His voice is strained and weak. The guards drop him on the bed, roughly pulling his legs up.

"Leave him. I will do it." I am not in a position to be giving out orders to the king's guards but my voice leaves no room for them to question me. They straighten and leave without saying anything else. I take over from them, gently hooking my hands under the prince's knees and arranging him comfortably on the bed. His skin is still half-wet with blood, and only a blanket covers him.

"I did not know you had turned," I tell him. An apology is layered underneath that I was not there with him.

He opens his mouth to respond but winces in pain, clenching his teeth together. I search the drawer for the lavender tonic and quickly find the familiar, purple bottle.

"This has become quite the regular occurrence," I say, sitting back down.

"The transformation?"

"Keeping you company during your recovery."

The prince smiles wanly as I tip the bottle towards his lips. I keep a careful eye to ensure it does not spill.

"And I am much obliged," he replies once he has had his fill. I place the bottle to the side and chew my bottom lip.

We fall silent. The sun begins its ascent, filtering through the gaps in the heavy curtains. Birds start their morning songs.

"What do you plan to do with me?" I ask. It surprises even me.

The prince lays there like I had lain with a fractured rib, both of us nursing the other back to health. I want it to be genuine, his concern for me, but I cannot deny the dead women who came before me. The ones he could not or *would not* protect.

The prince lets his head fall to the side, towards me, and we lock eyes. His hair sticks to his forehead with sweat and dried blood.

"I plan to keep you safe." His jaw is set.

My heart thumps rapidly, and I fight to keep my breathing even. He fixes me with the same intense gaze he had done before, as though he is looking into me. His eyes glance down to my lips for a moment and I am suddenly self-conscious. Exposed like a nerve. But the feeling is not unpleasant—the opposite, in fact, as a warmth crawls across my skin. I *want* him to look at me. I do not know what should happen next, but I know I do not want to leave.

The spell is broken when he shifts and grimaces in pain.

"More," the prince gasps, clenching his teeth and staring at the lavender tonic.

"O-Of course." I grab the bottle and tip more of the liquid past his lips. I find myself drawn to his mouth. The softness and fullness of his lips, despite the caked-on blood. I shake the thought from my mind and pull the bottle back. "Is this better, Your Highness?"

The prince blinks rapidly before exhaling through pursed lips. His body relaxes, the tension in his muscles easing as the lavender tonic works through his system. He sinks back into the bed.

"Sleep will find you soon," I tell him. "Rest."

To my surprise, he turns his head back towards me. His cheek rests on the pillow, a wonky grin on his face.

"Ha!" He gives a bark of laughter, loud and sudden. I jump out of my skin.

"Your Highness?"

"Thaaaat's not my naaaame," he drawls, giggling. I stare at him, bewildered. "Your Highness, this! Your Highness, that! But it is not my name, is it?"

"Um." I glance at the empty bottle of lavender tonic. I fear I may have poured too much. "No?"

"Correct!" The prince jabs a finger at me before rolling his head to stare upwards, a thoughtful expression on his face. "I would like to tell you my name, but...well..."

I wait for him to finish but he does not.

"Well, what, Your Highness?" I prompt and he bursts into another fit of giggles.

"Your Highness, Your Highness!" He laughs as though he has never heard anything funnier in his life. I decide to refrain from calling him by his title until he falls asleep, lest it trigger another mildly terrifying bout of laughter.

"Are you...feeling better now?" I ask, hoping a simple question might encourage a direct answer. But his eyes, large and shining, turn on me, and he breaks out into another lopsided grin. It reminds me so much of his smile, his genuine smile. I cannot help but grin back.

"Miss Shivani." He reaches out to grab my hand, holding it tight. "You are braver than I."

I laugh, thinking he is still joking, but his face has turned serious.

"I am not sure about that," I reply, shaking my head.

"You are," he insists. "You stand up to my father."

A heavy pit forms at the bottom of my stomach at the mention of the king. I give a half-hearted smile.

"I do not think that is brave of me," I reply, my voice small. I recall how often it has nearly claimed my life.

"Shivani," he says. He speaks my name quietly, with reverence. The sudden drop in formalities takes me aback, but he does not seem to have noticed his mistake. "You are brave every day you are here. I..." he stammers to a halt before squeezing my hand. "I admire you."

Butterflies explode in my stomach, and a deep heat crawls up my neck and over my face. I lower my eyes, bashful in the face of his sincere compliments. My brain churns quietly, trying to think of what I should say back. Should I tell him I admire him too? The way he perseveres through a brutal transformation so often? Or the way he has managed to live a life under the gaze of a cruel father and still have a soft heart?

I squeeze my eyes shut and decide to tell him all these things. How my heart flutters when he looks at me and how I look forward to each time we meet. I steel myself and open my eyes, but when I do, the prince is already asleep.

CHAPTER 19

Once a week, when the guards change shifts, two guards in particular end up working next to each other. Perhaps they are friends, or perhaps they are lovers—it does not matter to me. What does matter is they sneak off to abandon their posts for an hour because they, like myself, have learned they are unsupervised. Inez told me once over tea in the art room that the guard in charge likes to play tic tac toe with one of the older servants at the same time each week. I come across each segment of information individually, storing it away until they come together like a beautiful jigsaw.

For one hour each week, there are no guards outside of my door. I am free to roam. At least, the floor my bedchambers is on.

The first few times, I was too nervous to enjoy my limited freedom. I spend the time looking over my shoulder and jumping at every creak in my step. But the more I take advantage of the blessed hour and do not get caught, the more I relax into it.

Fascinated with the knowledge of more secret passageways littered throughout the castle, I begin exploring every item lining the corridor walls. Unsurprisingly, there are numerous portraits of the king—none of the prince or the late queen. Pale squares mark the walls, the ghosts of paintings the king had taken down. I wonder if they belonged to any of the monarchs before him.

I gently tug at a few of the portraits, but I find only flat walls behind them. I move onto the several shelves lined with pots of fresh flowers. I frown at them, wondering where they came from. The petals are soft like velvet, full and beautiful. They are not like the flowers found in Mossgarde with their tall stalks and small, delicate petals. I am reminded again of the prince and how he enjoys gardening. I resolve myself to ask about it next time I meet him—there must be a garden here somewhere.

I tap softly on the shelves, holding my ear close to hear any mysterious echoes which might give away the passage behind it. When that does not work, I carefully pull the shelf away from the wall. Instead of a secret passageway, there are yet more empty walls.

Sighing heavily, I flounce away. This floor of the castle is home to several other doors, all of them unknown to me. Curious, I open one of them and peek inside.

A bedchamber, identical in layout to mine, greets me. I cast a look around, but there is nothing of note, so I move on to the next door. This one is empty, bare of all furniture. I carry on until, a few doors down, I find something.

I swing open the door, ready to find yet another boring room, but this one is different.

It is a bedchamber again but much larger than mine. The air is stale, as though no one has breathed it for years, and the furniture is covered by white sheets. The curtains are drawn, leaving the chambers in deep gloom. I stare, lingering in the doorway.

I want to explore further, but I am unsure how much time I have left before the guards return. I cast a quick glance down the empty corridor.

One quick look, I think before stepping into the room.

It is as though I have stepped into a grave. The air is cooler than the rest of the castle, and the dust is thick around me. I shiver, arms prickling.

"What is this place?" I murmur to myself.

Pinching the sheets, I glimpse underneath only to find regular furniture. But the style is different to the rest of the castle—it is more ornate but not gaudy. It is familiar, yet I cannot place it.

The large object in the middle of the room

is clearly a four-poster bed, but I look under the sheet regardless, determined to turn over every stone. As I catch a glimpse, my pulse quickens.

The silk bedsheets were likely white at some point, but they have yellowed with age. But it is what is in the middle that catches my sight —a deep brown stain spreads across the centre of the bedsheet. Where the rest of the silk is still smooth and flat, the stain has turned it thick and stiff.

Blood.

I immediately drop the sheet, covering the bed once more. I want to turn and run back to my chambers, but I have not finished checking everything yet. I could wait another week for my next free hour alone, but...

I close my eyes. The stain on the bed will haunt me with questions. I need to find out as much as I can.

A sheet covers the wide bookcase against the far wall, so I hurry over. I did not want to leave anything disturbed, but time is of the essence, so I made a quick judgement—the room has not been touched for many years, so it is unlikely anyone will return. I tear the sheet down. It falls silently, leaving a plume of dust in its wake.

I am struck by the strangeness of the books. Instead of the uniform size and height of most books in the castle, these are oddly sized and do not fit together neatly. I tilt my head to read the spines and notice they are written in dragon text. They are dragon books.

I half-turn to look at the rest of the room, still covered in sheets. The style of the furniture now makes sense—it belonged to a dragon. Even as the pieces fit together, I am left confused. A dragon lived in Mossgarde Castle. I wrack my brain, trying to remember anything Aunt Meena told me about a dragon living in the castle, but I recall nothing.

I turn back to the books.

"Who were you?" I mutter, fingering the spines.

I come across a peculiar one, titled *Svellenta*, written in the common tongue. I have come across the word before during my studies, but the translation does not immediately come to mind. *Interesting*, I think and hook a finger on the top of the spine to pull it free.

A loud creak cracks through the air. I stifle a yelp and jump back. Mouth open, I watch as the bookcase splits down the middle and parts, leaving a dark tunnel. I stare at it, chest heaving. The low whistle of the wind snakes through the darkness. It must lead outside. My heart skips at the thought, and I take a shaky step forward.

As soon as I enter the secret passageway, I am plunged into darkness. I nearly lose my nerve, but the call of the wind steadies me. If this leads outside…No. I do not let myself think of that. Not yet.

I inch forward, my hands on the walls on each side of me. I expected them to be rough-hewn, like some of the other passageways, but the brick is smooth. As though it has been built this way instead of carved. I take a deep, fortifying breath and move forward. The floor begins to slope down, so I carefully pick my way onward. One stumble, and I do not know how far I will fall. Without my sight, all I can hear is my own shaking breath and the promise of the wind.

Time slips away from me as I walk, but I press on nonetheless. The ground levels out again, and I catch a pinprick of light in the distance. My breath hitches. I stumble on, faster than before, trying to reach it. The light grows and grows, turning a deep, hazy orange. The light of the late afternoon sun. The air becomes less stale, and I feel the tickle of a breeze around my ankles. I break into a run, tearing through the tunnel to reach the light. The outside. *The outside.*

I come to a halt at the end of the tunnel as the world opens up.

I am somewhere in Mossgarde, but I do not know where. The passageway leads onto a raised platform high above the swamp below. Insects buzz around me, the trees rustle in the slight breeze, their leaves half-orange. I look up, but I can no longer see the sky, blocked out again by the canopy of branches.

I stifle a sob, clapping both hands over my

mouth. I have done it. I have found a way out.

But I linger on the precipice between my prison and my freedom. *I should run*, I think. *Run from here and never look back. Run to my Aunt, run to the border of Mossgarde and onward again until I reach the Glass Sea. Until I reach Frostalm.*

I think of the snow hare.

My feet do not move. I stand with my fists clenched at my sides.

I think of Inez. Of Vanya. Eliza.

The prince.

I think of them all, and I know I cannot leave. To leave would be to doom them all to a lifetime of torment.

To stay would be to doom myself to the chopping block, another part of myself whispers angrily. And it is true. But it is not enough.

I turn from the exit and stride back the way I came. My fate is tied with theirs now.

CHAPTER 20

Winter arrives in a flurry of overnight snow and frost. Mock snow, Mossgardians call it. Thick enough to fall from the sky but melted to nothing by the time it reached the swamp. It never settles, but it is enough to chill the air.

I awake to a cold room, my breath turning to mist in front of my face. I blearily look through the window and see fat, heavy snowflakes falling. Already, there is a layer of snow forming along the windowsill.

I groan and throw my head under the covers, curling into the smallest ball I can. I instinctively make a checklist in my head of tasks to do—I need to save the swamp reeds from a hard frost and check the house for holes and drafts to stay warm inside. It takes me until the sixth task on the list before I quietly realise I do not need to do any of these things. I am not home. I have not been home for months.

I peek my head out of the covers to test the temperature again. It is chilly, but compared to the bitter cold of my father and I's home, it is bearable. Particularly with the thick, soft duvet wrapped around me.

"Good morrow, miss." Inez knocks at the door before entering with a breakfast tray. The smell of hot saffron tea and fresh bread wafts my way, luring me further from my warm cocoon.

"Good morrow, Inez," I greet her. I have not spoken a word of the secret tunnel I found to anyone. It is too important, and though I trust Inez, I cannot risk the information getting to any of the guards.

She places the tray on my lap with a smile. New breakfast foods have appeared—warm honey cake, hot cocoa alongside the tea, and strips of salted marsh rabbit. Food to keep you warm. My mouth waters as I inhale deeply, but the memory of last winter chews at me. My father and I would often go to bed hungry as not much grew in the swamp during winter. If we could not hunt the swift marsh rabbits or sparrows, we would be resigned to the dregs sold at market. Often, we only had enough money for a bruised pond apple or two.

I push the memory deep, deep down and start my breakfast. As usual, I split it with Inez, who sits at my bedside and eats with me.

"I will need to dress you today, miss," she tells me as we feast. "The prince has asked for you to accompany him on a walk this morning."

"A walk?" My heart thunders.

"Around the castle, miss," Inez clarifies before taking a bite of buttered toast.

"Oh." I gnaw at my bottom lip, excited to see the prince again but unsure of where in the castle he plans on taking me. There is also a nagging sadness in the back of my mind that I should not be enjoying such luxury as warmth and comfort when I know it is the condition of my imprisonment.

"What is it, miss?" Inez asks. Her eyes watch me keenly.

I sigh and push the tray away.

"Do you think me weak-willed, Inez?" I ask. She raises her eyebrows.

"Of course not, miss."

"You can be honest. I will not be cross," I tell her earnestly.

"I *am* being honest," she replies, shaking her head. "There is not one person who has met you who would think you weak-willed. Probably many other unflattering terms, if you ask some of the guards, but not weak-willed. What makes you ask?"

I gaze out the window, watching the snow fall. I remember standing on the windowsill three months ago, ready to risk my life just at a chance to escape. And now I am sitting in my cage, enjoying cake and tea.

"I have become complacent, Inez," I

murmur, not looking away from the window. "I have stopped fighting."

She places her warm hand over mine.

"No, miss," she says. "Fighting does not always mean throwing punches or flinging yourself out of windows."

I shoot her a sideways glance, wondering how she knew, but say nothing. She leans in.

"Sometimes fighting is just surviving."

I look down and smile. The snow hare scurries through my mind, limbs outstretched and eyes wide.

"You are right." I breathe deeply. "I do wonder, though…"

Inez looks at me expectantly, nibbling on her toast.

"If there was way a way to leave, would you?" I ask, keeping my tone light.

She blinks. Once. Twice. Three times. The toast remains in her hand.

"Leave, miss?"

I gesture around us.

"The castle. Would you leave?"

She opens her mouth once and closes it. Opens it again.

"This is my home," Inez says finally. "I do not know anything else."

"But to get away from the king would be worth it, no?"

"We can never get away from him, miss."

The words fall from Inez as casually as if

she were telling me about the weather, but they cause a deep fissure across my heart. *We can never get away from him.*

I want to cry for her, for all of them, for me, but I do not. Instead, I rearrange my face into something resembling neutrality and close my hand over the top of hers.

"It was purely hypothetical anyway," I say with a smile and Inez visibly relaxes, her shoulder sagging. "No point in discussing it any further."

"Quite right, miss," Inez replies brightly and reaches for a slice of honey cake.

Later, once we have finished our breakfast, Inez dresses me for my morning walk with the prince. Despite staying indoors, she insists the castle is too chilly to walk around in the simpler dresses—without a lit fire, the cold seeps through the brick.

She bundles me up in a pale blue dress with thick fabric, long sleeves and a soft, warm lining. I don thicker shoes underneath. It is not as practical as the queen's red dress, but it will keep me warm.

"This colour looks lovely on you, miss." Inez beams as she tucks my long hair under the collar. "What a pretty picture you are."

I blush and give a shy smile.

"Thank you, Inez." I twirl for her, but the heavy weight of the dress means the skirt barely lifts. Inez claps regardless, delighted.

"It is no wonder the prince is so smitten with you," she says before adjusting the buttons on my bodice. My heart flutters at her words, but I do not want to let it show.

"W-What do you mean?" I ask. I try for a casual laugh, but it comes out nervous and shrill. Inez gives me a knowing look.

"I see more than you think," she says coyly.

"Well." I sniff, trying to hide the secret thrill in my chest. "I think you might have the wrong end of the stick. The prince is most assuredly not smitten with me."

"Oh, I believe he is." Her expression turns stricken, her face tight. "Many girls have passed through this room. But this is the most he has ever requested their presence."

I frown and lower my eyes, my mouth twisted to the side. I pluck at the frilly trim on my bodice.

"Do not misunderstand me," Inez continues. "He made sure they were well looked after and tried his best to shield them from the king and himself. But since…"

"Since what?"

"Forgive me. It is not my tale to tell." She stands back to admire her handiwork. Before she dressed me, she had taken the time to wash and oil my hair so it shone like onyx. I must agree with her—the pale blue suits me, stark against the darkness of my skin. I wonder if the prince will like it too.

We sit with more hot tea until there is a knock on the door.

"I shall leave you to it, miss." Inez stands and curtsies.

As she leaves, the prince steps in. He inclines his head in greeting, hands clasped behind him and back straight.

"Good morrow, Miss Shivani."

He is dressed in emerald green velvet, complimenting his tousled brown hair and fair skin. His eyes match the steely grey sky outside. When he sets them on me, all the thoughts leave my head. He looks at me expectantly, and I realise I have not replied.

"O-Oh," I stammer and give a hasty curtsy. "Good morrow, Your Highness."

A playful smile tugs at the corner of his lips. His gaze briefly travels down my dress before snapping back up—I almost think he is about to say something when he half-turns away and gestures to the door.

"Shall we?"

I stifle my disappointment and nod.

"Yes. Let's."

Despite my warm outfit, Inez was right—the castle was cold. As soon as I leave the warmth of my chambers, the air hits my face. Regardless of the chill, I find myself enjoying it. The air is crisp and cool, fresher than anything I have breathed in a long while. I inhale deeply.

"Do you enjoy winter, Miss Shivani?" the

prince asks. I turn to him and see him watching me with kind eyes.

"No," I admit. "Not usually."

The prince contemplates this and extends his arm. After a moment of hesitation, I accept it and wrap my hand around his elbow. Even through my gloves and his thick sleeves, I can feel the firmness of his arms, solid beneath my fingers. I try not to think about it.

We stroll through the corridors leisurely, blanketed in comfortable silence. The guards stayed mostly out of our way, standing at attention against the walls. Their uniform has changed to a wintery white and blue, with thick fabric under their armour and comfortable gloves to protect their hands from the cold.

The prince leads us around a corner and another until we reach a steep set of stairs.

"Apologies, it is quite a climb," he says, gesturing for me to go ahead of him. "Have you quite healed?"

I instinctively touch my side, but the pain is almost entirely gone.

"I am," I reply, eyeing the stairs. "But will the climb be worth it?"

"It will." He smiles, his eyes twinkling.

I huff my way up the stairs, grabbing the top of my skirts and lifting them so they do not tangle around my feet. The prince patiently climbs behind me, stopping when I stop and going when I go. By the time we reach the top, my face is so flush, I no longer notice the cold. We meet an old wooden door marked with age.

"Very well, then," I gasp out, one hand on the stitch burning my side. "Show me."

I am reassured by the prince also being out of breath, his cheeks tinged with pink. He slides past me and twists the doorknob. I peek around him, but he moves in front of me, obscuring my view.

"Ah." The prince grins and wags a finger. "A surprise, remember?"

"Is this not it?"

"Almost, but not quite." He turns to me. "May I cover your eyes?"

I glance behind me at the narrow, spiral staircase where he led us. My throat is suddenly dry.

"Yes," I reply hoarsely.

He gives me a reassuring smile and places a hand over my eyes, moving behind me as he does so. His skin is smooth and warm, his touch gentle. I lean into him instinctively.

"Forward," he says softly in my ear. "A few steps."

I do as he instructs, tentatively taking a step and then another. His hand appears on my waist, halting me. Even with my eyes covered, I sense his presence close behind me. His chest brushes my shoulder blades. My breath hitches.

"Are you alright?" Concern laces his voice. "Is it your rib?"

"No," I breathe. "I am well."

His hand squeezes my waist at my answer. I am almost disappointed when he moves in front of me, keeping his hand over my eyes. I hear the squeak of a door hinge before a wall of warm, humid air washes over me.

"Okay," the prince says, removing his hand. "Here it is."

I blink at the sudden light. As soon as my vision clears, my jaw drops.

"Oh," I gasp softly. "Your Highness, it is beautiful."

We stand in a room made entirely of glass, circular and tall, with a domed ceiling. I am struck by the warmth and the smell—earthy and fragrant. Several terracotta pots of various sizes sit in various places, housing some flowers I recognise and some I do not. Towering ferns grow up one side, a wall of ivy lines another. A large table sits in the middle, laden with lines of small, square tubs. Each of them is filled with rich soil and dotted with vibrant green sprouts. A watering can sits in the corner next to a rake and two spaces, one short and the other tall. Morning sunlight filters in, drenching the flowers in a honey glow. I inhale deeply.

"Thank you," the prince replies, shutting the glass door behind us to keep the warmth in. I step in further, admiring a tall flower with velvety red petals. *This is where the flowers come from*, I think to myself, recalling the castle corridors filled with strange plants.

"Did you grow everything here?"

"I used to," he tells me, standing near the door while I wander. "I am sad to say I have neglected this place for a while, leaving the work to the servants. But...I have recently rekindled it."

I feel his eyes on me. I turn to look at him and catch his gaze once more, intense and warm.

"I have you to thank for that," he says.

"Oh." I find my mouth is suddenly dry. "You are welcome, then."

There is a beat of silence before he abruptly crosses the distance between us. I nearly take a step back but resist, squaring my shoulders and raising my chin instead.

"How are you finding your art room?" he asks innocuously, as though he could not have asked from the other side of the glasshouse.

"Yes, it..." I consider a curt, formal response but the prince is standing so close and watching so intensely, I cannot formulate one. I think of him dozed on painkillers and speaking candidly to me. I decide I do not need lavender tonic to do the same. "It has been a true sanctuary for me, Your Highness. I fear I would have lost my mind in this cage otherwise. You have my sincere thanks."

The prince looks at me for a long while before taking another half-step forward. Now he is close enough for me to smell the soap he used this morning—sweet and earthy—but also something dark and pleasant underneath. It is the smell of him, I realise. My heart sets off at a gallop as he towers over me. All sense of dignity leaves my body.

"Even though your father is a prick," I blurt out. Horrified, I clap a hand over my mouth. The prince's eyes widen, and his mouth parts slightly. There is a moment where I do not know what he will do.

And then his face breaks into a grin, and the glasshouse rings with his delighted laugh.

"Well said, Miss Shivani."

He turns to one of his plants and strokes the leaf tenderly. A fierce warmth radiates from my face, but I make an attempt to recover quickly, moving the conversation along from my strange outburst.

"This is your version of my art room, I suppose?" I ask, stepping away to squint at a squat, spiky thing.

"That feels accurate," he replies. "Although there is a tree which I like to visit also."

I recall the tree outside my chambers I tried to use to escape. The prince's presence there suddenly makes sense.

"It is quiet there," he continues. "The guards do not often patrol around it, so I am free to read in relative peace."

"Until someone decides to fling themselves off the windowsill."

The prince catches my eye, and I give a sheepish grin.

"I am only glad I was there to help," he says, ever the gentleman. "Shall we continue on?"

We spend the rest of the morning in the prince's greenhouse as he shows me his favourite flowers and the history behind each exotic plant. Their names roll off his tongue easily as he recants obscure plant knowledge with little effort. The part of me that thirsts for knowledge is in awe, and I find myself listening with eager interest.

We end up in a small gap between flowers where we can stand and look out through the glass. I blink at the view. We have climbed high, to the highest point in the castle. Snow coats the flat surfaces of the walls and catches on the ledges. The sky remains a hard grey but the snow has ceased falling. The prince points out a part of the castle walls where a tree pushes its way through the brick.

"I caught you…" He points. "Right there."

Even though I already know, the memory comes to me in a rush, like a harsh, cold wind. From this view, I can see the distance between the ledge I stood on and the tree. Whether it is real or a trick of the season, the branches of the tree look especially fragile. I swallow hard, trying not to think of what would have happened to me if the prince had not been there and I had truly jumped. My eyes trace down the ledge to the hard brick beneath. I picture my mangled body there, having undoubtedly missed the tree or fallen through the branches. I blanch.

"My apologies, Miss Shivani." The prince breaks me out of my spiralling thoughts. "I should not have shown you."

I inhale quickly, trying to dislodge the unpleasant images.

"It is quite alright, Your Highness. I-I made a jest of it first." I blink rapidly and look away, catching the prince's eyes. He takes my gloved hand in his, and my heart stutters.

"No, it was a dark time for you, and I do not wish to remind you of it. I can only imagine how much you have worked to...make the most of your situation here." He takes a deep breath. "I wished to take you to my favourite place in the castle, but I should not have mentioned the tree. I apologise."

I search his eyes and find only sincerity.

"Accepted, Your Highness." I incline my head, and he smiles, relieved. He turns to look at the plants, and, to my delight, his hand stays in mine. I try to steady my heartbeat and listen to him.

"The guards do not climb this high," he tells me. "It is the only true place I am able to find some peace."

I think of my art room and the peace it brings me. To be alone and unwatched in a sea of hostile guards and observing eyes. I started to understand the prince knew the value of that and wanted to give it to me unprovoked. Purely to share something he knew was important. A sanctuary.

"You have a kind heart, Your Highness," I tell him and squeeze his hand. He turns to me and I realise how close we are, nearly touching. The humid air is so tense I cannot remember how to breathe.

He raises his hand and nearly reaches for my cheek but hesitates. Instead, he slides his arm around my back and pulls me in. His face nestles at the nape of my neck. He holds me tight, hugging me as though I am a life raft in an unforgiving sea. After a beat, when I realise what is happening, I reciprocate. I wrap my arms around him and let myself melt against his chest. He is firm and solid—he brings me such a feeling of safety. I realise the art room is not my only sanctuary here. The prince is, as well. I do not know how long we stay that way, but neither of us wants it to end.

Eventually, the prince pulls back with a dazed expression.

"I..." he starts, but the words seem to stick in his throat. "I am due to turn tonight."

"Oh." I am unsure what I expected but it is not that. I clear my throat and take a step back. A flash of disappointment straightens my spine.

"I would appreciate your company during my recovery," he continues.

"I always accompany you, Your Highness."

"Regardless, I do not like to assume. You are always free to change your mind." He reverts to his usual formal position, hands clasped behind his back. His face has fallen into his accustomed neutrality except for the pink tinge in his cheeks. My mouth curves into a smile.

"Thank you, Your Highness." I chew my lip for a moment. "Has it…always been a regular occurrence? Your turnings?"

The prince sighs and rubs the back of his neck.

"At first, it was. Or so we thought. But soon, it would happen sporadically, sometimes even in my sleep. I became a danger to everyone around me."

He draws himself back as we both notice the resentment in his voice.

"I suppose it would not be a curse if it was easy to manage, would it?" He dips his gaze with a sad smile. There are a few moments of quiet while I process this.

"Your Highness," I say. "I am sorry you must suffer this curse. Especially…"

He brings his eyes back up until they are fixed on mine, boring into me in a way he does so easily. I take a deep breath and continue.

"Especially from your mother," I finish, keeping my voice soft.

He says nothing, but his eyebrows push up together in the middle, and his eyes shine with tears, glinting in the firelight. He looks so mournful, I cannot bear it and reach across for his hand, grasping it tight.

After a long moment, he speaks.

"I do not even hate her," he whispers. "I just wish I knew what I had done to make her hate me."

Tears begin to spill, sliding down his fair cheeks and falling from his jaw. He makes no move to rub them away, and so neither do I, allowing him this sadness.

"You were a child," I tell him. "A baby. You did not do anything, Your Highness. Do you blame me for my father selling me like I was a load of bread?"

He blinks at me.

"O-Of course not." He shakes his head. "Your father is a foolish, gambling, low-life cur, if you will pardon my language."

His sudden burst of fury on my behalf makes me smile despite myself and he gives a sheepish grin back.

"Sometimes, Your Highness, we are a victim of other people's choices. I promise you, you did nothing to deserve this curse," I tell him, giving his hand an encouraging squeeze.

"My thanks, Miss Shivani." He takes a deep breath and wipes the last of his tears away with the back of his arm. "My thanks for being a…"

He halts, his eyes moving from where our hands are bound up to my face. I blush under his gaze, but he does not finish the sentence. His lips remain parted but he has frozen, eyes uncertain.

"A friend," I finish for him.

He moves as if to say something but hesitates.

"A friend," he repeats eventually before releasing my hand.

CHAPTER 21

We fall into a comfortable routine. As well as my usual visits, each time the prince turns, I am escorted to his bedchambers to aid his recovery. Each time, it becomes a little easier to open up in conversation, and I can feel the same in him. He laughs more but also cries more, sometimes a few tears which quickly dry but sometimes great heaving sobs which rack his whole body. It is during these times I take to holding his hand tight and letting him release the sadness and the pain he has held. Sometimes, the anger, too.

In turn, I find myself laughing more and crying less. When I am not with the prince, I paint in the art room, creating vast landscapes and experimenting with the hundreds of colours I now have access to. Or I am with Inez, sharing afternoon tea and exchanging stories with hushed giggling.

Occasionally, I am slipped notes from the

kitchen, updating me on the latest gossip from Vanya and I send notes in return. I write recipes my aunt taught me with a promise to finish the tale of the siren and the witch when I am able to see her next. Each time I go back to my chambers, my *cage*, the anger and fury are a little less sharp when I know I have allies.

The secret passageway leading outside the castle remains stuck in my mind, like corn between teeth. I cannot use it, not without the rest of the king's hostages, but I cannot ignore it either. The prince, while his curse remains, will never leave. This knowledge troubles me, corroding our time together.

❋ ❋ ❋

I am in my art room one day, painting the morning sky, when the prince sends a guard to escort me somewhere.

"His Highness has asked it to remain a surprise, miss," the guard tells me when I ask where we are going. Curious, I follow him through the never-ending castle halls until we reach an area I have not yet explored.

The prince is standing outside grand double doors accented with gleaming silver. He gives a toothy smile when he notices me.

"Miss Shivani." He greets me with a slight bow, his hand on his stomach.

"Your Highness." I curtsy back before he

dismisses the guard. As soon as he leaves, the prince leans forward to brush his lips against my cheek. I inhale the scent of him, blushing as he draws back.

"So, where have you taken me?" I ask, trying to stifle the flutter in my stomach.

He merely smiles at me, the corners of his eyes crinkling, and opens the doors. As I step in, all the breath leaves my lungs.

A library. It is vast, three stories tall and lined with thousands of books. Each floor has its own walkway circling the shelves with ladders dotted around. The smell of books hits me all at once, the sweetness mixed with dust and age. I take a few more steps in and spin slowly on the spot, taking it all in.

"This is amazing!" My voice comes out louder than I intended and echoes around the vast room. "Sorry," I whisper, contrite.

"No, no." The prince steps forward to join me. "You are right. Even after seeing it my whole life, it never ceases to amaze me."

We look sideways at each other, smiling, as though we have a secret only we know.

"You are free to come here whenever you wish. I come here myself often, and maybe we can…" He trails off, and the tips of his ears turn pink. "Spend more time together."

"I would like that, Your Highness." My voice is even despite the millions of butterflies in my stomach. Although I know he views me as merely a friend, I have only grown fonder of him. His presence, large and soothing. The dark and sweet smell of him when he comes close to me. The slightly lopsided smile he gives when I laugh, as though pleased to have elicited such a reaction from me.

The gentle soul he houses behind the bars of his curse.

To calm myself, I turn away and begin wandering the library.

We spend several hours there, occasionally speaking in hushed tones about a book we have found or are hoping to read. The library is bigger than anything I could have even dreamed of, having only had access to the one-room library my Aunt owns. I try to ignore the dull ache at my temples at how much she would love to see this place.

The immediate possibilities of researching the prince's curse open up to me—the information we need could be right here.

The prince gravitates to the flora and fauna section and I accompany him as he tells me excitedly of his favourites. He is the most animated I have ever seen him, and his joy fills my heart. Afterwards, he guides us to the history section where my enthusiasm grows.

"Where did you learn to read so many languages?" the prince asks me as we peruse some thick texts on the history of sirens.

"My aunt," I answer absently, running my

finger along the spines. A few of the books are familiar but I mentally log some away to come back to later. "She is a magical woman and taught me many things."

"Really?" The prince cocks an eyebrow, intrigued. "She taught you magic?"

"She did." I cock my head to the side, reading the title of a book about siren songs. "She taught me how to read spells written in witchtongue."

The prince's eyes widen in understanding.

"Ah! I have found many books here which are written in an unfamiliar text. Perhaps they are spell books? Let me take you to them."

He slides his hand into mine and whisks me off, up two sets of ladders and several landings until we reach the very top floor. It is not as well-lit here, but it is warmer. A purple glow emanates from one of the bookshelves. My breath hitches at the sight of it.

"Here." The prince brings me to the glowing bookcase which, upon closer inspection, is only coming from one book. "This entire shelf is written in another language—even the letters are different from ours. I tried searching in the other books for a translation, but the only reference I found to it was the word faeth."

"Faeth," I mutter to myself. "It means magic."

"In what language?"

"Dragon," I whisper.

We fall silent, staring at the glowing book. I frown at the purple glow.

"Do you think it is safe to open?" the prince asks, taking a large step back from the bookcase. "I have opened it before, but maybe it...it has some kind of, uh, slow-acting poisonous magic—"

I shake my head.

"It is likely safe. Dragon magic—faeth—does not affect other people, only the wielder." I shoot the prince a reassuring smile before turning back to the book. "Which is why it is so interesting this book is clearly enchanted by au'mana."

If I was connected to my magic, I am sure it would be humming in tandem with the book. I reach out and grab it by the spine, sliding it out from where it is sandwiched between two other books. It is heavier than I realised and releases a plume of dust as it slips off the shelf. I raise my hand to waft it away and nearly drop it. The prince swoops to grab it.

"My thanks," I say gratefully, and we both carry it to the nearest table. It sets off another cloud of dust as we slam it heavily. The prince wrinkles his nose.

"I know," I say in disgust as I wave the dust away.

"No, it is not that." He sniffs the air. "Can you smell that?"

I pause, inhaling, but I cannot smell

anything other than old books.

"Salt," the prince confirms.

The book sits innocently on the table, bathing it in a lavender glow. Text is embossed across the top of the cover, along with distinct artwork. Realisation dawns on me.

"It is definitely enchanted then," I whisper, running my hand across the cover to feel the ornate ridges of the design.

"By witches?" the prince asks, frowning in confusion. "But the other texts called it faeth."

"No, no, look." I run my finger underneath the title. "They have a similar-looking alphabet, but this is definitely witchtongue—the letters curve more, whereas dragon text is more straight lines. This word here is au'mana, not faeth."

The prince peers over my shoulder.

"That is why it smells of salt," he says. "When au'mana is used, it has that smell. Correct?"

"Correct," I confirm. "Faeth does not have a smell. It has a…"

I stand up straight, my brain churning.

"What?" he asks, a look of concern crossing his face.

"It has a taste," I say, turning to him slowly. We stare at each other.

"Well, what taste? Snowberries?" The prince tries for a half-smile, but it quickly drops when I do not respond.

"Your Highness." I try to swallow but my

mouth has gone dry. "I am sorry to bring this up, but...your mother..."

The prince stiffens, and a muscle in his jaw twitches.

"What about her?"

"Was she a dragon?"

There is a beat of silence before the prince laughs nervously.

"Do not be absurd. How could she possibly be a dragon? Think of the logistics of it," he tries again for a joke, but I shake my head.

"No, Your Highness, a dragon *descendant*. Before, I told you faeth only affects the wielder. This means dragons can alter their appearance into something more...human-like. They carry all the magic of their ancestors but they look no different than you or me, unless they choose to shapeshift, although it often takes decades to learn how to do so safely. I have never met one before, of course, but I have studied them immensely—" I am babbling now, overwhelmed by the knowledge as my mouth tries to keep up with my brain.

"Shivani," the prince cuts me off, raising his palm. "What are you trying to tell me?"

I shift from one foot to the other, trying to formulate a tactful sentence.

"I believe your curse is dragon magic, Your Highness," I say. "You cannot smell faeth like you can au'mana, but...you know it is there. It tastes like blood." I recall all the times I have spent with the prince while he has turned, the coppery tang sitting uncomfortably on my tongue. Because there was faeth in the air. "I believe your mother was a dragon, and she used her magic to curse you."

"But..." The prince swallows hard, his throat bobbing. "But how is that possible? You said dragon magic cannot affect other people."

I cringe at my earlier blanket statement.

"It has been known to happen." I spread my hands, contrite. "Curses are...different. Their very nature defies the rules of magic, which is why they are *extremely* rare. The wielder must not only be a master of their magic, but they... they must be a truly broken person to draw on such strong hatred."

The prince's shoulders sag, crestfallen.

"My mother could only curse me because she hated me that much."

My mouth gapes uselessly as I try to find the words to comfort him.

"I am so sorry, Your Highness." It is all I can think to say.

He stares at the floor for a long moment before taking both my hands in his.

"My apologies, Miss Shivani," he says, his old formalities slipping in. "I feel I need to be alone for a while."

I watch him as he presses his lips to the back of my hands, my mind desperately scrambling for something, anything, which might help. But I have nothing.

"I am sorry." His voice breaks, and my heart snaps clean in two. Before I can reply, he leaves.

CHAPTER 22

Month Four

Inez and I share our supper in the art room, bundled under blankets against the chill.

She brings us a spread of roasted rosemary sparrow, garlic potatoes, and a bowl of carrots and watercress cooked in butter. Vanya has sent up extra portions of saffron spiced cookies, as per my recipe, alongside a note signed by the kitchen staff. I place the note delicately next to my bed, treasuring it, and smell the warm scent of the cookies. I ignore the churning nostalgia and sadness it brings, knowing my Aunt is not the one making them with me.

Inez and I sit in front of the glass wall, looking out over the treetops as the sun dips below the horizon. The sky is a vibrant mixture of pink and orange, spread like watercolour. We eat in silence, content with watching the world outside.

"This would make a beautiful painting," Inez comments before biting into a crispy potato.

"It would," I agree. "I am hoping to commit it to memory so I may paint it tomorrow."

She looks over at the various canvasses sitting against the wall, each one a window into another world.

"I think you would fetch a pretty penny for those, miss." She nods at them.

"Really?" I had never considered selling them—I painted for an escape and for peace more than anything. "I do not know if they are grand enough for that."

"Oh, I think they are. They would fit right in on the walls here in this castle. I cannot imagine a grander place."

I look sideways at her, then, curious.

"Have you ever wanted to see anywhere else other than this castle?" I ask, schooling my features and keeping my tone light.

Inez pauses, a forkful of sparrow halfway to her mouth before she replies, "No, I do not know anywhere else. I do not know what I would do." She puts her fork down and sighs. "My brother was always the adventurous one," she says, her eyes unfocused. I wait for her to elaborate, but she says nothing, lost in thought.

"Did he live here with you?" I ask, taking note of the past tense she used and treading carefully.

"Yes, our whole family lived here. We

have for...well, as far back as my grandmother, at least. Although, back in those days, servants were not required to stay in the castle and could leave for their own homes at the end of their working day," she replies. "Anyway, now it is just me left. Apart from my mother, but she was allowed out of the castle for her retirement. I like to imagine she is relaxing in a sweet little cottage somewhere."

Inez smiles sadly but it slips off her face, replaced with a forlorn look.

"He was a guard here, although he always had finer dreams," she says, her voice small. "My brother, I mean. Well, a guard in training. He was ten-and-seven when...when he was supposed to..." Inez stammers to a halt, her breathing ragged. Her eyes are shiny with tears, and her hands shake. I immediately put my plate on the floor and reached across for her, grabbing her hand with both of mine.

"Eight years ago," she says hoarsely. "When the king took his life from him."

Inez's tears flow freely. I move to kneel in front of her and draw her towards me in a tight embrace.

"I am so sorry, Inez," I whisper to her as she sobs into my shoulder. "I am so sorry."

"Lucian," she cries. "His name was Lucian."

We stay that way, hugging and rocking while she cries his name again and again.

* * *

Later, when the moon in high in the air and the castle falls silent, I toss and turn in my bed, unable to sleep.

Inez's story haunts me, and a great sorrow wells in my chest when I think of what she went through. Each time I close my eyes, I see her face as she recalls her brother's death. No—*murder*. I cannot stand it.

Without thinking, I throw the covers back and get out of bed. Slowly, I creep across my chambers and open the door, peeking through the gap. The hall is empty and quiet.

I sneak out and find the secret passageway leading to the prince's chambers. It is empty of servants, so I hurriedly make my way through it before I can stop myself. On the other side, a guard lingers in the halls, but his back is turned. Silently, I creep out from behind the secret door and cross the few meters to the prince's chambers. His door is unlocked, so I quickly open it and slip inside before I am spotted.

"Shivani?" The prince sits on his sofa in front of the hearth, reading. He stands up as soon as he sees me. "What are you doing here?"

"My apologies, Your Highness," I puff, out of breath from hurrying and from nearly being caught.

The prince glances down my body before

quickly averting his eyes. It is only then I realise I have not changed into my proper clothes, and I am still in my flimsy nightgown.

"Shit!" I gasp. "Oh, Saints, my apologies, I-I do not know what has come over me."

I whip my head around, looking for something to cover myself with. The prince picks up a heavy blanket from his bed and crosses the room to me. Keeping his eyes on my face, he wraps it around my shoulders until I am covered from the neck down. Shame burns my cheeks.

"I will leave, m-my apologies." I make to turn around but he still has a grip on the blanket, holding it across my chest.

"Shivani," he says, his voice serious. "What has happened?"

I look up at him, his eyes wide and full of concern, and I want to tell him but resist.

"It is not my story to tell, Your Highness." I shake my head. "It…it has just shaken me, that is all."

The prince studies my face, lips drawn into a thin line.

"Very well," he says, a deep line between his eyebrows. "But you do not need to leave if you do not want to. You are always welcome here."

I linger hesitantly. The prince's room is warm and familiar compared to my cold, lonely bedchambers.

"I would like to stay, please," I say, and he inclines his head.

We sit on opposite sides of the sofa as he keeps a respectable distance, although all I crave is his touch.

"What...were you reading before I interrupted?" I gesture at the book in his lap in an attempt to distract myself.

The prince holds it up, showing the cover. The room is deep in gloom except for the glow of the fire, but I recognise the looping letters and rambling title.

"Witchcraft?" I raise my eyebrows.

"Indeed."

He gently places a bookmark between the pages before closing the book. I find myself hypnotised by his hands, large and strong but handling a book so delicately

"I realised my knowledge of witches and au'mana is quite poor," he continues. I blink away my thoughts and listen. "Seeing as you yourself are a witch, I thought it wise to investigate further."

"Why is that?" I ask.

He shoots me a confused look, one brow raised.

"To know more about you." He speaks as though to say 'of course'. A rush of affection flows through me as my cheeks warm. Between the heat of the fire and the prince's words, I find my whole body growing warmer, in fact.

"And have you found anything interesting?" I wring my fingers together to stop myself from grabbing and hugging him. He straightens, an excited smile on his lips, and sits an inch closer to me on the sofa.

"Much indeed! I have learned your magic flows from an organ next to your spine. An..." He opens the book and scans the page, finding the word he was looking for. "...Ophid, is that correct?"

"It is." I give him a small round of applause and he beams. "Although mine has been... dormant, I suppose, for quite some time." An ache throbs in my chest, and I resist the urge to reach out to my au'mana again, knowing it will only disappoint me. The prince blinks.

"Dormant?"

"Yes." Bitterness tinges my voice. I run my tongue across my teeth. "Ever since I was brought here. I thought it might have been drugs at first. I am not so sure anymore. The only thing I am sure of is I cannot use my magic. And I do not know why."

"I am sorry," the prince says softly, reaching across to lay his hand on top of mine. I inhale deeply and recall the way he hugged me that day in the gardens.

"Your Highness?" I enquire tentatively. "Would you...would you hold me?"

I feel foolish as soon as the words leave my mouth, but the prince only smiles kindly and opens his arms. I shuffle over, still wrapped in my blanket, and curl up next to him. He rests his arms on me, pulling me even closer, and lays his cheek on the top of my head.

"I would do whatever you asked of me, Shivani," he whispers as I sink into him. Each muscle I had not realised was tense begin to relax, and I close my eyes. Safety. Comfort.

"Thank you, Your Highness," I breathe as my eyelids become heavy.

"My name is Theo," he replies in a soft, low voice.

Theo, I think, before tipping past the precipice of sleep and drifting off into a dragon-filled slumber.

❖ ❖ ❖

I dream of my father, the sound of his heavy breathing when he returns from the public house. I brace myself for his barbed words, but instead, two huge wings sprout from his back. He towers over me as I curl into a ball, pretending to sleep to avoid his wrath. I dream of the snow hare, heart thumping, muscles burning, terror-ridden.

I awake with a start. My eyes shoot open, and I blink quickly, trying to remember where I am. The orange glow of an early sunrise pours through the window. I realise I am still on the sofa, half-lying against the prince. He has slumped onto the arm of the sofa and is softly snoring, his arm propped under his head. I am afraid to move in case I wake him and our embrace is over.

My head is cosy against his chest. His muscle is firm under my cheek, and my pulse stutters. I close my eyes and try to memorise this moment, the scent of him so close to me, the warmth I can feel from his arm around me, the security and safety of being curled up next to him.

"Good morrow," he says, and I jump out of my skin.

"G-Good morrow, Your Highness," I stammer, wondering when he had woken up.

"Theo," he reminds me, and I can hear the smile in his words. His voice is slightly different, thicker and slower. I realise, with a thrill, that it is his morning voice. It is an intimate thing to hear someone when they first awaken and have not put on their mask for the day.

"Theo," I repeat, feeling how his name rolls in my mouth. To address a man of nobility by his given name, particularly so when they are royalty, is generally reserved only for close family and spouses. It is widely accepted to be a private acknowledgement. I wonder what it means that he has given it to me—the obvious answer does not seem likely.

Neither of us moves from our positions, warm and comfortable but scandalously close. His hand trails delicately across my upper arm while we doze. His fingers barely brush me, but it feels like a deliberate movement, and that is enough to cause an eruption of goosebumps along my neck. We are lying in a position you would expect from a married couple in the privacy of their own home, but not two people who are...merely friends.

The thought sours me, and I shift my position away from him until I am sitting upright. The prince—*Theo*—looks at me quizzically.

"My apologies, Shivani," he says, pushing himself to an upright position as well. "I did not mean to make you uncomfortable."

"No, it is not that, it..." I pull the blanket tighter around me. "We should not have been so close, like that, when you only view me as your friend."

Theo stares at me.

"It is not right," I press on. "You should... reserve such things for someone you choose to court."

"Shivani." He furrows his eyebrows. "I am courting *you*."

My heart leaps into my mouth. My stomach falls through the sofa. My brain stutters to a halt.

"Huh?" I exclaim stupidly. Theo shakes his head, laughing.

"I thought you knew?" He spreads his hands and shrugs. "Did you truly think we have spent the last few months as friends only?"

"I...well...yes!" I splutter, springing to my feet. My blanket slips, and I fumble to pull it back up. Theo, still laughing, stands up to help me. He gently tugs it back over my shoulders before letting his hands rest there.

"My apologies." He smiles remorsefully. "I thought I had made my intentions clear, but...I admit, I do not have much experience."

"Oh. Well...I suppose neither do I." I think back to the men who had propositioned themselves to me in varying degrees of crudeness and shudder at the memories. I think of Eoin.

There was never the pretence of a courtship with Eoin. Sex, attraction, and intimacy are not always one and the same, I learned. I could not force romantic feelings, though I tried for a time, thinking if sex and attraction were there, the rest would follow. But it never did.

This feels different. This is the missing piece that allowed me to be so bold with Eoin and so bashful with the prince. Why a tumble with Eoin made no mark on the rest of my day, but merely locking eyes with the prince is enough to suck the air from my lungs.

Intimacy.

"Then I would like to make it clear now." He reaches up to brush his thumb across my cheek. Instinctively, I lean into his touch. "I feel very strongly for you, Shivani. To be candid, I do think of you as a friend—my *closest* friend. But not just that. You are special to me."

His hands move down to mine and grasp them. He brings them up to his lips and plants a kiss on my knuckles. I shiver with delight. When he looks at me, his eyes are bright and clear.

"I feel the same," I breathe. I am relieved and terrified all at once at finally verbalising what I have been harbouring. The fear of rejection and the sorrow at unreciprocated feelings melt away. I look up at him, tall and broad but gentle and sweet, and we smile at each other like fools.

"Would you join me for dinner tonight?" Theo asks, rubbing his thumbs across the back of my hand. "Not as mere friends?"

"Yes. Of course." I nod dumbly, trying to ignore the blood rushing in my ears, my cheeks aching from the size of my grin.

"Then, I look forward to it." He beams at me, and my heart has never felt so full.

CHAPTER 23

I spend the day sitting down, standing up, and sitting down again in quick succession. My brow will not stop sweating, and I wring my hands just to feel like I have something to do.

Inez is patient with me, listening to my anxieties as I spew them at her in an incoherent mess.

"I did tell you the prince was smitten with you, miss," she teases.

"Well, in hindsight, yes…I suppose it was obvious." I give a sheepish smile as she works on my hair, pinning it in place.

As soon as I told her I was to dine alone with the prince dinner, that we were officially courting, she was all abuzz and pulled out a series of beautiful dresses. She has truly outdone herself this time—my hair is arranged in an ornate pattern, half-pinned up but with some of my dark curls falling down each side of my face. She has washed and run oils through my hair so it is sleek and shiny, catching the light when I turn.

The dress she chose is dark purple, studded with jewels and ran through with intricate lace. The bodice hugs my figure in a flattering cut, clinging to the curves of my body before flaring into a floor-length skirt. She has dusted my dark skin with a powder that makes my cheeks glow gold. I stare at my reflection, dazzled that I could look like this.

"I should like to dress this way more often." I smile, turning my head this way and that to admire the glow of my cheekbones.

"For another dinner?"

"No, just...for no particular reason," I say. "Other than for my enjoyment."

"That sounds like a fine idea, miss." Inez nods agreeably and re-adjusts one of my curls.

"And I would like you to join me." I turn to her.

"Me?"

"You." I grin. "I admit, the whole routine seemed farcical to me, even insulting that I should be prettied up like a package for the prince. And, I suppose, that was the king's intention. But with you, I have realised there is a beauty to it...like a ritual, careful and peaceful, moving from each step to the next. I would like to share this with you—if you will let me?"

Inez smiles bashfully before nodding.

"That sounds lovely, miss," she replies

before stepping back. "Truthfully, I enjoy the ritual of it as well. My mother would often teach me how to dust my cheeks just so or to plait my hair into these beautiful designs. She had a magic to it…"

My ears prick at her choice of words, my au'mana humming.

"A magic?" I query gently, pretending to fiddle with the pins in my hair.

"Yes…" She smiles sadly. "Lucian had it as well, but our mother passed before she could teach him anything."

Inez stares vacantly, and I stay quiet, allowing her to speak.

"Sometimes, she would make things glow. It was wonderful," she recalls, with a fond look. "She wrote everything in her journal, but it was in another language, so I was never able to understand it."

Another language? If Inez's mother made things glow, it must be witchtongue. A wave of familiarity and kinship washes softly over me, calling my name.

"I may be able to read it," I say, treading carefully with my words. It does not appear Inez is aware her mother and brother were witches. "I am quite good with languages."

"Oh?" Inez's eyes light up. "The letters are different to ours, though."

I turn to smile at her. I think of my own mother and how I have nothing of her, besides her temperament. It must pain Inez to have something of her mother's that she cannot understand, especially if she has no au'mana to bond them.

"That is quite alright, I am sure I can translate it for you. It is the least I could do for your kindness and friendship."

Inez beams at me, her hands clasped in front of her mouth.

"That is most generous of you, miss."

"Not at all, Inez." I wave her off. "Bring me her journal, and we will go through it together. I would love to know more about your mother. What was her name?"

"Ruya," she replies. "Her name was Ruya."

❋ ❋ ❋

When I step into the dining room, I realise it is lighter than it has ever been. A thousand candles circle the room, elevating it from its usual cavernous dimness into a well-lit chamber. The long table in the middle, usually laden with a feast, has been reduced to two sets of plates and cutlery sitting opposite each other at the head. One of them is in front of Theo. He stands up when I enter and dips his head.

"Good evening, Miss Shivani," he greets, only a hint of the smile he reserves for me playing on his lips.

"Good evening, Your Highness." I curtsy

back. He walks around the table to draw my seat back for me, tucking it under me as I sit, before returning to his place opposite me. The candlelight flickers across his face, setting his grey eyes aglow. He leans across slightly.

"You look beautiful as ever," he says quietly, avoiding the echo of the room.

"My thanks," I reply, cheeks warming.

Servants bring out our dinner—a main course of thick lentil stew, flatbreads loaded with butter and garlic, and baby potatoes cooked in salt and fennel. The smell is divine, and I inhale it deeply.

"This looks amazing, Your Highness." I gaze at the dish.

"I asked Inez to inform me of your favourites. I heard you have been teaching our kitchen staff some new recipes," he replies with a playful glint in his eye, ladling the lentil stew and placing it on my plate. "I was hoping this evening would be most enjoyable for you."

I suppress a shudder of glee at this show of affection. I chide myself for somehow not realising he has been doing similar things for several months. Now I know his feelings are the same as mine, I fully submerge myself in it and allow it to flow freely, rather than attempting to squeeze them in a box.

Only one thing gnaws at me—Theo, despite putting on this decadent display of his intentions, remains rigidly formal anytime we are not alone. I dip the flatbread into my stew, wondering if perhaps he is embarrassed of me. I am a commoner and a prisoner, and it is likely he is expected to marry a woman of nobility whose father has not sold her to pay off his debts.

I shake off this fear, determined to enjoy the evening. Theo holds up his goblet of wine.

"A toast," he says. "To allies and sanctuaries."

I clink the rim of my goblet against his, and he smiles at me warmly.

"How are your paintings coming along?" he asks before scooping a large spoonful of baby potatoes onto his plate.

"Wonderfully, Your Highness. I have decided to try my hand at still life."

"What about your landscapes?"

"I still enjoy them, but I think it is good to start pushing into other areas." I shrug. "It would not do to stay in a bubble of comfort forever."

"Indeed," Theo replies, looking thoughtful. "There is an art dealer who visits the castle on occasion, hailing from Frostalm. I should like to introduce you to him."

My heart skips at the mention of Frostalm.

"An art dealer?" I raise my eyebrows. "Whatever for?"

"For your paintings, of course." He laughs before taking another sip of wine. A guard coughs behind me, and Theo's smile immediately drops. Confused, I turn around, but there are only the usual guards standing in position.

"What is it?" I ask.

"Nothing." He half-smiles and continues eating.

The atmosphere shifts. I chew my lip, contemplating whether to bring the conversation back to the art dealer. Theo focusses on his food, eating quickly, so I decide to let the topic lie.

We eat in silence for the next few minutes before sitting back to allow our plates to be cleared.

"My thanks," I tell the servant, and Theo does the same.

He fidgets with the collar of his tunic while I sit opposite him, awkwardly rigid. The usual ease of our conversation has evaporated.

"The hour is late," I eventually say, the silence unbearable. I stand up from my seat, scraping the chair back. "I should head back to my chambers. Thank you for dinner, Your Highness."

I curtsy and swiftly exit the dining room before he can say anything back. Tears well up, threatening to spill, but my irritation manages to hold them back. I hike up the skirt of my dress to walk quickly back to my chambers, feeling ridiculous in my frivolous outfit.

"Wait!" Theo calls behind me. I hesitate, half-turning, before deciding against it and powering on. "Shivani, please. Wait."

He eventually catches up to me, slightly out of breath.

"Yes?" I snap, turning on my heel to glare at him.

"I...I am sorry for the way the evening went."

"You should be sorry. You are the one who caused it." I ball my hands into fists, my vision starting to swim with tears. "I do not deserve to be treated like...well, I do not know. A secret? An embarrassment?"

"You are not an embarrassment," he says firmly, reaching for my hand, but I snatch it away.

"Sweet words are meaningless when you act in total contradiction to them."

"I know, I...I am sorry." He glances over his shoulder, eyes wide, before turning back to me. "Please allow me to visit your chambers tonight."

"Really?" I scoff. "Absolutely not."

"Just so I can explain myself and..." he reaches out his hand, palm up. "Apologise properly."

I look at his open hand, an invitation for me, and sigh. I drum up every well of trust I have in him and put my hand in his.

"Fine," I say quietly. Theo's shoulders sag with relief before he brings my hand up to kiss it.

"Thank you, Shivani," he says.

I say nothing and turn, stalking back to my

chambers and leaving him in the corridor.

CHAPTER 24

I wish I had Aunt Meena to talk to. Or Inez. Or even Vanya.

I pace my room back and forth, thoughts churning in my head. I do not know if I have any right to be angry at Theo or if I am simply overreacting. *Hysterical*, my father used to say. The word never used to bother me, but now it jabs at me like a thorn. Maybe Theo does have a rational explanation for his behaviour, and I should be putting my trust in him. Or maybe he is another version of his father—cruel but in quiet and insidious ways. How are you supposed to tell a beast from a man when they look the same?

I shake the last thought out of my head. If I am not my father, then Theo is not his. It is unfair of me to compare him when he has so far only been a gentleman and given me no reason to think he has an ulterior motive. I press my fingers to my temples, sighing. It is difficult to toe the line between healthy scepticism and complete paranoia.

Luckily, my tangle of thoughts is interrupted by a soft knock at the door.

"Enter," I call.

Theo steps in, quietly shutting the door behind him. It is late into the night and the last thing we need is to alert the guards with unnecessary noise. Even him being here, in my chambers with me alone, is crossing a line. It would break the illusion I am at his beck and call, cowed to the prince.

I fold my arms across my chest and jut my chin out.

"Well?"

Theo fidgets awkwardly before gesturing to the bed.

"May I have a seat?"

I look between him and the bed before unfolding my arms with a sigh.

"Yes." I nod and sit next to him. The bed sinks slightly under both our weights as we sit side-by-side, stiff and upright.

"Firstly," he half-turns to me, "I am truly sorry. I would never want you to feel as though I am embarrassed of you, and I am angry at myself for doing so."

"Theo, you act as though you are a different person when we are not alone. I do not understand it, and it is thoroughly vexing." I lean forward and put my face in my hands, frustrated.

"I do not know which side of you is real."

"All the sides of me are real," he replies, and I sit up to look at him. "When I am in sight of the guards, I am…I *have* to be the prince and nothing else. Many of the people who work here understand my father is not a good man, but the guards…the guards report things to him."

Worry starts to gnaw at me.

"What sort of things?"

Theo's shoulders are hunched, and his face looks stricken.

"Who I am close to," he answers quietly.

I swallow hard, trying to dislodge the lump in my throat.

"Is it just the guards?" I ask, thinking back on the times I have spent with the kitchen staff and the servants. "Does anyone else report things?"

Theo shakes his head.

"It is just the guards. The servants are invisible to my father—he does not even consider them unless for torment."

I nod slowly, allowing myself a deep breath to calm my nerves.

"Shivani, I cannot have anything happen to you. I cannot," Theo continues and reaches across to grasp my hand tightly. "Please, the guards must not know."

I press my lips together before squeezing his hand back.

"Why did you not tell me?" I ask. "I would

have understood. I *do* understand."

"I thought I could keep the illusion for the guards intact but I did not think how it would make you feel." He hangs his head. "For that, I am so sorry. I…I wish I had an excuse, but it was simply a short-sighted mistake. I was too focused on trying to keep you away from…it does not matter. I am sorry."

Theo looks at me, his eyes wide and earnest. A flood of affection for him washes through me for all he has done for me. I reach out and brush a brown lock from his forehead. He catches my hand and presses his lips against my palm, keeping his eyes on mine. My pulse quickens.

"Thank you for telling me," I say. "You do not need to keep things from me."

"I only…I wanted to protect you from the truth of it."

I shake my head.

"I do not want that." I turn further towards him, twisting my torso. "Theo, if we are to court, you need to understand we are on equal ground."

His eyebrows furrow.

"Of course—"

"Which means," I continue, raising my voice slightly, "when you have these worries or concerns or anything else, you come to me with them before you decide to do anything on my behalf. We are partners."

Theo blinks, the slightest trace of surprise on his face.

"Partners," he repeats as though testing out the word, and a smile curves his lips. "Yes, I like that. Although, if I am being candid, I believe you may be a more formidable force than I. It is more likely you would be the one protecting me."

He gives me his lopsided grin before reaching out to cup my face. His hand is warm against my cheek, and I lean into it, my worries from the evening evaporating.

"Theo," I breathe, and he raises his eyebrows expectantly. "Would you stay with me tonight?"

Without breaking eye contact, he nods.

"Always."

He begins to pull me closer, but I stop him.

"Just…" My heart is thumping so hard against my ribs, it may burst out at any moment. "Just like the last time where we…I-I mean to say, I do not want to…"

I am suddenly intensely embarrassed, trying to formulate the right words without being too assuming or crude. My face warms as I attempt to stammer out a sentence. Theo stands, smiling.

"You are in control, Shivani," he tells me. "We will do nothing unless you choose to do so."

I blush, relief rushing through me.

"Well, I…I would like to change first." I laugh nervously. "I do not think my dinner dress will be the most comfortable sleep attire."

"I believe you may be correct. Although I did not think they ever looked comfortable." Theo grins before turning and walking to the washroom. "I shall be in here with the door closed. Call me when you are ready."

As soon as he shuts the door, I quickly inspect it to make sure he is telling the truth, which, of course, he was. And that is when the panic sets in.

My boots and stockings are simple enough to remove but Inez dressed me *because* it was a dress which required an external set of hands. The bodice is laced tightly at the back. I manage to twist my arm and grab the ribbon between the tips of two fingers, but when I yank at it, I realise it is held firmly in place with a complicated knot.

"Ugh!" I groan, throwing my hands down in frustration.

"Are you quite alright?" Theo calls from the bathroom.

"No, um, yes!" I lift up my skirt, trying to see if I can pull the whole thing up and over my head.

"No and yes?" he answers.

"It…is…complicated!" I reply, each syllable punctuated with a yank upwards. When that fails, I let the skirt fall back down. "Saints!"

"Shivani?" Theo calls again, knocking on the bathroom door. "Can I come out?"

"Yes," I say miserably, and he steps out

after a moment. He raises an eyebrow when he sees me.

"So, you have opted for the dress as sleep attire?"

I glare at him.

"No. I...well, I cannot seem to take it off." I raise my hands and let them fall to my sides. He regards me with an amused look.

"Would you like me to help?" he asks.

"Is that proper?" I reply, even though having him sleeping in my bed while unmarried makes it a moot point.

"It is practical." Theo shrugs.

Exasperated, I put my hands on my hips.

"Very well! My dignity went out of the window long ago, apparently." I turn and put my back to him so he can unfasten the knot. When he steps behind me, I feel his warm breath on the back of my neck, and I close my eyes as goosebumps spring up.

I vaguely feel him moving the ribbon through the thick fabric of my bodice, but I am distracted by the closeness of his mouth to the nape of my neck. He reaches up to brush my hair over the front of my shoulder, which I believe makes it easier for him to see what he is doing, but for me, all the feeling has left my legs.

My knees buckle slightly, and I catch myself almost immediately, but Theo places a hand on my waist to steady me. His hand is warm even through the dress, and his grip is firm. I fear my legs will give way again at any moment.

Fortunately for me, he manages to untie the knot and I feel him pulling the ribbon back, unlacing it in one smooth movement. The bodice eases its grip on my torso and slides down slightly. I put my hands on my chest, holding it up.

"There," he whispers and I desperately try to clear the fog appearing in my head. He steps back as I turn.

"My thanks," I say hoarsely.

He inclines his head before retreating to the washroom, closing the door behind him. I am left feeling…I am not quite sure what. I want him to go in the washroom while I change to retain my modesty, but I also want him to stay and remove the rest of my dress for me, using the same soft but firm touch he used before. I close my eyes, picturing it.

"Shivani, are you ready?" he calls through the door and I jump. How long have I been standing here, daydreaming?

"One moment," I call back, flustered. I drop my dress and hurriedly replace it with my nightgown. I have several to choose from, and in a moment of madness, I pick the most immodest one available. The white fabric stands in stark contrast to my mahogany skin, with a low neckline and a hem falling just short of my knees. The clinging fabric hugs the shape of my hips and breasts in a way that is completely indecent. I think how scandalised anyone would be knowing I was willingly wearing this in front of a prince, unmarried and alone at night in my chambers. A tumble between commoners is one thing, but to act this way with royalty is entirely different. Instead of the expected shame, there is a secret thrill, not altogether unpleasant.

Although…would anyone be truly scandalised? The king sent me to his son for this exact reason, after all. I make the decision to cast off my worries and do exactly what I want.

"You may come out now," I call through the door, trying to keep my tone light.

I wait for him, hands clasped behind my back as he steps through. When he does, he freezes in the doorway, mouth open and eyes wide.

He first catches sight of my nightgown before his eyes snap up to fix on mine. He says nothing for a moment, his mouth closing and opening several times. I wait patiently for him to gather his bearings, trying not to show how pleased I am.

"You are…dressed," he eventually says, his voice thick. He manages to drag his eyes up to mine and glues them there.

"Yes," I say simply and turn to climb under the heavy covers of my bed.

Theo seems to shake himself out of it and follows me, but his ears are tinged with pink, and he now avoids looking at me completely.

"I must apologise," he says, rubbing the back of his neck. "I do not have any night clothes with me."

"Oh, I suppose not." I sit up in bed, contemplating this. "Well...what would be most comfortable for you?"

Theo's face turns a bright shade of crimson, and he shuffles uncomfortably.

"I am afraid it would not be decent, Miss Shivani," he says, his awkwardness allowing his old formalities to slip back in. My lips shape the letter 'o' as I realise what he means. I think about it for a moment before coming to a decision.

"Theo," I say firmly. "I think we are already far past modesty for modesty's sake. I believe you would not do anything untoward, regardless of how either of us is dressed. Or...undressed."

The last few words come out in a breathy husk as my mind is invaded with images of Theo sleeping nude. I try my best to push them out but I cannot deny the look he is giving me has emboldened me in new ways.

"Well..." He hesitates a moment, and I hold my breath. Slowly, he reaches up and starts unbuttoning his tunic.

I know I should look away, but I find myself enraptured. Theo keeps his eyes on me while I watch his fingers move further and further down his tunic. It opens, and he shrugs it off, leaving his white undershirt. I look at him then, a question in his eyes. I give a small nod.

Theo's fingers reach to the bottom of his undershirt, and he tugs upwards. I inhale sharply as his bare torso is exposed, fair and smooth. The muscles in his stomach and chest move hypnotically as he pulls further up, sliding the undershirt over his head and letting it fall to the floor.

I unabashedly drink in the sight of him —the smattering of fair hair across his chest, trailing down to his stomach. He is somewhere between soft and defined, and I fight hard not to reach across and place my hand on him. I swallow hard.

He pauses and waits for me. After a moment, I nod again.

This time, his fingers slide to the buttons on his trousers, making my breath catch. The room is silent except the sound of my racing heart in my ears. He undoes each button slowly, watching me all the while, waiting for me to stop him. But I do not.

The last of his buttons come apart, and he hooks his thumbs under the band of his trousers. Slowly, he pushes down before stepping out of them. The only thing left is his drawers —loose white fabric which narrows and ends at his knees. His hands hover on the band of them where they are tied low around his hips, showing the cut of his muscle before disappearing under the fabric. I never knew how the bottom of a man's stomach could be so attractive. Again, his eyes find mine and ask the question.

"Stop," I say, my voice barely above a whisper.

As soon as I say it, Theo moves his hands away. My gaze travels from his kind eyes to his strong jaw and further still until I am staring at his bare torso. I am aware I am being lustful, but I cannot bring myself to care, and Theo stands patiently by the bed. The corner of his mouth upticks, a hint of a pleased smile.

"Just like last time," I tell him before reaching for the corner of the covers nearest to him and throwing it back.

He accepts the invitation, sliding into bed next to me.

"I am not expecting anything more from you than you are willing to give," he says and stretches his arm onto my pillow. I shuffle closer and rest my head on his chest. He is warm and firm beneath my cheek, and I find myself relaxing almost immediately. Hesitantly, I place my hand on his stomach, and he responds by placing his hand on top of mine. I lace my fingers between his, and he curls his other arm over, pulling me closer. I am overly aware all that lies between us is the flimsy fabric of my nightgown and his drawers. I try to steady my breathing.

"You are sure I am not…" I struggle to find the right word. "Teasing you?"

He chuckles softly.

"I could lay here with you for the rest of my life and be happier than I have ever been, Shivani," he says and rubs his thumb against my hand.

Pleased, I close my eyes and listen to his heartbeat. It is racing faster than I thought it would be. I slide my leg over his until his thigh is nestled between mine, and his pulse speeds up even further. I wonder if he is as nervous as I am.

Safe, warm and comfortable, I drift off in the middle of my thoughts.

CHAPTER 25

Saint's Day arrives in a flurry of colour and cheer.

The entire castle staff are invited into the throne room to hear the king's speech before the celebrations can begin. When Inez takes my hand, leading me into the stream of servants as everyone makes their way to the throne room, I am surprised.

"But I do not worship the Saints," I whisper to her.

"It does not matter." She shakes her head, smiling. "Everyone is welcome on Saint's Day."

She links her arm with mine, and we follow the rush of people, the atmosphere buzzing around us. People are dressed in their usual staff uniforms—a bleak grey—but for today, the king has allowed them to pin fabric flowers to their clothes and paint their faces and arms with vibrant ink. They beam at us, singing and laughing, as we allow ourselves to be pulled towards the throne room.

I hope there are enough people around me for me to blend in, especially with the flourish of colour around me, but the king lays eyes on me straight away. I stand in the crowd, and we stare at each other while he lazes leisurely on his garish throne. There is the slightest curl to his lips.

And then Theo steps into the room, dressed in his usual jewel-toned royal clothes, but there is a small flower pinned to his chest. A new wave of excitement ripples throughout the crowd as he stands next to his father, hands clasped behind his back. He sees the king watching me and bends to whisper something in his ear. Whatever it is, the king finally breaks his eye contact, and I release a pent-up breath.

"Good people," the king calls out, voice echoing through the room. The crowd immediately falls silent, their obedience overriding their joy for the day. "Please take this day as a token of my generosity to celebrate the Saints in all their glory."

I begin to tune him out, not interested in him turning a religious day into something he has "gifted" his staff. I glance at Theo instead, who has his eyes firmly fixed on a distant point. It hurts, but I understand why.

"What a load of tripe," Inez mutters to me, close enough so only I can hear her. I smother a smirk.

The king eventually concludes his self-gratifying speech and exits with a sweep of his cloak, not bothering to look at me this time. I expect Theo to do the same, but instead, he makes his way into the crowd, weaving through the clamour. I realise he is walking towards us, squeezing past people apologetically.

"Your Highness," Inez and I greet him in tandem. A few of the servants look at us quizzically, but most are too intent on following the festivities.

"Miss Shivani, Miss Inez." He nods at us both.

"It is good to see you again, Your Highness," Inez tells him, her voice earnest. Theo's face softens.

"And you, Miss Inez," he replies. I blink, surprised at the friendship between them, but there is something sad there as well. Neither of them says anything more so I decide not to pry.

"What are you doing here?" I ask him, jerking my chin at the king's doorway. "I thought you would be leaving with him."

Theo wrinkles his nose slightly in disgust before quickly wiping the expression from his face.

"My father will not be here for the celebrations."

"Oh?"

"He is heading for Swordstead, now the storm has cleared." Theo gives me a pointed look.

"He will be gone for several weeks."

"Well, I should think so—Swordstead is on the other side of the country." Inez frowns. "I thought he had given up on this journey to the werewolves. It is unlike him to travel so far."

I cast my mind back, recalling how often the king has left his fortress but I cannot remember even once. My brow furrows.

"Indeed." I tap my chin before turning to Theo. "Do you know why he is so insistent on visiting Swordstead?"

Theo spreads his hands.

"I did not ask."

"Well...will the guards not be suspicious of you spending time with me so publicly?" I ask, glancing nervously at the numerous guards positioned around the room. Their eyes glint.

"Who said I was spending time with you?" He winks at me before clapping his hands loudly. The rest of the servants turn to look at him, eyes wide and curious.

"My friends!" he calls, and I am surprised at how well his voice commands the room. "Happy Saint's Day!"

At this, they begin cheering. Theo patiently waits while they settle, a faint smile on his lips.

"I would love the opportunity to celebrate with you all, if you will have me?" he asks the open crowd. The crowd does not hesitate, swallowing him into the masses with firm claps on the shoulder and an abundance of flowers pinned to his tunic. Theo laughs and thanks them, allowing them to welcome him into the crowd. Inez gives me a smile and a sidelong look.

"His Highness has never before joined us for Saint's Day," she tells me as the crowd begins to move, sweeping us through the corridors.

"Indeed?"

"Oh, he always treats us right, do not mistake me. Polite and kind to all the staff." She watches him chatting easily to one of the gardeners. "But he was closed off."

"Because of the curse?"

"Yes. And…" Inez lowers her eyes, but before she can say anything else, the mass of servants pulls us into the dining room.

The usual cavernous room is now lit up with strong, bright torches. Several stalls line the walls where staff have made their own wares. As the crowd thins out, spread around the room, Inez and I stroll past tables laden with jewellery, food, and other trinkets. Most popular are the fabric flowers as they are the easiest to make—small strips of colourful cotton or silk folded in a way to imitate petals and then fastened with a pin. Inez picks one out for me—a beautiful purple flower—and pins it to my dress.

The hall fills with the smell of baked goods and I find a stall selling saffron cookies. Vanya stands behind the table and inclines her head at us.

"Miss Shivani." She folds her arms. "I must thank you for the recipe."

She gestures to the biscuits, delicately baked and presented in neat rows.

"Of course." I grin, happy at the mere sight of something so familiar and close to home. "They look quite incredible. My aunt would be impressed."

A ghost of a smile crosses Vanya's face.

"I did not think witches worshipped the Saints," she comments, but not unkindly.

"And you are correct." I smile and point at a cookie. "May I?"

"Of course."

"Who do you worship, out of curiosity?" Inez asks, taking another cookie for herself.

"Well, no one, I suppose." I take a bite and savour the buttery crumble. A rush of homesickness sweeps over me but I push it away, blocking it with obscure facts. "Did you know that 'Saints' are what dragons called the old gods?"

Vanya raises an eyebrow, intrigued. Inez reaches for another saffron cookie.

"Dragon magic is drawn from meditation and peace of mind. Often, this went hand-in-hand with their religious practices, like praying," I continue, pleased at having someone, other than Theo, who listens to my ramblings.

"So, their magic is drawn from the Saints?" Vanya probes.

"Correct! Or at least, it is widely believed to be so. This whole county used to be populated with dragons, in fact, before they migrated to Coalsburgh. Their culture still lingers." I gesture at the rest of the festivities. "Like Saint's Day."

Vanya gives a thoughtful look to the crowd before leaning forward over the table.

"Let me show you something," she tells me, expression unreadable. Inez and I share a glance but follow Vanya regardless as she leads us away from the bustle of the crowd.

She opens a secret passageway, a slim door disguised as brickwork. Vanya presses two fingers against one of the bricks, and the door pops open with a click. Vanya and Inez step in first.

"Wait!"

The three of us whip around, expecting guards, but it is only Theo. My shoulders sag with relief. He jogs over to us, slightly out of breath.

"My apologies." He nods at Inez and Vanya. "Do you mind if I join you on this excursion?"

Vanya looks at me, eyebrows lowered in uncertainty.

"Unless it is...private?" Theo asks, sensing her hesitation.

"Is it, Vanya?" Inez turns to the other woman.

"Of course you may join, Your Highness," Vanya eventually replies before ducking into the passageway. Inez shrugs at me and follows. Theo gives me a questioning look, but I spread my hands.

"Shall we see where this leads?" I say.

Theo smiles and gestures to the passageway.

"After you, Miss Shivani."

With Theo at my back, I climb inside, and he closes the door behind us.

It is dark, with no lit torches. I fumble around in the gloom and nearly fall, but soft hands catch me.

"Careful, miss," Inez's voice is close in front of me. "Hold my hand and follow me."

I feel her palm as her hand clasps mine. Behind me, I reach for Theo. His fingers weave between mine and hold me tight. Like a daisy chain, we move through the darkness with only each other to guide us.

Whereas the other passageways led us through the castle and ended up in other corridors, this one deposits us in a hidden section. A lone room.

We climb out of the passageway, blinking at the sudden light. The room is bathed in a purple glow, the torches on the wall flickering with lavender fire. They line the small, circular room—it is only just big enough for the four of us but with a high ceiling. I gaze up at the torches, surprised.

"An enchantment," I whisper, watching the hypnotic purple flames.

"Oh!" Inez exclaims with a wide smile. "My mother used to be able to do that. Turn things purple, I mean."

"She put a spell on them, using witch magic," Vanya tells her evenly. "They will never go out."

"Well, enchantments do not last forever. They only last until the object is broken or the person who cast it dies." I squeeze Inez's hand. "It is proof your mother still lives, enjoying her retirement."

Inez's eyes water as she beams at me.

"Thank you, Miss Shivani."

"So, this was your mother's secret room?" Theo turns slowly on the spot, taking it all in.

"No, Your Highness," Vanya says and her voice softens. "It was your mother's."

Theo's head snaps to look at her, his eyes wide. The muscle at his jaw dances, but he says nothing.

"How do you know?" I ask Vanya, brushing a reassuring hand across Theo's arm. He catches my hand before I can pull away. Vanya and Inez pretend not to notice.

"This was her altar to the Saints so she could pray in private." Vanya indicates to the far side of the room. Theo and I step closer to inspect it.

A table has been carved out of the wall, rough but sturdy. Small statues line up like soldiers, each one painted a different colour. I pick one up delicately, curious.

"That is the Celestial," Vanya murmurs over my shoulder. I turn the figure this way and that, watching the silver and blue dance in the light. "Saint of wisdom and intelligence."

"And charisma." I place it back gently. "It is who silver-tongued dragons prayed to."

The rest of the figurines match the other Saints—The Idol, Nephel, and Shivanya. I pick the last one up, admiring the details carved into the clay. It is heavy in my hands.

"That is my Saint," Vanya tells me, nodding approvingly. She makes the sign of Shivanya, tapping her forehead and her throat in quick succession. "And my namesake."

"You pray to justice?" Inez pipes up, peering around me. "An admirable choice."

"I agree," I say, placing Shivanya down again where she stands proudly. "She is my namesake also. My father is not a witch—he followed the Saints and chose my name before I was born."

Bitterness sits uncomfortably in my mouth at the thought of my cowardly father naming his only daughter after the Saint of justice. I run my tongue across my teeth to rid myself of it.

"I can see why. She was known for her iron will." Inez smiles at me and I manage to dredge up a smile back.

I cast a sidelong glance over the purple

torches. Yet another remnant of witchcraft in this castle. I slot the information away next to the enchanted book and the hidden escape tunnel. Vanya, too, has her place in my mind next to the other mysteries. I eye her as she lingers next to the altar, an unreadable expression on her face.

I turn to see Theo planted firmly on the other side of the room, watching us with interest but making no move to come any closer. He fidgets awkwardly.

"Perhaps it is time we make our way back to the festivities," I suggest, and relief floods his face.

"I agree." He nods and, without hesitation, steps back into the passageway. Vanya and Inez follow closely behind. I give one last look at the queen's secret altar—her lovingly crafted statues and the enchanted torches on the wall. I chew the inside of my cheek, thoughtful, before turning my back and leaving.

CHAPTER 26

A week later, Theo turns.

I am summoned to his chambers in the early hours of the morning when a few stars are still stubbornly twinkling in the orange sky. When I arrive, he is lying in his bed in a familiar bloody state. I hurry over to him. Even though I have become accustomed to this routine, concern still floods my mind. His turning has become less and less frequent, and I worry it is the calm before the storm.

"Theo." I grasp his hand. "I am here."

He smiles weakly at me, his cheek pressed against the pillow.

"A silver lining to this curse," he wheezes. "You have a reason to visit me."

"I would visit you regardless." I brush his matted hair from his forehead.

"Ah, yes, the agreement." The corner of his mouth tugs upwards, and I roll my eyes at his ability to tease even during intense pain.

"Let me fetch the lavender tonic," I say, but he stops me as I move.

"No, wait." He licks his chapped lips. "It is a little easier tonight. The pain is less sharp."

I eye him dubiously.

"Are you quite sure?"

"I am. But..." He winces. "I am rather sick of sleeping covered in blood."

"Oh." I look him over. It was often low on the priority list to clean him up when he was suffering so greatly, and he usually waited until morning to wash. "I see. Shall I take you to the washroom?"

"Truthfully, I would like the castle baths. But I do not know if I can make it that far." He glances at the door.

"Do not worry about that. I will help you," I say, standing up. "The hot water may ease your pains also."

He gives a heavy sigh and waves a hand weakly.

"Very well," he says. "I trust your judgement."

I give him a reassuring pat on the shoulder and stand. The baths are not far, only a few minutes' walk away, but in Theo's current state, it will likely feel like a lifetime for him. I scoop an arm under his upper back and lift, helping him onto his feet. He groans, gritting his teeth. I hope I am right about the hot water.

We inch through the halls, taking regular

breaks so Theo can catch his breath. I sense the guards eyeing us, but pay them no mind.

"Not much further," I soothe him and recall a story I read in dragon text long ago to distract him. "Do you know the dragons of old built many communal baths?"

"Indeed?" he breathes. His face is pinched, but he cocks an eyebrow, intrigued.

"They believed the water had healing properties, as it was so vital to life," I continue. "They carved great bathhouses out of the side of mountains, bathing in the hot water secretly buried there. Supposedly, there are still some that remain. It is said the hot water springs were the inspiration for dragon magic as they learned how to heal themselves through it. Healing turned to other forms of manipulation, which turned into shapeshifting."

"Faeth," Theo mumbles, putting the pieces together. I nod encouragingly.

"Faeth. The ability to change yourself through prayer."

Theo ruminates on this quietly, some of the tension easing from his expression as the story distracts him.

I feel the warmth emanating from the castle baths before we reach it. Steam pours from between the gaps in the doors, swirling against the cooler air in the castle.

"We have arrived, Theo. You made it," I tell him, but he is only able to give me a shaky half-smile.

We stumble into the baths, quickly closing the door behind us to keep the warmth in. The air is hot and humid, and the steam is thick. There is a marble runway around the entirety of the large room, shelving various bottles of soaps, shampoos and empty jugs, with steps descending into the baths. Candles, protected from the moisture, hang in glass boxes from the ceiling. The water looks inviting—clear and blue against the white marble—as the steam dances across the surface.

Theo is only wearing his drawers, roughly pulled onto him by the guards when he turned back, so we do not bother to undress him. I help him as he stumbles down the steps into the hot water. His legs nearly buckle beneath him, but I catch him in time, wrapping my free arm around his waist. He is heavy, but I am determined.

"M-My apologies," he gasps, grimacing.

"I want to hear no apologies from you," I tell him firmly. "Your only focus is healing."

We reach the water and, using every muscle I can draw upon, I ease him slowly in. He inhales sharply through his teeth as the hot water touches his feet and then moves further up his legs until finally settling at his chest as he sits. Crimson swirls through the water like red paint as the blood is soaked from his skin. He tips his head back and sighs.

"Yes," he says, eyes closed. "This is helping.

Perhaps the dragons were onto something."

Relieved, I sit on the step above him and submerge my feet and calves in the water. I wiggle my toes, savouring the sweet burn of the water.

The blood is gently sloughed from Theo under the water, but the part of him above the surface stays stubbornly stuck.

"Would you like me to help clean your face and neck?" I ask him. His eyes flutter open and find mine.

"If you would be so kind," he replies, a hint of his spirited smile on his lips. "But you will need to come in with me."

"I am fully clothed." I laugh.

"In your nightgown." He shrugs. "It will withstand some water."

I roll my eyes good-humouredly.

"Very well." I place my hands palm down on the step and push myself off, sliding into the water next to him.

It is hot but not uncomfortably so. After a second or two, I acclimate and the warmth seeps into my bones pleasantly. I turn to Theo and scoop water into my hands, pouring it over one of his shoulders.

"Closer," he murmurs, looking at me through half-shut eyes. "Please."

"How close?" I whisper, reaching across to pour more water on his other shoulder.

As an answer, his hands move under the

water to grip my thighs. In one swift movement, he pulls me across until I am kneeling over his lap, my thighs on each side of his. I gasp with the sudden movement and his eyes open fully.

"Is this alright?" he asks, his hands still on my thighs. His fingertips press pleasingly into my skin.

"Yes," I breathe.

I slowly move my hands from under the water up to his bare chest, washing away the angry red. He closes his eyes again, tipping his head back but keeping his gentle grip on me, holding me to him. I move further up until I run my fingers across his collarbone, feeling the dip between the ridge of the bone and his neck.

I continue up slowly and start to work on the sharp angle of his jaw. The skin is not as smooth here, spiked with fair stubble that I, for some reason, enjoy even more. I dip my hands in the water, washing his jaw of blood before returning to his face. His eyes remain closed, his expression peaceful.

I look at his lips, chapped and bloody, and a bout of nerves springs up inside me.

"Theo?" I whisper. "Are you still awake?"

"I am," he replies without moving.

"Would you like me to keep going?"

The corners of his lips tug upwards.

"Please," he says.

I hesitate briefly before obliging. Making sure my hands have been cleaned and soaked, I bring my thumbs up to his lips and brush them slowly, moving from one corner to the next. I move gently, mindful of his aches and pains, washing away the last remnants of blood. I think about how his lips would feel against mine.

I linger a few seconds too long and have to tear myself away. His hair is still matted with blood, so I use that as a reason to move on. I lean to grab one of the smaller jugs and a jar of sweet-smelling soap.

"Keep your head back," I tell him, voice hushed. It does not feel like a place for raised voices—too quiet and intimate.

"As you wish," Theo murmurs and his thumbs begin to stroke the fabric over my thighs. My nightgown is already thin and being under the water has made it feel as if it does not even exist at all. I exhale and focus on my task.

I dip the jug in the water to fill it before carefully tipping it over Theo's hair. A river of red runs from the step into the water. I slide my fingers through his hair with one hand while pouring water with the other, pretending I am trying to get the blood off when, really, I want to feel the thickness of his hair between my fingers. Theo's lips part as he exhales softly.

When his hair has been soaked, I scoop two fingers into the soap and apply it, using both hands to lather. I can feel his scalp beneath my fingertips and apply some pressure as I move.

Theo groans as I do so.

"Is that painful?" I ask, immediately releasing him.

"No." He gives the tiniest shake of his head. "It is wonderful."

I smile and resume massaging the soap through his hair, working it up into a red lather.

"You are wonderful," he breathes, nearly indecipherable.

My heart fills. Smiling, I pull one of my hands away to pick up the jug. I re-fill it and pour fresh water, rinsing the suds and blood away. After several repeats, his locks are shiny and clean, the colour of dark honey again. Despite being wet, his hair is thick in my hands, and I run my fingers through it once more.

"There," I say. "You are cleaned."

Theo opens his eyes then and keeps his gaze on me.

"My thanks," he says, and one of his hands releases my thigh. He brings it up to the side of my face, cupping my cheek. I know what he wants to do, and this time, I want him to do it. He slides his hand into my hair, tenderly gripping the back of my head, and I allow him to pull me in towards him.

His lips are still wet from the water but soft and warm against mine. I melt into him, my back arching as I press my chest against his. My hand finds the nape of his neck, and I hold him there, wanting and needing him closer.

When his lips part mine, I give no

resistance. His tongue slides against mine briefly, shooting a jolt through my body. A warmth spreads inside me which has nothing to do with the baths. Theo's grip tightens a fraction on the back of my head, his fingers tangled in my hair, and a gasp escapes me. There is barely an inch between us and still it feels like I am not close enough. I press myself closer and Theo responds in kind, his arm wrapping around my waist. The world melts away around us. I only pull back when I am breathless.

Theo looks at me with a lopsided smile, his eyes somehow glazed and sharp all at once, his cheeks tinted pink. He traces the pad of his thumb across my jaw.

"You and I," he says, his eyes not leaving mine.

Looking at him there, beautiful and kind, I know I am in love.

CHAPTER 27

Month Five

News about the king spreads fast.

I am painting in my art room, lost in the process of replicating the vase of flowers sitting in front of me. Flowers the prince has sent for me, vibrant and beautiful, grown in his garden. Tubes of paint are scattered on the ground and the table as I dip my brush in a particularly striking shade of dandelion yellow and swipe it across the canvas. I am feverous, fixated on my task as the rest of the world around me ceases to exist. I do not hear Inez until she is right next to me.

"Miss Shivani!" She waves a hand in front of my face, startling me out of my bubble.

"Oh." I blink. "Inez. Good afternoon."

"It is evening now, miss," she corrects me.

"Is it?" I turn my head to look out of the glass wall. The sun sinks below the horizon, and the first of the navy blue night sky slowly crawls in. "Oh dear, I seem to have lost track of time again. Apologies, did I miss you for dinner?"

"Never mind that, miss." She shakes her head before pausing. "Although, yes, I should fetch you dinner if you have not eaten yet. But that is not what I came here for."

She bends over to grab my hands. Her skin is warm against mine, but her brows are furrowed.

"What is it, Inez?" I ask, turning away from my painting, concern rising.

"News of the king has arrived," she says, and my stomach drops.

"Is he returning to the castle?" I ask. "I thought we had longer."

"A rider from Swordstead met him halfway. He...I am sorry, miss, but he is bringing home a bride for the prince."

Nausea bubbles in my stomach. A deep ache forms in my chest, like a storm cloud, dark and troubling. I try to say something but there is a ringing in my ears blocking out all my other thoughts.

"Miss Shivani?" Inez grasps my hands tighter.

"I am alright," I manage to say, my voice quiet. "When does he return?"

"A month," she replies. "I am so sorry, miss."

"In time for my six-month sentence to

end," I say bitterly. *In time for him to remove my head.*

I stay still for several moments, my brain churning. Inez watches me, a ball of nervous energy.

"Will you take a note to the prince for me, please?" I say eventually. "We...I need to talk with him. Urgently."

"Of course, miss," she replies, standing. "I will find him immediately."

After I hastily scribble a note and send Inez away, I stand alone in the middle of the room. I clench my fists hard enough for my nails to dig into my palm and fight back tears. My ophid is tense, and I wish, now more than ever, I could reach my au'mana.

"I will figure this out," I say out loud to myself. "I will."

I take a deep breath and unfurl my fingers. Once my breathing has calmed, I hurriedly make my way to my chambers. I will need to speak to Theo first, but if that fails—for reasons I do not allow myself to think about—I will escape. I know the castle layout better, I know the staff, I can think of a better plan than last time. I have the secret tunnel. My skin itches at the thought of leaving everyone behind and I clutch at my neck, agitated. I only hope my note reaches the prince soon.

But when I open the door to my chambers, Theo is already there.

"Shivani," he says and his voice is laden with relief and sadness. He crosses the room immediately and scoops me into his arms, burying his face in the crook of my neck.

"You received my note already?" I ask, wrapping my arms around his back.

"Note? I have been here for hours, waiting for you," he replies, drawing back. His eyes are wet with tears, his cheeks blotchy.

"Theo..." I reach up to push his tousled hair back before cupping his face.

"You have heard then? I always knew news spread fast amongst the staff, but I did not realise how fast." He gives an attempt at a smile, but it crumbles immediately, and he begins sobbing. I pull him back into an embrace, making soothing noises and stroking the back of his head. I am a fool for ever thinking he would turn his back on me for another.

"The king will not return for a month," I tell him. "We have time to think, to plan."

"You have a plan?" he mumbles into my neck, voice thick with tears.

"Well, of sorts," I say before pulling away. "We will think of something together, yes? However long it takes, there will be a solution."

He nods, wiping his tears away with the back of his arm. His lashes are stuck together, and his eyes are puffy. My heart goes out to his sensitive soul.

"You are much more pragmatic than I,"

he says, blinking his eyes dry. "I would have wallowed here forever if you had not come back."

I laugh before bringing his face to mine. I press my lips against his as his arms wrap around me.

"And I would not have lasted as long here without your kind heart," I tell him as he presses his forehead against mine. "Let us stay here tonight and not think any more of it. Tomorrow, we will wake with fresh minds and clear eyes."

He exhales and nods before I lead him to my bed. Even with the threat of the king's return, once I am slotted in his arms, sleep comes easily.

"You and I," he whispers before I slip into darkness.

* * *

As soon as I awaken, my mind is made up. I lay buried in the crook of Theo's arm, eyes wide, listening to the sound of his steady heartbeat. When he does not awake after a few minutes, I carefully extract myself and sit up in bed. Theo stirs with a grumble.

"Theo."

"Mhmm?" He does not open his eyes but turns towards me, wrapping an arm around my hips with his face half-buried in his pillow. I swallow past the dry lump in my throat.

"Theo," I repeat. "There is a secret tunnel in the castle."

"There are many secret tunnels in the castle," he mumbles into the pillow.

"No, listen." I lick my lips. "There is one that leads *outside*."

Theo does not move for a moment, but his eyes shoot open. They swivel in my direction.

"Show me."

The guards eye us unhappily as I lead Theo to the bedchamber I found, but they say nothing. They often keep quiet when the king is away. When I open the door, the room is the same as I remember. I pray no one has been in since.

Theo steps in and looks around, eyebrows furrowed.

"Curious," he says. "The tunnel is in here?"

By way of an answer, I cross the room to the bookcase and pull the handle, disguised as a book. With a loud clunk, the bookcase splits, revealing the tunnel. Theo's jaw drops.

"Saints," he whispers. "And you are quite certain it leads outside?"

I nod my head vigorously.

"I walked the entire length of it."

"But the castle...I was told it stands on stilts above the swamp?"

"It does." I rub my temples, a headache forming, but I catch Theo wrinkling his nose. "Wait. What do you smell?"

"Salt," he says, narrowing his eyes at the tunnel. "Another enchantment?"

I whirl to stare at the bookcase. There is no

glow…or perhaps there is, but we cannot see it from inside.

"The tunnel must be invisible to those outside the castle." I chew on my thumbnail. A witch lived in this castle, of that I have no doubt. So much of it has been enchanted in ways no unknowing person would be able to tell. I think of Inez's mother, Ruya, and wonder what part she had to play in this.

"This is incredible," Theo says, breaking me from my thoughts. "You can leave, Shivani."

"Leave?" I turn back to stare at him. "I cannot leave."

He looks at me as though I have grown an extra head.

"But you must. My father is…is going to kill you." Tears spring to his eyes. "Do you not understand?"

"Of course I understand. It is *my* head that will roll," I say, and it comes out harsher than I intended. I inhale deeply. "I will not leave you to suffer under him any longer. I will not leave any of you."

"But—"

"Theo!"

His mouth clamps shut and his hands ball into fists.

"I do not want you to kill yourself for me," he says, his voice strained and his nostrils flaring.

"Theo," I say slowly. "You do not decide

how far I will go for you. That is my choice and mine alone."

Tears spill down his cheeks.

"But you will die," he chokes out. "If you leave now, you can *live*. You can find somewhere safe, be free of this place. Find…find someone to love and marry and be happy."

I sigh and step towards him, taking his hands in mine. He is right—I can flee and survive, as the snow hare does.

But I am no snow hare.

"You need to understand this. I stay, not because of what I feel for you, but because it is the right thing to do. True, I can leave, and maybe I will find a new home. But I would be tormented for the rest of my life knowing I turned my back on people I could help. Because I *can* help. This curse…the answer is close. I know it is."

Theo squeezes his eyes shut, trying to blink away tears. He grasps my hands tightly and takes a deep, shuddering breath.

"What…what must we do?"

I slip one of my hands away from his to close the tunnel door. The bookcase slides back together, the wood slotting into each other perfectly.

"We need more information."

❈ ❈ ❈

The first stop is the library.

"So, how does this apply to our current predicament?" Theo asks as we scour the shelves. I pull out various books that look like they have potential and stack them in Theo's arms.

"Woefully little is known about your curse," I reply, cocking my head to read the title of a thick, green book. "But what we do know is the king uses it to control you. You have never left the castle, never talked to anyone else in the kingdom besides the staff here, and it gives him an excuse to lock you up in that awful dungeon."

"The dungeon is to protect people from me," he retorts before pausing. "But I concede to your point."

I smile sideways at him. "Curses are rare indeed, but they can always be broken. We need to figure out how to break it."

"What about true love's kiss?" Theo grins at me. "Perhaps we should try that."

"We have kissed plenty of times, and none of them have broken your curse." I shake my head playfully.

"Ah," he says and I hear the smile in his voice even without looking. "So, you do love me."

I freeze, my hand halfway to a book. My heart is suddenly thunderous. The dust from the bookshelves lodges itself in my throat and I choke on it.

"I...I..." I splutter.

Theo laughs and leans forward to kiss my temple.

"I jest," he says before nodding to the bookshelf. "You believe one of these will give us the answer?"

I cough awkwardly and take the opportunity he gives me to change the conversation.

"Y-Yes," I stammer. "I believe so. If we can break the curse—"

"We can leave," Theo finishes for me. "Together."

I smile.

"Together."

When I decide we have enough books to start with, we make our way to one of the tables, and Theo drops them heavily. Many of the books are in the common tongue, but several are written in dragon text. The only exception is the purple book of au'mana.

"The answer is in here somewhere," I mutter. "It must be."

I briefly consider sending for Aunt Meena —if anyone knows anything about dragons, it will be her. But it would be too dangerous, both for her and for Theo and myself. If anyone discovered we were *actually* trying to break this curse, my head would be on a spike by the morning.

I leave Theo to trawl the other books while I wade through the dragon text. I am not as fluent as I used to be and some of the words I cannot understand, but I try to piece it together with context. I find a section detailing dragon curses, but none of the descriptions match what happens to Theo. And they all emphasise how rare they are, only being used once every thousand years by some anomaly of a dragon.

Frustrated, I slam the book shut and pull over another.

"Nothing, I assume?" Theo asks, licking his finger to turn a page. I am temporarily distracted by the sight of his tongue and have to internally scold myself—this is clearly not the time.

"Nothing," I reply with a heavy sigh. "I do not understand. Dragon curses are rare because of the sheer intensity of emotion required to transfer their internal power to another. Dragons use meditation to draw on their faeth, which requires peace of mind rather than high emotions. It often takes decades to master. It just does not make sense how you were cursed."

I put my head in my hands, elbows propped on the table.

"What about witch curses?" Theo asks, glancing at the purple book.

"Well, witch curses are *slightly* less rare because our au'mana is drawn from powerful emotions," I say. Theo perks up, but I shake my head. "But they can only enchant or curse inanimate objects, not living things. Even plants are immune. Besides, we already know your mother was a dragon, not a witch."

Theo slumps back.

"So, we have reached an impasse," he says.

"No," I reply firmly. "No. There is something that will help us. We...we just need to keep looking."

Desperation slips into my voice—I notice it, and Theo looks at me, noticing it as well. He pauses before sitting forward again.

"Then we will keep looking," he says and opens another book.

We read and find more books and read and find more books until the castle falls silent and the night sky takes over. The candles burn low, casting a dim glow, which makes it difficult to read.

"I think we will need to finish for the night," I eventually say, breaking the silence. I raise my arms above me and stretch them, ridding myself of the ache in my joints from being sedentary for too long. My ophid protests—I have never gone this long without using it, and I know the strength in it is waning. Theo looks as tired as me, with dark circles under his eyes.

"We will try again tomorrow," he says with an encouraging smile despite his fatigued features.

✻ ✻ ✻

We stay in his chambers for the evening, as we have been doing each night since the baths.

As he falls asleep, I lay with my head on his chest, unable to join him. There are so many thoughts in my head. My brain is a hive of bees, each of them a different thought buzzing around incessantly. I run my finger in circles on Theo's chest, eyes wide in the dark, thinking.

What are the facts? I ask myself. *Start there.*

The facts are that Theo transforms into a beast, seemingly at random. It is a curse placed on him by his mother at birth, who was executed shortly after by the king once he had realised what she had done. This information niggles at me, but I cannot think why, so I file it to the side and move on.

The curse is dragon in origin, of that I am certain. The taste of faeth when Theo transforms and his mother's altar confirms she was a dragon, so she could only have used dragon magic. But was it her who cursed him? Again, I am stuck on this piece of information. It could not have been anyone else unless someone snuck in while he was a baby...and if they did, why? Was it a grudge against the king or perhaps the queen?

I groan, my thoughts dragging me down a hole I am struggling to climb out of. There are too many unknowns, and I endeavour to find out more information of Theo's birth tomorrow. I eventually fall into a fitful sleep.

When I awaken, it is late into the morning, and I feel as though I have not slept at all.

The sun spills through the window, bathing us in a golden glow. Theo is still asleep, the covers pushed down to his hips. I sit up blearily.

"Theo?" I say, my voice still hoarse from sleep.

"Mmm," he replies, unmoving. I take him in, the shape of his arms and the definition of his shoulders. I place a hand on his chest and find he is warm.

"Good morrow," I say fondly before planting a soft kiss on his collarbone.

He doesn't reply but wraps an arm around my waist, resting it there.

"You will need to visit the library alone today," I tell him. "I have other investigations to do."

"Hmm?" he says, a line appearing between his eyebrows but otherwise remaining still.

"I will see you later on this evening in your chambers." I kiss his cheek before slipping out of his hold. I leave a note for him on the bedside, knowing he most likely did not register anything I told him, and make for the servants' quarters. The thought of our mornings together being taken from us fills me with renewed vigour and determination courses through me. I will break the king's grip on our lives if it is the last thing I do.

CHAPTER 28

I take the secret passageway to the servants' quarters to avoid the guards.

The passage is dark and narrow, but I am well-travelled in several of the secret pathways of the castle so I press on confidently. I sneak out of the other side, behind a large painting only a few metres from my destination —the servants' quarters.

Inez is awake when I arrive, in the middle of her breakfast with the other staff. She stands up when she sees me, her eyebrows raised.

"Miss Shivani!" she exclaims, placing her tea down. "What are you doing here? We were not expecting you."

"I need your help," I tell her before inclining my head in greeting to the others. "My apologies for the interruption."

"Miss Shivani," they greet me back with friendly waves. Vanya sits with a kitchen porter, playing cards while they eat. Her face remains stoic but she nods at me, mouth full.

"Of course," Inez says and we leave back through the secret passageway, this time entering a different section which ends up close to my art room. It is only when we are alone and the door locked behind us that I speak.

"My apologies for interrupting your breakfast," I say, but she waves it away.

"Is this about the king's return? Then it is important enough to miss some toast. How can I help?"

We take a seat at the paint-filled table, and I try to organise the thoughts scattered in my brain.

"Theo—" I start before clearing my throat. "*The prince's* mother, you knew her?"

Inez is taken aback by my question, her eyebrows raised.

"The queen? Well...I suppose I did, but it was so long ago. She passed when I was a young child," she tells me. "Why do you ask?"

I lean my head on my hand, one finger pressed against my temple.

"I am not quite sure yet but there is something about the prince's curse which has been nagging at me," I say, chewing my lip. "It does not make sense. We have been researching thoroughly, and there is no known curse which matches the prince's. So how did she do it?" I pause. "*Did* she do it?"

Inez tenses.

"You think the queen was not responsible?" She blinks at me, the gears turning in her brain. As if on instinct, she looks over her shoulder even though we are the only ones in the room. "Well, then, *who*? Not the king, surely?"

"No...No, I do not think so. He is cruel enough, certainly, and I believe he has enough hate in his heart to perform a curse. But he is not magically inclined...is he?" I look at Inez expectantly.

"I do not believe so, miss." She shakes her head. "He has never made anything glow purple, at the very least. But magic can be hidden, can it not?"

"Sometimes..." I sit, thinking. "No. There are not infinite types of magic, and I fully believe the king would have exploited it if he had the ability to do so. The hold he exerts over others is entirely due to his status and not a magical ability. No," I conclude. "It could not have been the king."

Something else catches my brain, but I cannot quite see it. What would the king do if he were magically inclined? I shake the thought away, deeming it irrelevant.

"So, it was the queen then?" Inez asks.

I make a vague sound, unconvinced.

"Would anyone else have been around or had access to the prince when he was a baby?" I ask, considering the theory of someone sneaking in while he was still in his crib.

Inez thinks for a moment before shaking her head.

"The prince has been sheltered, even within these walls," she tells me, gesturing around us. "And the staff were prevented from assisting the queen during the birthing process."

I give her a questioning look.

"The king believed she would survive if she was fit to." A look of disgust crosses her face. "The young prince was kept confined for the first several years of his life, even from the staff, due to the dangerous nature of his curse."

I sit back and ponder this.

"It was the queen then," I say with a sigh. "It could not have been anyone else."

Inez is quiet for a moment before speaking.

"I am sorry I could not be of more help, miss," she says, patting my shoulder. "I was too young to remember much of the queen, and the king got rid of the staff who did know her."

My ears prick up at this.

"He got rid of them?" I repeat. "Why?"

"The queen had many friends amongst the staff. I suppose the king did not want her allies around him after what she had done."

My eyebrows furrow.

"So...she was well-liked?"

"Yes, miss."

I stare at her dumbly. The queen being popular with the staff was not a thought that had ever crossed my mind. I picture her from the tales we have been told for twenty-five years and all I can see is a bitter, vindictive woman.

"But how?" I ask. "If she was this horrible wretch capable of cursing her own son?"

"I suppose a lot of evil people are quite charming when they want to be." Inez shrugs.

"But with the staff?" I brood over this. "I cannot understand. There are so many missing parts to this story."

Inez regards me with sympathy as I rub my temples.

"Do you want to stay for lunch, miss? I can ask Vanya to rustle something up for you," she offers.

"No, thank you. I think I am going to clear my head," I say, standing.

There are too many moving fragments in this puzzle, and my mind begins to slow, bogged down by it all.

"Oh, I do have something for you before you go." Inez brightens before pulling something out of her apron.

She presents me with a small notebook bound with strong leather. It gives off a tell-tale purple glow, albeit faintly.

"Your mother's journal?" I ask, accepting it from her. There is the slightest hesitation in Inez before she lets it go.

"Yes, I…Perhaps we can go through it together soon?" She tears her eyes away from it to give me a hopeful smile. I press the book to my chest.

"I will treat it with the utmost care, Inez," I assure her.

The creases in Inez's forehead smooth before she curtseys a farewell. I tuck the journal into a secure drawer in the art room, the only one which has a lock. I keep the key safe in one of the hidden pockets of my dress and make my way to Theo's glasshouse to clear my head.

The air in the castle grows warmer, although there is still a brisk edge to it, leftover from winter. The cold season never lasts long in Mossgarde.

I climb the mountainous steps up to the greenhouse, needing a moment away from the guards. When I reach it, I find Theo already there.

He sits at the large table in the middle, several pots of soil in front of him and an open gardening book to one side. I open the door with a loud creak, and his head whips up.

"Ah." His shoulders drop in relief, and his face brightens. "Good morrow, Shivani."

"You are not in the library?" I ask, sitting beside him.

"I was," he sighs. "But I was beginning to feel overwhelmed. I needed a moment."

I smile, sympathetic.

"Apologies for disrupting your peace," I tell him, but he shakes his head.

"I am pleased to see you." He leans forward

to press his lips against mine. No matter how often we kiss, it still causes a flutter in my stomach. "Did you find anything useful in your investigations?"

"I am afraid not. Apart from learning the queen was well-liked amongst the staff, which contradicts everything else we know."

"She was?" Theo is as surprised by this as I was.

"Supposedly, yes. It is why your father got rid of the staff who knew her."

Theo chews on the inside of his cheek.

"Back to the library, then?" he asks, moving away from the topic. He slots his bookmark between the pages of his book and closes it.

"Back to the library," I confirm, rubbing an aching spot on my forehead.

We spend the rest of the day sifting through any books which even slightly appear like they may have useful information. I learn more about dragon culture, diet and religion than I ever thought I would, even when my aunt helped me to study. I think to myself, with bitter irony, I would have no issue passing the Frostalm exam now.

"Did you know tattoos are a crucial part of dragon culture and have been used for centuries?" I ask Theo.

"Yes, we found that out yesterday," he replies, not looking up from the page. His head is leaning on one hand, his elbow propped up on the table.

"Did we?"

"We talked about how it explains my back tattoo."

"Oh." I remember one of our many conversations in the gloom of the library. "We did."

Theo's tattoo was likely a product of his curse, given the word in dragon text embedded in the swirling pattern. He had shown me his tattoo when I asked and I managed to replicate the word onto paper for us to study. It was not a familiar word to me, so I could not translate it to the common tongue, and none of the dragon books made reference to it, leaving us with another fruitless endeavour.

"I think we might be going in circles." Theo clasps his hands and sets his brow against them. "I cannot read anymore."

"But we must not give up," I insist.

He raises his head.

"I know, but we cannot keep going without rest, either." He spreads his hands, and my shoulders sag, defeated.

"You are right," I say. "What do you suggest?"

Theo thinks for a moment.

"Meet me in the greenhouse this evening," he says mysteriously. "I will show you."

CHAPTER 29

The evening air swirls in through the open castle windows and bites at me as I wrap my shawl tighter around my shoulders. The halls are quiet as, thankfully, the night patrols are made up of about half the guards as during the day, and I make my way towards the greenhouse via several winding hidden passageways.

The hall leading to the narrow, spiral staircase is lined with the outline of where several paintings used to be. I wonder if I could convince Theo to let me hang one of my paintings. With a jolt, I realise how foolish the thought is—the king is on his way with an arranged bride. This is not my home.

I press on, head down. When I arrive at the greenhouse, Theo is already waiting for me.

"Shivani." He inclines his head, but I barely hear him. I gawk at the scene he has created.

Lit candles litter the ground, sitting on

small brick platforms. Fresh flowers surround us, bundled together in bunches of various shades of pink and red. In the middle of it all, the table has been pushed back to make space for a den of thick blankets and pillows, cushioning us against the hard ground. A basket of biscuits, sandwiches and assorted finger foods sits patiently.

"What is all this for?" I laugh incredulously, walking up to him. Theo takes me in his arms. They are strong and firm around me.

"For you," he replies simply. "Because I…"

He falters, his mouth half-open as though the end of his sentence is lodged in his throat. I blink up at him expectantly, but instead of speaking, he swoops down and kisses me.

After a moment of surprise, I snake my arms around his neck and kiss him back. His tongue slips deftly over mine, and a familiar warmth spreads through my body. I pull him closer and graze my teeth over his bottom lip. He moans into my mouth and draws back, breathless. He stares at me, eyes wide.

"What?" I breathe. "What is it?"

"N-Nothing," he replies, but he is shifting uncomfortably. "I just…require a moment. To cool down."

Confused, I look around.

"But we are in a greenhouse." I laugh. "It is warm in here."

"No, Shivani." He shakes his head with a

grin. "Not in…that way. I was…I mean to say, my body was…responding. To us. To you."

"Oh," I say softly and glance down. I am amused to see his cheeks turn pink, although my face also grows warmer. "Well, then…shall we eat while you…" I gesture vaguely at him. "Cool down?"

"I think that may be for the best," he agrees, letting out a relieved breath.

We sit on the blankets, tucking ourselves together while we tear through the basket of food. We quickly make use of a flagon of snowberry wine and spend the next few hours talking and laughing with ease. The anxieties of the last few days begin to dissolve.

"I have the impression you think me a naïve soul, Theo," I tell him before taking a final bite of a cucumber sandwich.

"Not at all," he replies, reaching over me to take the last slice of fudge. "Why do you think that?"

"Earlier, when you could not find the words to tell me you were…well…" I look him up and down. "Hard."

He chokes on his fudge.

"S-Saints," he splutters, thumping his chest to dislodge it from his throat. I laugh, whacking him on the back to help.

"Are you quite alright?" I ask as he recovers his breath. His cheeks are flushed, although I am unsure if it has to do with what I said or the near-death experience with his fudge.

"Yes, thank you." He takes a deep gulp of air. "Apologies."

"No, no, the apologies should be mine. I did not realise you were so delicate."

"Delicate!" he exclaims, laughing. "Hardly so. Rather, I am a gentleman. A gentleman who was not expecting his lady friend to be so crude."

He grins, nudging me with his shoulder.

"It is not crude for a lady to know what to expect." I sniff, although I cannot stop myself from smiling back.

"True, but with the way you have been with me…I suppose I did make an assumption."

"In what way?"

"Well, every time we have been together closely, you are…" He casts his eyes skywards, thinking. "Overcome."

I stare at him, wondering if I should be offended.

"Would you be so kind as to elaborate?" I ask sweetly. Theo catches my look and gives a contrite smile.

"I do not mean to say you have no effect on me because I assure you, you do. There have been many times where I have thought about…" He trails off, glancing at me, and clears his throat awkwardly. "Anyway. I mean to say, you allow me to take the lead often."

Seemingly satisfied he has explained himself well enough, he looks for my reaction.

"And you believe that is due to inexperience?" I query, one eyebrow cocked.

"An assumption," he repeats. "Which was wrong of me. Regardless, your experience or lack of experience matters not."

"Indeed," I say, pausing. "Admittedly, I have not accepted many suitors, but…I have never quite felt the same way with anyone else than I have with you."

Theo looks sideways at me.

"Romantically?" he probes.

"Yes." I swallow. "And other ways."

His face breaks into a sly smile.

"The feeling is mutual," he replies, turning towards me. "Truth be told, I have only ever felt something similar to this with one other person…but that was a long time ago."

"Oh?" I say, intrigued. "May I ask who?"

Theo tilts his head up, looking at the stars through the glass. For a long time, I do not think he will reply. And then he sighs and slides back until he is lying down, his arms tucked under the back of his head.

"I was seven and ten," he says, eyes fixed on the night sky. I lay on my back next to him. "I became friendly with one of the guards. Or, well, he was a guard-in-training, I suppose. The same age as me."

Something familiar twigs in my brain, but I ignore it and listen.

"He was often stationed outside of my

chambers, and eventually, we would make small talk, and then it would move onto...something more than everyday conversation. It was the first time I felt like someone was on my side, an ally, and the conversation flowed so easily. I began to look forward to seeing him. He would accompany me on trips to the gardens or when I could not stand to be around my father any longer and took my meals in my room...he would be there. He...he was my first kiss and my first love."

Theo's throat bobs as he swallows before taking a deep breath.

"Anyway. The rest of the guards did what they were there to do, which was to report what I was doing to my father. I knew something was wrong when he left without saying goodbye. For days, I thought it was something I had done. I had *said* something or-or *done* something to offend him and drove him away." He blinks away tears, his eyes fixed on the sky. "And then my father had me watch him walk to the guillotine. He was bruised a-and bloody, and *Saints* knows what they did to him in those three days in between because he was a shadow—" Theo's voice breaks, and he takes a moment before he continues. "He was a shadow of the person I knew."

Tears slide down his temple. He sniffs before wiping them away.

"His head was on a spike until the crows

pecked it clean. I have one window in my chambers, and my dear, dear father put him on the spike right outside." He spits these last words bitterly.

My heart aches listening to his tale, but I know it is nothing compared to how Theo must feel. I put a hand on his arm and squeeze.

"I do not have the words to console such cruelty," I whisper. "I am so sorry, Theo."

I go to him, wrapping an arm around his stomach. He responds, turning and holding me tight.

"I do not fear my father's wrath on me," he tells me, his lips moving against my neck. "I fear his wrath on you. I will not let him touch you."

I do not respond, allowing Theo this space to grieve. But a storm roils inside my chest, so strong it makes my hands shake. In my mind, it is certain—for what he has done, it is *my* wrath the king needs to fear.

CHAPTER 30

Theo and I stay out in the greenhouse until the sky begins the lighten. I hold him until his tears dry, and we stay in comfortable silence, side by side. We watch the stars slide across the sky and eventually fade, our hands clasped.

When he is ready, we make our way back to his chambers, moving stealthily through the secret passageways to avoid the watchful gaze of the guards. We only bump into one person —a startled kitchen porter who nods to us and moves on.

We are exhausted by the time we reach Theo's chambers, and he promptly collapses into bed. I wearily drag myself behind the screen to change into one of the several nightgowns I have brought to his chambers previously, and by the time I make it to bed with him, he is softly snoring. I look at him, splayed out under the covers and mouth slightly open, and feel a rush of fondness. I climb in next to him and try not to think about the time we have slowly counting down, the blade of the executioner's axe ever-looming above my neck.

※ ※ ※

The next day is, unsurprisingly, spent at the library. Inez brings us breakfast and tea as we push our way through book after book after book. Both of us, despite being avid readers, are beginning to get sick of the sight of them. After slamming another useless book shut, I sit with my face in my hands, trying to hold back the flood of tears threatening to spill. Without my au'mana, I only have my knowledge and even that is proving worthless.

"Shivani," Theo says, his voice low and soothing. "I think it is time for a break."

I groan in response, not moving. I hear his chair scraping back as he rises and moves to stand behind me.

He bends to murmur in my ear, "I will help you."

Strong hands squeeze my shoulders. He kneads at the tense muscles there until I am forced to relax. I drop my hands from my face and sit up.

Theo's thumbs push firmly but gently, and I close my eyes, enjoying it despite my frustrations. I twist my neck slightly, feeling every squeeze.

"Good?" he asks, and I nod, keeping my eyes closed. He continues on for several minutes, until even my ophid relaxes, before brushing my hair to the side. His lips are gentle on the nape of my neck.

"Mmm." I smile, moving my head to the side to allow him better access to the soft skin there. He responds by grazing his teeth lightly over it and following up with more tender kisses.

"Shivani," he whispers, his hands on the outside of my upper arms. "There is something I would very much like to do...but stop me if you do not want to."

My pulse quickens at his words.

"I will," I whisper.

"Sit on the table for me," he instructs, his voice soft but dominating. Immediately, I comply, turning to push myself up onto the table and facing him.

He nudges himself between my legs, capturing my face in his hand and bending to kiss me. Although familiar, there is something different this time, something exciting and exhilarating and new. It makes my heart race and anticipation course through my veins.

"Tell me to stop, and I will," he mumbles against my mouth before moving down, leaving a path of kisses from my jaw to my chest. He continues, further and further, until he is kneeling between my legs.

He looks up at me questioningly, storm grey eyes alight, and I reach down to run my hands through his thick, soft hair. I am nervous but it is swiftly overtaken by my wanting.

"Do not stop," I breathe.

He smirks and, with ease, pulls one of my legs up onto his shoulder. The skirt of my dress rides up, exposing the bare skin of my thigh above my stockings. He kisses the skin there tenderly, teasingly, looking up at me all the while. I am out of breath even though I have barely moved, and there is a scalding heat throughout my body.

Theo hooks my other leg onto his shoulder before pushing up my skirt. I cannot take my eyes away from him as he leans forward, and his head disappears under the fabric. A beat later, I feel the warmth of his tongue along the most sensitive part of me.

I gasp and grip his hair harder. He takes his time as though savouring me, and each movement of his lips sends a jolt through my body. My moans echo through the library. I pull my skirt up and his eyes stay on mine, looking up and watching me, watching my reaction to him. Theo devours me, and I let him.

He strokes me with the flat of his tongue, deftly, *hungrily*, as though he is a man starved. He moans against me, sending vibrations of pleasure along my spine. While one hand grips his hair, the other desperately claws at the table.

And then I feel something. He reaches up to press a finger against my entrance, hard and thick in contrast to the softness of his mouth. I instinctively tense but he is gentle, sliding his finger in slowly. Inch by inch, he sinks inside me before drawing back. His tongue sweeps across me, dipping between my folds before circling my sensitive bud. It brings me to the edge.

"Yes," I gasp, shuddering as wave after wave of pleasure crashes through me. My body jerks, my back arching with each surge, but he does not release me until I am too sensitive to continue. "S-Stop."

He immediately pulls away, and I collapse back onto my elbows against the table.

"Saints..." I huff, chest heaving. The only sound is my laboured breathing as I close my eyes in bliss.

"Are you alright?" Theo asks, rising to his feet. He leans over me, stroking my cheek.

"I...I cannot feel my legs," I tell him and we laugh, open and loudly, endorphins flooding my brain.

"Would you like to stop?" he says. Half-recovered, I sit up and kiss him, tasting myself on his lips. He is pressed against me, and I can feel the bulge he is harbouring. It makes me want him more.

"No," I say. "I want you to take me."

Theo says nothing but kisses me harder. There is a new fervour to him, an urgency. I reach down to free him.

He moans at my touch, and I feel him throb. He is warm and solid beneath my fingers, and a warmth pools between my legs again, preparing for him. I guide him towards me, and he grabs my hips, his fingers digging in hard enough to leave bruises. Theo pushes himself against me, where his finger had been just minutes before. I tense up but relax quickly with the familiar strength in his arms around me. He pushes in a few inches, and I clamp around him as though I do not want him to leave.

"Saints," he hisses through clenched teeth, and I pull my head back to look at him.

"Are you alright?" I ask, concern lacing my voice. But when I look at him, his eyes are glazed over with lust.

"You feel amazing," Theo groans, drawing back slightly only to push in further. I grasp the back of his neck, anchoring myself as he pulls my thigh up higher.

He fills me, stretches me in a way that is both pleasant and painless. He draws back, and I wrap my legs around him, pulling him deeper until he is fully sheathed. His hips move unhurriedly, back and forth in slow, deliberate movements to make sure I adjust to him. My breathing turns ragged as he rubs against a spot inside me that makes my thighs tremble.

Theo picks up his pace, moving with a renewed urgency, shaking the table beneath me with every thrust. Each time he withdraws, my body pulls him back.

"More," I plead, and Theo obliges, grabbing me under my thighs and spreading my legs further. Holding me open for him. His jaw is tense, his eyes on mine. Each stroke sends new waves of energy through me.

"Fuck," he gasps, tilting his head back. The muscles in his arms and back are hard as boulders, his breathing is uneven—I know he is close. When he next looks at me, there is a question in his eyes.

"Inside me," I breathe. "Please."

At my words, Theo shudders violently and lets his head fall forward onto my shoulder. His grip is hard, keeping me as close as possible. He moans, eyes squeezed shut. I slide my hand up to the back of his head and hold him to me as he finishes, kissing his neck softly.

When he recovers, he lifts his head, eyes dazed. We smile and press our foreheads together.

"I do not-," Theo closes his eyes briefly, swallowing hard. He breathes deep before trying again. "I wish I had the words for what you mean to me," he whispers. "I cannot describe it."

"Theo-"

"Please." He pulls back to lock eyes with me. "Please let me try."

Silently, I push back his honey dark hair matted to his forehead and give him an encouraging smile. Theo takes a trembling breath.

"There is no end to the admiration I hold for you. Your mind, your courage, your absolute determination is nothing short of remarkable." Despite his nerves, the words fall so naturally from his mouth. Theo reaches up to brush the pad of his thumb across my cheek. "If souls could speak, mine would be calling out for you. I do not pray to the Saints but I would pray to you. I would fall at your feet without question, I would crawl across the deserts of Coalsburgh, I would swim across the Great Oceans for you. Saints, Shivani, I will wring this curse from my bones so I can be with you."

I do not realise I am crying until I feel the tears slide down my cheeks. Theo brushes them away, his own eyes shiny but clear as glass. He beams at me with his lopsided smile.

"I love you," he whispers.

My heart swells. My au'mana, even quietened, hums softly. Calling to him. Calling to his soul.

"I love you, too," I say, and I know I will give everything I have to defend him.

CHAPTER 31

Month Six

The king has arrived, along with the poor girl from Swordstead, at The Magenta Inn. When I query what this means with Inez, she gives me a sad look.

"They are a week away at most, miss," she answers.

"A week?" I screech. "But they were not due to return for three weeks!"

"I believe it may have been a mistranslation." Inez taps a finger off her chin. "The note came from Swordstead and werewolves written language is quite rudimentary."

I sink into my seat, staring into the void.

"Fuck!" I scream suddenly, causing Inez to jump. "What are we going to do? We have no plan, and our research has gone nowhere."

The image of the tunnel invades my mind.

I push it firmly to the side.

"We do still have a week to think of something. Oh! Perhaps you could make a case for remaining in the castle as staff? Instead of…"

She trails off, unable to finish her sentence. The suggestion makes me gag, to be stuck under the king's thumb as his servant while also watching Theo wed someone else. But I am rapidly running out of options.

"Maybe," I admit. "It could give us more time to…I do not know. Do *something*."

I sigh heavily and stand, picking up the leather book I had taken back from my art room.

"My apologies, Inez, we can go through your mother's journal together tomorrow morning," I tell her, the weight of it in my hands. "Tonight, I need to…think."

"Of course, miss."

"Is…is Vanya available?" I ask. I recall the queen's altar she took us to and wonder what else she knew about the queen.

"I am afraid not, miss. I believe she accompanied Eliza to the nurse after a nasty burn."

"Ah. I will call for her in the morning then. Send my regards to Eliza, please, if you see her."

"Of course, miss." Inez bobs a curtsy and leaves.

I sit on my bed, hunched. The weight of a thousand grains of sand trickling through the hourglass rests on my shoulders. I desperately wish for Aunt Meena's help and try to imagine what she would say.

Look at the facts. Remember your studies. Keep your head clear.

I let my face fall into my hands and groan. None of that helps me now. Once again, the tunnel pushes itself into my mind, and I sit up abruptly.

The tunnel. My escape. I glance out of the window, judging how high the moon is. With a rough estimate, I have several hours before the sun comes back up, and I need to be back in the castle. And I *will* come back.

After I have seen Aunt Meena.

I fasten a thick cloak around my shoulders, a worry gnawing at me that I may be putting her safety at risk. I cannot let anyone in Mossgarde see me lest they report it to the king. I pull on comfortable boots and wait at my door, listening for the guard shift change.

As soon as the guard stationed outside walks away, his armour rattling down the halls, I slip out before the next one can arrive. The unused bedchamber is several doors down, so I scurry over as quickly as I can, my boots silent on the carpeted floors. When I find it, I sneak in and close the door softly behind me, just as the next guard arrives around the corner. I wait, holding my breath, until the sound of his footsteps passes. Only then do I creep over to the bookcase.

Nervous about the noise of the tunnel

opening, I wait a while longer until I am sure the guard is outside my chambers and away from this room. Breathing deep, I pull the hidden lever and watch the tunnel shudder open. I nearly turn back but resist, pressing my lips together.

I will return.

I take a deep breath and charge into the tunnel.

* * *

I have forgotten how humid the air is in Mossgarde, how close it presses in around you. As soon as I step outside, tears threaten to spill. It is dark, but I recognise every sound of the swamp and the taste of the air. I clap a hand over my mouth and swallow my sobs, pressing them down for another day. Instead, I take a long, shaky breath and focus on finding Aunt Meena.

I am unsure where the tunnel has deposited me and turn slowly on the spot, trying to recognise anything around me. The moon casts slivers of silver beams through the canopy, ineffective against the darkness. Even as my eyes begin to adjust to the gloom, I cannot see much. Cursing, I gingerly take a step off the wooden platform and begin walking forward, wary of the soggy ground giving way to deep bogs that would swallow me whole.

After a few minutes of frustratingly little progress, I come to a halt. Something is different. I freeze, wracking my brain to try and understand, when a tingle crawls up my spine. I shiver, thinking an insect has gotten into my dress, but it is not that. It...it is my ophid.

I draw myself up to my full height—my ophid stretches and uncoils like a cat waking from a long sleep. Hardly breathing, I reach out to my au'mana. It washes over me, warm and welcoming.

My magic has come back.

With shaking hands, I pull my au'mana forward. The purple glow, flickering like fire, trails from my spine over my shoulders and to my palms. I hold my arms in front and let it light my way.

With the help of my au'mana, I eventually stumble upon the edge of Mossgarde. A well-worn jetty dips into the swamp water where two crocas rest. Their protruding eyes swivel in my direction as I clamber onto the jetty, but they otherwise pay me no mind. I retract my magic, using the light of the lamps to guide me instead.

Further into town looms the yellow glow of the public house. I head in its direction, creeping quietly across the wooden bridges linking the platforms. I recall the last time I walked this way, on my way to Aunt Meena's library to study—when I still thought I was going to Frostalm. Old anger bubbles up like hot tar in my stomach.

This time, when I pass the public house, I

do so in the shadows. I hear the faint rumblings of laughter but nothing uproarious, thankfully. I zip from shadow to shadow before hurrying across the last bridge. I do not stop until I reach Aunt Meena's library and slam the door closed behind me.

At once, a knife is pressed against my throat. There is no hand holding it, but it glows dark purple, hovering by itself in the air.

"Auntie!" I cry out as loud as I dare as the blade bites into my flesh.

"Shivani?" a familiar voice replies from the dark.

The knife clatters instantly to the ground, the glow evaporating. Strong arms scoop me up as my face is pressed into Aunt Meena's soft shoulder. I inhale the scent of her. She does not let me go.

"I missed you," I say, and she replies with a sob.

"Saints, I did not think I would see you again," she says, pulling back to cup my face. Her cheeks are streaked with tears, and her hair is greyer than last I saw her. "Your father...that cur..."

"It does not matter now. I need your help."

"Of course, child, of course."

Aunt Meena ushers me over to a stool while she sits on a stack of thick books. The purple of her wooden leg peeks out from under her skirt as she crosses her ankles. I hurriedly fill her in on the castle, the prince, and the curse. Her frown deepens as I go on.

"It does not sound like any curse I have ever heard of," she says, and I sigh heavily.

"I know."

"And you are sure it is a curse?"

"Yes." I pause. "What else could it be?"

Aunt Meena gives me the same look as when I answer an easy question wrong.

"And what about your au'mana?" she continues.

"It is blocked. It *was* blocked. They drugged me—" My voice catches, and I take a steadying breath. Aunt Meena grasps my hand, quiet fury under her tight features. "They drugged me at first, but then...I do not know. Something else blocked it. This is the first time I have been able to use magic since I was taken."

As if to reassure myself, I reach out to my au'mana. It hums in response.

"Well, a witch lived there, did she not? Inara's mother?"

"Inez, yes. Why?"

"Another witch would be the most likely candidate for blocking au'mana," Aunt Meena says. "Regardless, you have escaped now. We can leave this wretched place behind and never look back."

She stands up and begins rifling through her things, pulling out books and crockery and stuffing them into bags.

"Auntie, wait."

"We need to leave before the sun is up, child. Before they realise you are gone," she says, and then quieter, "We need to keep you safe."

"Aunt Meena, I need to go back."

Her hand freezes halfway to a jar of fermented reeds. It wavers, but she does not say anything.

"The people who live there…they have no one to help them. Even if we leave, there will be another woman sent to the chopping block next year. And the next. It will never end."

Her hand drops, and I watch her shoulders sag, her back still to me.

"Someone needs to stop him." There is renewed conviction in my voice.

Aunt Meena sighs so deeply, it feels like even her soul is tired. Eventually, she turns to me. I meet her eyes and do not look away.

"Iron will," she says with a sad smile. She crosses the room to grasp me by the shoulders. "You stop him, Shivani, and you take everything down with him."

CHAPTER 32

I return to the castle with a few hours to spare before the sun comes up. As soon as I step into the tunnel, there is a shift somewhere in my body. Something I am unable to place. It takes me a long moment to realise I am, once again, cut off from my au'mana. The knowledge is painful but less sharp than before; now, I know it is not permanent. The existence of the tunnel itself has lessened the barb.

I trudge upwards in the dark, exhaustion slowly overtaking my limbs, but I press on regardless. Aunt Meena's voice echoes in my head—*another witch*. The only witch I know for certain lived in the castle was Inez's mother, Ruya. I press my lips into a thin, determined line, the image of her diary burned into my mind.

I reach the end of the tunnel as it opens into the gloom of the abandoned bedchambers. But when I step inside, a shape moves in the darkness.

I nearly yelp but stop myself in time, grabbing the edge of the bookcase. Vanya steps closer, moonlight cast across her face.

"What..." I gape, a hand on my chest to slow my thundering heart. "What are you doing here?"

She only narrows her eyes at me and crosses the space between us. I flinch, but she reaches past me instead, touching the bookcase tenderly.

"You have gained more use from this than we ever did," she mutters, gazing at it wistfully.

"Who?"

She turns her piercing eyes on me.

"Inez told me she gave you Ruya's diary. Have you read it?" she asks. There is the slightest crease between her brows.

"No. Not yet." I squint at her, frowning. "Why?"

Vanya only sighs and turns away.

"You do not have long," she tells me. "Now the king has a bride for the prince. He has no need of you."

"Why a bride?" I ask quickly before she can leave. "Why now?"

"The king is not stupid. He is only growing older, and his son will take his place one day—he needs a queen he has control over. Swordstead will be in his debt for the money he has paid for her."

My tongue withers in my mouth.

"I have time," I say weakly. "Before he arrives."

Vanya looks at me with such pity, tears well in my eyes.

"He does not need to be here to have you killed," she says before opening the door. "Are all witches born with more honour than sense, I wonder?"

At once, my tears dry. I look at her sharply, frowning. A missing puzzle piece dangles in front of me.

"What do you know of other witches?" I ask.

Vanya's eyes glint in the darkness, and then she is gone.

By the time I chase after her, the halls are empty. I look in both directions, but there is no Vanya or any guards. Frowning, I hurry back to my chambers to retrieve Ruya's diary. It sits innocently in the middle of my bed, where I had left it. I clutch it to my chest, relieved, before opening it.

The handwriting is small but distinctly witchtongue, with looping letters across the pages. I flip forward through the dates until I reach about nine months before Theo's birth. There are some spells written, some comments about her day and complaints about the king. I spot Vanya's name a few times across the pages and decide to come back to it later. The queen's name, too, is mentioned often. The three of them, it seems, were close.

I spend the rest of the night reading fervently. With Ruya's story, the last piece of the puzzle clicks.

✣ ✣ ✣

I awake to desperate banging on my chamber door. I jerk up from where I am slumped across the bed, Ruya's diary still in my hands. I snap it closed and hide it under the pillow.

"Miss Shivani!" a male voice from the other side of the door shouts. A guard. He follows it up with more thumping.

"Yes, coming!" I call back, jumping to my feet and swinging open the door. Instantly, I know something is wrong.

The guard stands, panting, his eyes wild behind his helmet. Dark crimson is splattered across his chest, covering the king's crescent.

"The prince," he gasps.

"What has happened?" Alarm turns my voice shrill. "Is he alright?"

"It...is best if you see for yourself," he answers before turning. I curse and follow him, hiking up my skirt to half-jog.

The guard hurriedly leads me to the dungeon, where the familiar stale air invades my nostrils. The taste of blood sits uncomfortably in my mouth. I can hear the prince, turned and roaring viciously.

"He has turned again so soon?" I ask breathlessly as we traverse the narrow stone stairs.

"It is worse than that, miss," he replies, his voice grim. "He turned around noon yesterday and has not come back since."

"He has been this way for over a day?" I exclaim, aghast. "How? Why?"

"That is what we were hoping you could tell us," he says. "You have an affinity for him. We have seen it."

His words curdle my stomach, spoken as if from a spy. We come to the bottom of the steps and into the dungeon.

Theo is angry, angrier than I have ever seen him in this state. He thrashes against his cage like a wild animal, furiously swiping at the bars. There are deep cuts running along his arms and face and several sections where his scales have chipped off.

"What have you done to him?" I whisper furiously, whirling on the guard. He holds his hands up.

"Not us, miss," he replies. "He has done that to himself trying to escape."

As he speaks, Theo throws his head back, unleashing a terrible roar that makes both the guard and I slam our hands over our ears. When he is finished, he resumes his assault on the bars. Even after I remove my hands, my ears are ringing.

"What?" I yell at the guard, seeing his lips move.

"I said we need to get him under control," the guard replies, raising his voice. "If he is in this state when the king returns—or kills himself—the king will have our heads."

I look at Theo, blinded by wrath, and recall Ruya's diary. It makes sense. His mother's magic, the word printed across his back in dragon text, which I could not quite recognise. I turn my tongue over in my mouth, tasting blood. Faeth is thick in the air. I know how to fix it. How to fix everything.

I glance at the guards around us—I cannot tell him the truth here. I need to get him back to his chambers, back to safety and away from the king's spies.

"Did the prince know the news about the king?" I ask. "Did he know his father is only a week away from returning?"

"Well, yes," the guard replies, looking at me quizzically. "The prince is always the first to be informed of any news."

Without hesitation, I stride over to the bars.

"Wait!" the guard calls, but I ignore him, walking up to the outside of Theo's cage. He pounds his fists against the blood-stained metal.

"Theo," I say firmly. "We have only had a setback. We still have time to figure this out. We are not giving up."

He turns to glare at me with venomous yellow eyes. I do not look away and take a step closer.

"You and I," I whisper to him.

He blinks, the narrow slits of his eyes expanding. I press a hand against my chest.

"Listen," I say softly. *Listen to my soul.*

Recognition sparks in his eyes.

SNAP.

A wet crack echoes through the dungeon, followed by another. Theo howls painfully as his body contorts, bones and muscles snapping and rearranging. His scaley skin tears open, making way for the human skin underneath. He hunkers down, curling into a ball on the ground.

"Open the cage!" I order the guard standing slack-jawed behind me. He jolts, alarmed, before springing into action, running over with the keys in his hand. As soon as he pulls the door open, I scramble in, falling to my knees next to Theo.

"It is alright," I soothe as the guard throws a blanket over him. He sobs and shivers as I bring him up the stairs and to his chambers.

"How did she do that?" the guards whisper to each other as we leave.

"Witch magic?"

"No, it was…something else."

They stand out of our way, suspicion and accusation in their eyes. I ignore them and go through our routine—making him comfortable in bed, tipping lavender tonic past his lips and holding his hand until he falls asleep. It is only when he is snoring softly that I allow myself to sit back and think about what the truth truly means.

You are out of time, Vanya's voice whispers in my mind. Theo's unexpected turn gave me a grace period, but it will not last long. I grasp Theo's hand and will him to recover before the guards decide I have outlived my usefulness and come for me.

CHAPTER 33

I wake up with a start. I am in Theo's bed, alone.

I blink the sleep away and half-sit up, looking around his chambers.

"Theo?" I call.

"I am here," he replies, stepping out of the washroom with a towel wrapped around his waist. He is still wet from bathing and he throws a second blood-stained towel to the side. "We need to get ready."

I rub my eyes blearily.

"What can you mean?" I ask, my brain addled from too little sleep lately.

"To leave." He says it plainly as though it is obvious. My heart stops. The memories of the last few days come back to me in a tsunami, pushing me beneath the surface.

"Theo—"

"It is too late. My father will have ordered your head by now, with this…kidnapped woman in tow. You must use the hidden tunnel and leave. Now."

I shake my head, both my hands in my hair.

"I cannot," I say, my voice pleading. "There—"

"Shivani." Theo crosses the room and sits on the bed next to me.

Water droplets from his hair trail down his temple to his scruffy jaw. His eyes are red-ringed and laden with dark bags. I grit my teeth.

"Please," he says. "I do not know how much time we have before the guards—"

"I am not leaving without you," I say firmly. "I will not leave you to the king."

"I must stay, Shivani." He reaches across to squeeze my hands. "I am a danger to people outside these walls. I remember what the guard said to you last night—I had turned and I was not turning back. What if it becomes permanent? What if—" he falters, voice breaking. "What if I hurt someone? What if I hurt *you*?"

"No, no, no." I shake my head. "Theo, this has been all wrong. The whole time, we have understood everything wrong."

"What can you mean?" He frowns.

I scramble over the bed to kneel next to him, gripping his hand. I do not know how to explain myself clearly, the words becoming jumbled in my mind.

"The-the curse," I stammer. "It—"

"Excuse me, Your Highness," a guard speaks from the door, entering without us knowing. Theo stands immediately, pushing me behind him, but when we look closer, there are several more guards in the hall.

"What is this?" Theo asks, voice low. I clench my fist to stop my hands from trembling as they fix their eyes on me. My au'mana vibrates against the block between us, agitated.

"King's orders, Your Highness," one of the guards speaks. There is a tinge of apology in his voice, but it is drowned out by the steeling of his shoulders. "She does not need to be here when your bride arrives."

Theo straightens, and the muscles in his back tense.

"Even after what he did to Lucian," he says quietly. "You are still loyal to him."

They shift uncomfortably, eyes darting. *Lucian*, I think. Inez's brother. Theo's first love. I close my eyes briefly, chest aching. When the guards do not reply, Theo's hands ball into fists at his side.

"Cowards!" he spits at them. "You betrayed one of your own, and now you..."

His voice breaks, and he glances over his shoulder to look at me.

"I am sorry," Theo half-sobs. "I have failed to protect you."

"No..." I whisper, reaching for his hand, but Theo's head whips back around when the guards start to move toward us.

"Stop!" he shouts at them, drawing himself up to his full height. They falter slightly before pressing on, and Theo steps forward to meet them. "Stop this, now!"

They ignore him completely this time, one of them grabbing his arms to twist him away. He throws them off with ease but the guard is replaced with two others. One kicks Theo behind the knees, buckling his legs and forcing him to kneel. He tries to jerk himself out of their grip, but another comes forward to subdue him.

"No!" he cries as the rest of them swarm me.

Anger and adrenaline kick in. I reach blindly behind me and find the smooth surface of a wooden chair. I swing wildly, breaking it over a guard's head. It explodes into broken wood and splinters as the guard goes down with a yelp. I seize the opportunity and sprint across the room, trying to make for the doorway but it is crowded with more guards.

One of them grabs me from behind, wrapping his arms around my stomach and lifting me while another tries to get a hold of my legs. I shriek and kick out, my heel connecting with his nose. There is a sickening crunch and a spray of blood as he falls back, clutching his face.

"Do not touch her!" Theo roars, and there is something terrifying in his voice. Something deep and inhuman.

I catch his eyes in between the sea of guards, and they are wide and ringed with fear. Fear for me. Fear for seeing my head on a spike outside his window. I know what is going through his mind, and I know what is going to happen. I try to call to him, but it is too late.

A scream erupts from his throat and rips apart his body. His skin splits, and tears as scaly spikes and terrible boils push through. He grows and grows. The guards subduing him are violently thrown to the side.

"Theo!" I yell as the guard's grip on me drops in shock. The rest of them scatter, shoving each other out of the way to try and escape.

"The beast is here!" one of them calls as they scramble. I ignore him, fighting against the wave of guards, trying not to get knocked over and crushed underfoot.

Theo roars so loud the furniture quakes, and I clap my hands over my ears. The guards cry out and drop to the floor, stunned and deafened. He moves to swipe at them, but I throw myself in front of him.

"Stop!" I shout, holding up my hands. "Look, I am alright. I am alright. No harm has come to me."

I pat my body as if to demonstrate. Theo draws back, his yellow eyes on me, a snarl plastered across his long, twisted snout. He stares at me a moment, the slits of his eyes dilating. A gurgle escapes from somewhere in his chest.

"Ssssss…" he opens his mouth and groans. "Ssshhhh…"

I slowly drop my hands, watching him.

"Shhh…Shhhivaaaanii…" He speaks as though there is glass is his throat, low and jagged. I nod encouragingly.

"Yes. Exactly. You and I." I step forward, reach up on my tiptoes, and place my hand on his scaly stomach.

"Saints…" one of the guards mutters behind me. "The thing can speak?"

"He is not a thing," I say firmly, not turning or taking my eyes off his. "He is still Theo."

"Shiv…ani," he says again and this time, it is not a painful groan but closer to a voice, gravelly and deep.

"Theo." I smile at him, feeling the warmth beneath his scales.

He leans forward, stretching out a gnarled finger. I grasp it gently with both hands.

"Do you know why dragon text is so hard to read?" I ask the room, not expecting an answer. "Because they did not need to write often. Dragons spoke to each other, passing down their tales and their histories orally. But important things—things they wanted to preserve—they would not write them on paper but on themselves. They tattooed patterns and stories in ink on their wings."

Theo's stomach rises and falls as he

breathes steadily, his golden eyes aglow. I watch them as grey swirls like smoke in his irises until the angry yellow is gone. Until all I see are his eyes, soft and sweet. The guards are silent, watching.

"You are not cursed, Theo," I tell him. "You are a dragon."

CHAPTER 34

Theo does not turn back immediately. He sits quietly, cramped against the walls and ceiling of his chambers, his breathing quiet but rumbling. I sit with him after ordering the guards out. With Theo behind me, eyeing them hungrily, they make no argument and flee quickly. I contemplate the possibility of one or more of them informing the king, but by the time a raven reaches him, it will be too late for him to do anything.

Because I finally have a plan.

Theo does not ask questions straight away, and I do not force information on him. I rest my head against one of his large forearms, and I let him have his peace.

※ ※ ※

After an hour or two, I hear the familiar

wet snapping sounds of his body turning back. But instead of his skin splitting and tearing, his scales and spikes start to drop off softly. He groans and winces, but it is nothing compared to his usual screams. I watch him slowly shrink to his regular size, and when he is finished, he is not bloody but clean. The scaly skin he has left behind sits innocently like a coat he has taken off, dry and husk-like.

"Are...are you well?" I ask tentatively. He flexes his fingers, staring at them.

"Yes," he replies, his tone surprised, before turning to look at me. "But I have questions."

I hold back a smile.

"It would be strange if you did not. I cannot promise I can answer everything, but..." I slot my hand into his, weaving his fingers between mine. "I think I finally understand what happened to you. And your mother."

Theo swallows hard and squeezes my hand. I breathe deep and begin.

30 Years Ago

Honora watches him from the Mossgarde town square with stars in her eyes.

The prince is handsome indeed, grinning and waving to the crowd. Honora is just another face amongst many but there is a moment, however brief, where he looks at her. Their eyes meet, and the prince's smile widens ever so slightly. Her closest friend, Ruya, squeezes her hand.

"He looked at me," Honora whispers to her. "*Me*."

The girls, only seven and ten, giggle and clutch each other. Honora's cheeks ache from smiling, but she cannot help it. Her quiet town has never been so alive.

They watch with giddy glee as the prince dips his head, accepting his father's crown. The crowd cheers, long and loud, for their new king. Despite the fragile health of his father, the king turns his back to him, facing the adoration of the crowd. His eyes meet Honora's again, and this time, he does not look away.

27 Years Ago

Honora smooths the fabric of her gown, turning this way and that to inspect her stitching. It is the grandest dress she has ever made, and she worked until her fingers bled. But it is worth it. She will bleed as much as she must for love.

Ruya buzzes around her, adjusting

Honora's hairpins and adding more blush to her cheeks. Several items hover in the air, tinged with a purple hue. Ruya plucks at them, pulling them from the air as she needs them and letting them float away when she does not.

"Are you nervous?" she asks Honora.

"No," she replies with a coy smile. "I could not be happier."

"You can be both happy and nervous."

"Are you nervous, Ruya?"

"Well..." Her friend steps back, examining her work. "I have never worked for a queen before."

"I am your friend before I am your queen," Honora says, taking her hands. "That comes before all else."

Ruya smiles, her eyes crinkling, and wipes away a stray tear.

"A true love tale," she says, her chest swelling with pride. "All of Mossgarde is here to see your wedding."

Honora inhales deeply, settling the butterflies in her stomach.

"I am truly lucky, Ruya. To think, I nearly joined my grandparents in Coalsburgh..." Honora trails off wistfully. "I may never become Ascended in Mossgarde but I am happy with that."

A comfortable life. The thought makes Honora smile.

"If you are happy, then you have made

the right choice. The king loves you more than anything, and soon, you will be a queen."

"Yes. He loves me." Honora turns to look at herself in the mirror. Her dress sleeves are long, running down to cover even her wrists. A dull ache in her chest reminds her of her promise to the king—she would not show her tattoos on their wedding day. *Unsightly*, he had said. *They distract from your beauty*. When she had protested, his eyes became sad.

If you loved me, you would do me this one favour. For just one day.

And she does love him. So much so that it hurts sometimes, a sick feeling in her stomach. She runs the pad of her thumb over her fingers, feeling the callouses there from making her wedding gown. She has bled for him already, and she will do so again.

Honora tugs down the sleeves of her dress and smiles at Ruya.

"I am ready."

26 Years Ago

"How is she?" Vanya asks, concern etched into her face. By way of an answer, Ruya collapses to a sitting position on the side of her bed, hunched over.

The servants' quarters are quiet, with only a handful of others either sleeping or murmuring quietly to each other. Ruya's hands quake, her au'mana flickering weakly in the palm of her hands. Vanya wraps an arm around the other woman's shoulders, squeezing her. When Ruya looks up, her eyes are ringed with dark.

"You are exhausted," Vanya tells her, a deep crease between her brows.

"I cannot stop," Ruya whispers back.

"You must rest."

"I will," she says wearily. "It is just...we are so high from Mossgarde, and the tunnel needs so much magic."

She sinks forward again with her head in her hands. Vanya rubs her back, Ruya's ophid taut there.

"Honora is strong. She can fight—"

"He wants her pregnant."

Vanya falls silent, her throat constricting.

"What?" she croaks out.

"I heard one of the guards," Ruya says miserably. "He...if he succeeds, she cannot shapeshift. It is too dangerous for the baby."

"She will be unable to fight back," Vanya finishes quietly. "Has she said anything?"

Ruya shakes her head.

"Not since that night," she says, remembering the blood and claws. The night Honora finally told him 'no.' "She is barely lucid. The lavender tonic addles her mind."

Vanya clenches her fists. Ruya slumps forward, head in hands.

"We have been fools," she whispers, a sob stuck in her throat. "How could we ever have trusted him?"

"No." Vanya turns to grab her friend by the wrists, forcing her to lock eyes. "The blame is with him. Not Honora, nor us. If he were a good man, we would not be in this mess. Do you understand?"

Through tears, Ruya nods.

"We need to proceed as planned," Vanya continues, releasing her. "Before we are out of time."

25 Years Ago

The castle is quiet as Queen Honora slips out of her bed in the dead of night.

She is wearing an outfit she made herself, tight enough to stop any snagging but flexible enough to be comfortable. Dark as the night sky to creep through shadows undetected. Her chestnut hair is pulled back and tied, trailing down her back.

She glances at her bookcase, standing tall and silent in her chambers. She knows the secret it holds, but…she cannot. She must find Ruya and Vanya first. She awoke with cold sweat across her brow and dread in her chest. Her baby kicks, unsettled, as panic shoots through her veins. Something is wrong with him—she is certain of it. She needs her friends.

Honora eases open her chamber door, wary of the creaking noise it makes, and peeks through the halls. The guards are on their shift change, she knows, and there is a small window of a few minutes where there is no one stationed outside her door. She clutches her swollen stomach and moves as quickly as she can to the hidden door behind a large landscape painting. Ruya had told her about the passageways the servants used to get around quickly, and she had kept the knowledge firmly in her mind, biding her time. She closes the hidden door behind her softly.

The passageway is dimly lit, with only a few small torches dotted across the walls, but she has always had keen eyesight in the dark. It does not deter her. She strokes her stomach, heavy and uncomfortable, and whispers to the baby.

"We can do this," Honora tells him—and herself—before she strides on. Her jaw is set.

The only sound is her laboured breathing mingled with the damp drips of the brick walls. The air is thick with moisture, making it harder for her to breathe, especially with swollen feet and a sore back. Nevertheless, she grits her teeth and continues.

When she reaches the other end of the passageway, she knows she will be outside the kitchens. She presses her forehead against the door, catching her breath for a moment and listening on the other side. The guards do not patrol this area often, so she should be safe. But there is always a chance one is passing through…

Honora shakes this doubt out of her head. It is not a useful thought and she does not have space for things which do not help her. She takes another deep inhale before cracking the door open slightly.

As she does, she becomes aware of a wetness at her feet, and her thighs glide off each other as she moves forward. Glancing down, she sees the puddle of fluid on the passageway floor. She stares at it, her resolve wavering. She is running out of time.

You are Honora, she tells herself. *Daughter of dragons.*

The image of her husband flashes through her mind and her nerves harden into steel. *He has taken my life from me*, she thinks, *but he will not take my baby's.*

The corridor is silent and dark, the torches burning low. She narrows her eyes and surveys both ways before creeping out. Honora wastes no time and hurries towards the servants' quarters, where she knows they have their own entrance. And exit.

She is almost there when she feels the first sharp pain just below her stomach. She halts, squeezing her teeth together to stop from groaning, and presses a hand against the wall. It passes after a few seconds, and she blinks, taking deep, quiet breaths. She knows what is happening, but she cannot afford to stop. She must push on.

She walks on shaky legs as sweat begins to form on her brow. She wipes it away irritably and makes it to the servants' quarters as the next contraction kicks in. This time it is worse, like someone has reached inside her and grabbed her womb with a tight fist. A whimper escapes her lips before she presses them firmly together in a thin line. She stops, clutching her stomach as sweat runs down the sides of her face. She cannot wake the servants. She needs to make it to the exit.

She stumbles on, gasping, her legs threatening to crumble beneath her at any moment. She sees the exit and Ruya standing in front of it, waiting for her. She tries to raise a hand, but the contractions are coming quickly now and lasting longer. Ruya spots her, bent over double and rushes over.

"Your Highness," she gasps, horrified. "We must get you to your bed!"

"No," Honora moans through gritted teeth. "No, there is no time. We need to leave—ah!"

She cries out and collapses, but Ruya manages to catch her.

"Honora, please, think of the baby." Ruya scoops an arm under her back. She can hear the servants begin to rouse from their sleep.

"I *am* thinking of the baby!" Honora cries. The pain is too great, her face is contorted with it, and all sense of stealth has left her mind. "He cannot be born here. I will not let the king have him!"

Honora is on the brink of blacking out, her vision sprinkled with bright spots. The servants have woken and are concerned, gathering around her.

"What is wrong with the queen?" a small voice asks. A young girl stands, rubbing her eyes.

"Go back to bed, Inez," Ruya tells her firmly before turning back to Honora. "We need to get her somewhere safe. Now!"

The servants immediately oblige, putting Honora's arms over their shoulders and taking her back. *No*, she wants to scream, *do not take me back.*

They bring her to her chambers and help her onto the bed. She tries to claw her way off it, but they hold her tight.

"The baby is coming, Your Highness," they tell her. "We need to deliver him."

"No, no..." Honora sobs as another wave of pain wracks her body. "I need to save him."

Ruya's face is streaked with tears but she

makes soothing sounds for the queen, wiping her sweat-soaked forehead with a cool cloth. She wants to pour her au'mana into something to help, but there is nothing to ease her now. Honora's stormy eyes begin to glow a furious gold, bright as molten glass, the fear and pain overwhelming her.

"Your Highness!" Ruya cries. "You cannot turn!"

Honora growls with lengthening teeth.

"The baby!" her handmaiden pleads. "You will hurt the baby if you turn!"

Immediately, the gold is extinguished, and the buds of her transformation shrivel. Honora succumbs to huge, heaving sobs. Defeated.

And then she hears him. Goosebumps spring up along the back of her neck as dread crawls up her spine.

"Everyone out." The king stands silhouetted in the doorway, his voice cool.

The servants hesitate, glancing between each other.

"I said, out!" he booms. "If she is fit to survive this, she will."

The servants jump and scatter, but Ruya shoots a venomous look at him.

"No," she snarls, keeping hold of Honora's hand. "She needs help to deliver him safely. I will not leave her."

The king fixes her with an even look.

"You think I am unaware of your

machinations behind my back? Whatever you have concocted, I hope it was worth your head," he says, his tone almost bored. Two guards walk forth and wrap their grip around Ruya's arms.

She shrieks and kicks at them, drawing on her au'mana. The room begins to glow purple, every sharp item around her turning to point at them. They hover ominously, a protective bubble around the witch and the queen. The king, eyes narrowed, flicks his hand.

A guard darts forward and pushes a wet rag against her mouth. Ruya squirms out of his grip and flings her au'mana. The sharp objects fly at the king, who falls back with a startled cry and a clang of armour. When he stands up again, a letter opener has sliced his cheek open. He touches it with a shaking hand, blood on his fingers.

"Close her magic off! Now!" he barks.

The guards hold the wet rag to Ruya's mouth and nose. She tries to claw at them, but the other guards pin her arms back. She coughs, inhaling the foul drug, and her au'mana vanishes. The glow disappears, and the items drop back down again with a clatter. Impotent, Ruya is dragged away as she fights desperately to reach her magic again.

Honora watches, eyes wide and red-ringed, but can do nothing. The baby is coming. She can feel him. He is going to rip her apart, but she does not care. She only wants him to be safe.

The king gives her one last apathetic look and slams the door closed, locking it behind him. Honora unleashes a scream from the bottom of her soul through her body.

Prince Theo is born in wrath and blood.

The sheets are soaked red. Her son is crying for her, and she wants so much to reach for him, to hold him, but she cannot lift her arms. Exhaustion sweeps her, and she nearly closes her eyes.

No, she whispers to herself and snaps them open. In the corner of the room, cloaked in gloom, two figures stand. Their faces and bodies are covered, adorned in white silk, akin to marble statues. They stand and they watch and they do not move. Not yet.

Reapers.

Honora knows what this means. She looks back at them and shakes her head. Even if she has lost her battle, she feels her power swell. Ascended.

Her gaze swivels down to Theo. She will not be able to save him so she must protect him instead.

Honora summons every well of energy she has left and leans forward to pick him up. He is slippery with blood, but she holds him close, putting a supportive hand under his head.

"Oh, Theo..." she whispers. Even as she speaks, she can taste the faeth around her.

Looking at him then, she smiles despite

the pain and fatigue. He settles down, gurgling, and tiny scales appear and disappear along his skin. She presses a kiss to his forehead, her tears spilling freely. She inhales slowly, closing her eyes and clearing her mind.

In the lonely dark of the room, with her baby clutched to her chest, Queen Honora hugs him close and draws on her Ascension. She whispers in dragon speech, her home tongue, a spell she hopes with her whole heart will work. She rocks back and forth, the words sliding and rolling over her tongue. Dark marks form on Theo's back, spreading like smoke across his skin. She speaks and speaks until the mark is complete. She presses one last kiss to his forehead and utters the last word that will seal it.

Svellenta.
I love you.

CHAPTER 35

Theo says nothing as he listens. He is curled up underneath my arm, eyes wet, and takes a shuddering breath. When I am finished, he stays quiet.

"*Svellenta*," he says after a while. "That...is that the word on my back you did not recognise?"

"Yes," I say softly. "It was never a curse. It was a gift."

"A gift," Theo repeats, his voice cracking.

"She knew you were a dragon, like her, and wanted you to be able to defend yourself against...him." I stroke his hair. "But shapeshifting takes decades to learn and control. I do not know the full extent of it myself, there is so much about the rest of the world that is not written in books. But this Ascension... I believe it is a stronger magic which dragons can achieve. Honora used it to gift you shapeshifting. To defend yourself."

Theo nods numbly.

"The turnings were not at random," he whispers, almost to himself as though thinking out loud. "But whenever I was threatened."

He sits up slightly, wiping his eyes.

"Is this why it is so painful? Because it was forced?" he asks.

I rub my temples, dredging up old dragon knowledge hidden in the deep crevices of my mind.

"I believe so...all the books made reference to dragons using meditation to draw on their faeth. I suppose when used out of anger or fear, it is...a lot less peaceful," I answer as best I can. "In time and with practice, I believe you will be able to clear your mind at will and use your faeth painlessly."

Theo falls silent, processing this.

"I think we should use today for rest," I tell him. "You have...learned a lot of overwhelming knowledge in a short space of time."

"But my father." Theo shoots up to a sitting position. His lip is curled in anger. "He...he," Theo stutters, his hands balling into tight fists. "He killed my mother!" he yells, and his eyes begin to blaze gold. "He let me believe she hated me when this entire time...Saints, she loved me. My mother loved me." His voice falters and cracks, his anger rapidly dissolving into sorrow. He slumps back against me.

"It is alright," I whisper, trying to keep my voice as soothing as I can, even though I also want to turn my wrath on the king. For now, though, is it not what Theo needs.

"How do you know all of this?" he asks, sliding down until his head rests on my lap.

"Inez gave me her mother's diary—she wrote about everything that happened that night." I brush a lock of his hair from his eyes.

"But the king ordered her head. How did she write about that night?"

I hesitate, wondering if I should share everything else I learned or if I should let Theo ruminate on everything he has already discovered. I decide on somewhere in the middle.

"He did not follow through, as it turns out. And so she wrote about everything that happened afterwards. It…" I lick my lips. "It has given me what I need."

"What do you mean?"

"I have a plan, Theo," I whisper. "Not just for both of us, but for everyone in this castle."

He shifts onto his back and looks up at me.

"You do?" His voice is soft, as though he is afraid to believe me. I nod and clasp his hand, a bittersweet smile on my lips.

"I do. But first, you will rest."

"But I—"

"*Rest*," I repeat. "When you awaken, we will finally loosen the grip that bastard has had on us all."

✢ ✢ ✢

Theo sleeps until the late afternoon when the air begins to cool and the sun starts its descent. We have not been disturbed all day except for a servant who brings us a tray full of food.

"From Vanya and Inez," she tells us in a small voice, eyes darting nervously to a sleeping Theo. "And the rest of us in the kitchens."

"Thank you," I tell her from the floor, Theo's head still resting in my lap. She hesitates, lingering in the doorway.

"You might not remember, miss," she says, fidgeting. "But you prayed with me on Saint's Day. I had dropped the plate of biscuits and, well…it is a small thing, really, but you were very kind about it and helped me clean up."

I remember her now, a young girl nervous in the presence of the prince. My cheeks curve in a smile, remembering that day.

"If you need anything from us…the servants and the kitchen staff, I mean," she continues. "Well, you need only ask. Anything at all."

Her eyes widen and she leaves briskly, as though afraid to have said too much. But I am grateful—it will make our next task even easier.

Not long after, Theo rouses from his deep slumber. His face grimaces as he rubs his eyes sleepily.

"Shivani?" he says, voice thick.

"I am here," I tell him, running my hand

along his chest reassuringly. "Are you rested?"

Blearily, he nods and hauls himself up to a sitting position. He groans, stretching his arms high above him. I take the opportunity to draw my legs back up, easing the cramp in my calves.

Theo sighs heavily, looking around his chambers as though seeing it for the first time.

"So." He looks at me. "What is the plan?"

I give a small, determined smile.

"Let me show you." I get to my feet and stick out a hand for Theo. He accepts it, grasping me firmly and standing. His eyes glint.

"Lead the way."

We slip into the secret passageway leading to the servants' quarters—the same one Honora used to try and find her friends. When we emerge from the other side, we find two guards lingering in the hall. Their heads whip towards us as we clamber out from behind the landscape painting.

"H-how—" one of them stammers as they both stare at us.

"Move!" I bark, and they instantly scatter, running in the opposite direction from us down the halls. Theo grins at me with a thoughtful look in his eyes. "What?"

"Nothing," he says unconvincingly, but we do not have time for me to argue, so I continue on, marching us to the servants' quarters.

It is mostly empty when we arrive, with only a young boy I recognise as a kitchen porter.

He jumps at our presence, eyes glued to Theo.

"He will not hurt you," I reassure him, wondering how quickly news of Theo's attack against the guards spread. "You have my word."

The boy glances at me, relaxing slightly, but there is a tremble in his limbs. Theo steps forward and kneels.

"What is your name?" he asks, voice soft.

"J-James, Your Highness," the boy stutters back. His eyes dart to the door.

"A strong name." Theo smiles at him warmly. "I am a friend of Shivani and of Inez."

James looks to me for confirmation, and I nod.

"What...what do you want here?" he asks, a nervous waver in his voice.

"I have a very special task for you," I tell him, and his face lights up. "We need Inez's help. Would you be able to find her for us and send her here?"

"Inez?" His eyebrows furrow in concentration. "Okay, I think I can find her for you."

"Thank you, James." Theo stands up again. "We are most grateful."

The young boy grins, pleased, and scurries out of the room. Theo turns to me once he has left.

"What does Inez have to do with our plan?" he enquires.

I immediately start scouring the walls, but

large, heavy beds line the room, stacked on top of each other.

"She was here when your mother tried to escape. She might remember what the servants' quarters used to look like."

"Used to?"

I run my hands over the brick, searching.

"Honora planned to flee through the servants' entrance."

Theo casts his eyes skywards, thinking.

"The servants do not have an entrance—the king makes everyone stay in the castle." His eyes light up with understanding. "There used to be a door here."

"Exactly." I fall to my knees, bending over to look under one of the beds. "Which the king bricked up after Honora tried to escape through it, ordering everyone to stay on-site. Well, everyone he did not execute."

Nausea churns in my stomach at the idea of such a massacre, and Theo wears the same queasy look on his face. I breathe deep, putting the thought to the side and focussing on our task.

"But we have the secret tunnel. Why do we need to find an old doorway?" Theo asks. He inspects the walls with me to try and help, although he does not know what he is looking for. A pure-hearted action from a pure-hearted man.

"My auntie taught me this trick with her

au'mana. A way to enchant buildings without casting a spell over the entire thing," I tell him. Deep longing fills my chest. I take another deep breath and continue. "She enchanted a single brick, and the whole building fell under the spell."

"Ah, so we are searching for a brick," Theo declares before chewing his lip. "But why?"

I open my mouth to explain, but we are interrupted by Inez bursting into the room.

"Oh, Miss Shivani!" she gasps, her usually neat bun fraying with loose hair. "When I heard the prince had turned and—"

"Inez." I step towards her. "I am well. Theo is well."

I gesture towards him, and Inez blinks.

"Your Highness." She dips into a curtsy, but there is a softness to her features. I think of Lucian, the person they had both loved and had cruelly ripped away from them. Theo gives her a small, sad smile.

"We need your help, Inez," he tells her. She looks between the two of us.

"Me?"

"It will sound silly, but...do you remember where the servants' entrance used to be?"

Inez cocks her head, frowning. "The servants' entrance? Well, yes...but it has long since been bricked over."

"We know but..." I lick my lips and glance at Theo. "There is a brick in particular we need to find."

Inez's eyebrows shoot up and she gives a nervous laugh. "A brick?"

"Please, Inez." I step forward and clasp her hands. "Do you trust me?"

She looks at me, her jaw set. "Absolutely, miss."

With determined swiftness, she steps around me and hurries to one of the many beds.

"Here," she tells us, pointing at the wall. "It was here."

"Help me with this bed, Theo." I push up the sleeves of my dress.

He grasps one of the metal bars on the headboard while I grip underneath the bottom. Together, we haul it away from the wall, the feet scraping loudly across the bare floor. Behind us, several other servants and kitchen staff have gathered in the doorway, watching curiously. I ignore them and stand in front of the exposed wall.

It is faint, but I can see where the arch of the old door used to be. There are subtle cracks in the wall, running over and between the brick. I run my fingers across it, but there is no purple brick. Regardless, my ophid thrums, and I know there is au'mana nearby.

"There is nothing here," Theo says, shoulders sagged in disappointment.

"No," I disagree. "There is. I can feel it. There is more than one layer of brickwork."

"Then what do we do?" Inez asks, wringing her hands. I know the servants' eyes are on us as they mutter and speculate amongst themselves. I stand back and regard the wall.

"We break it."

CHAPTER 36

We spend several hours chipping away at the wall. A few servants step in to help us, banging kitchen tools or garden shovels against the solid brick, but we only succeed in sending a few small chips of brick pinging off. After some time, Theo pulls me to the side.

"I think I know how to break the wall," he tells me in a low voice. I brighten, but he shakes his head. "But I do not know if I can do it."

He looks at his hands, flexing them uncertainly.

"You want to shapeshift." It is a statement more than a question. I lower my eyes. In his dragon form, Theo could easily break through the wall, including the enchanted brick, releasing the spell on the castle. But would he be able to control it?

"I think…I think I would like to visit my mother's altar," he tells me. "Would you come with me?"

I step onto my tiptoes, snaking a hand around the back of his neck and pulling him towards me to press a kiss against his forehead.

"Of course."

I explain to Inez that we have an idea and will be back as soon as possible. She wishes us luck, and we hurry past the throng of servants and make for Honora's altar.

It is as we left it during Saint's Day—dust coats the surface, small statues of the Saints standing patiently, their shadows dancing in the purple light. I take Theo's hand in mine and send a prayer to Honora. *I will not let him take your son.*

Theo steps forward on unsteady legs, letting out a shaky breath. He lingers in front of the altar awkwardly before turning back to me.

"What...do I do?" he asks, his cheeks burning red. "I know I should know this, but..."

I move to join him, lightly holding both his hands so we face each other.

"There is nothing for you to know, Theo," I tell him, voice hushed. "I have only read about the practice, but I believe it is simply...something you feel."

He chews his bottom lip, uncertain

"What if I do it wrong?"

"You cannot do it wrong—it is a personal experience. Whatever you do, it will be right for you," I assure him firmly. "Your mother gave this gift to you so you would not need to spend decades learning. The knowledge is within you."

His eyelids shutter, and he exhales in one long, slow breath. Our hands stay loosely clasped, and I follow him as he kneels on the floor. There is a small rug in front of the altar cushioning us against the hard ground. I close my eyes as well, listening to the flickering torches and Theo's steady breathing.

I lose track of time as we kneel there, joined at the fingertips, sitting in peaceful quiet. When his fingers change from soft to hard, lengthening across my palms, I keep my eyes closed. The tips of his claws rest along my forearms, and I feel the weight of his presence in the room, even without looking at him. His breathing becomes heavy, with a grumbling undercurrent from deep inside him. Scale rasps against the stone floor. I remain still, his hot breath coming from somewhere above me, fluttering my hair.

"Shivani," he speaks, and he sounds like Theo, only deeper. I open my eyes and look up at him.

* * *

The staff still chip away faithfully at the wall when we return, several of them sitting with water flasks and small snacks while they wait their turn. But flasks freeze on their way to their mouths and jaws drop as Theo and I walk back in. Even Inez, who turns with a welcoming smile on her face at first, looks at us with wide eyes, her smile fixed in place.

I step over the threshold first, with Theo following closely behind. He ducks his head under the doorway as he does, falling forward onto all four claws with a solid thump. His golden eyes are ablaze as he stalks in. The servants stare, motionless.

This time, he is not a beast covered in boils with twisted bones and warped beyond recognition. This time, he knows who he is and what he has been given.

This time, he is a dragon.

His scales are the colour of morning haze, lucent gold even in the dim light, smooth and flat. His claws are long and sharp, the painful knots gone. His snout is straight, and his deep-set eyes keen. He is beautiful.

"My friends," Theo says, his voice rumbling across the room. Several people take a step back. Inez steps forward.

"Your Highness." She hides the tremor in her hands by pulling her sleeves down and inclines her head in greeting.

"Miss Inez," Theo replies, lowering his large head. I watch as the other staff glance at each other, unsure, but some of the terror ebbs from their eyes. "Miss Vanya."

Vanya steps forward to match Inez, nodding politely. Her posture is rigid as always, but she curtseys, dipping low in respect. Slowly, the other servants follow suit, mumbling their greetings and bowing.

"My friends," Theo repeats, and his voice, despite the inhuman growl running beneath it, is earnest and distinctly his. The staff's shoulders begin to drop, less guarded, and listen.

Theo glances back at me, and I nod, placing an encouraging hand on his scaly arm. His chest rises as he takes a long breath.

"For too long, I have stood and watched my father abuse you," he says, and his words ring loudly against the silence of the servants. "For too long, I have failed to protect you for fear of his wrath. I have failed to use the protection my..."

His voice falters, and he takes a moment to compose himself.

"I have failed to use the protection my mother gifted to me to defend myself against him and to defend *others* against him. His evil thrives, not because he has power, but because others watch and do nothing. Like me...before today." He fixes them with a golden gaze. The servants lean forward now, transfixed and nodding eagerly. "I have been sleeping, but now I am awake. And I am ready to fight."

Theo crosses the room to the bricked-up doorway in three thunderous steps. The servants gasp and stumble back as he rears up, twisting his body and swinging his weighty tail with a grunt. It slams against the brick, exploding it into a cloud of dust and rubble.

I cough and wave the brick dust away from my face, squinting at where the wall had been. As it settles, the large hole exposing the castle grounds outside remains. And there, amongst the rubble, a single brick lays intact, glowing purple.

Heart thumping, I scamper over and pick it up, pushing the other bricks aside. Inez and Vanya tentatively peer over my shoulder.

"Is that what we were looking for?" Inez asks, brick dust smeared across her cheek. I nod silently. *This is it*, I think.

"Why is there an enchanted brick in the servants' quarters?" Vanya kicks a broken piece of debris from her path. It skitters across the floor as the others look on. I turn to them, bathed in the purple glow.

"Inez's mother was forced into enchanting it," I tell them, looking at Inez with a sympathetic half-smile.

"Why?"

"Because it enchants the whole castle. It stops any witch in here from using their au'mana. This is why I could not fight back. It is why no one could fight back." I grip the brick tightly, my fingertips turning white. "But it is not part of the castle anymore."

My ophid hums, calling to me.

I feel Aunt Meena's hand on my shoulder,

warm and firm. On the other shoulder, an unfamiliar grip. Even though I have never heard her before, I know it is Ruya.

Show him who you are.

Au'mana unfurls through my body.

I close my eyes and reach out.

CHAPTER 37

The king returns in the dead of night, his croca-drawn carriage and accompanying party scaling up the castle under the moonlight.

He strides into this throne room, posture straight and shoulders back with several guards trailing behind him. I stand to the side, silently watching from the shadows.

Everything is prepared. The servants evacuated through the secret tunnel with all the belongings and food they could carry. The castle stands empty and cold, except for the king's loyal guards, but by the time they notice, it will be too late.

The king stops short when he sees Theo lounging on the king's throne with one knee bent and one leg stretched out, his cheek resting against his fist. The king comes to a sudden halt halfway across the room and regards his son with one eyebrow raised.

"Child," he says evenly, "That does not belong to you."

Theo does not reply and instead fixes him with a stare. The king narrows his eyes slightly but gives no other sign of moving. After a beat, Theo slowly stands from the throne.

"Good," the king says, clapping his hands together and smiling. His beard has grown long and straggly during his journey, but his clothes are untarnished as usual. "Now, I am sure you are excited to see what I have brought you—those fatheads at Swordstead did send a raven, yes?"

"Yes," Theo replies quietly, standing in front of the throne still. His hands are balled into fists behind his back.

"Excellent. Even halfway, it is a horrid place. Far too damp and cold. But they are in dire need of an ally," the king continues. If he notices Theo's quiet rage, it does not bother him. "Some civil war or famine or something. Anyway, they had no female heirs to send so they allowed me some other high-born girl. It will need to do—for too long have you been dithering about, making doe-eyes at that commoner witch. But now she is gone..."

The king snaps his fingers, and the throne room doors open with a loud groan. Two of his travelling guards march in, hauling something between them. No, *someone.*

My hand shoots up, hovering in front of my mouth in horror. Theo presses his lips together, jaw clenched. To others, he is standing with his regular upright posture—to me, I can see every muscle in his body is tensed, like a coiled spring.

The guards drag the girl in, her feet stumbling. Her dress is caked in dirt, and her hair is long and wild. She looks around with wide, red-ringed eyes swivelling around the room, her lip quivering with the effort of holding herself together. A surge of rage swells inside me, and I instinctively take a step forward before having to stop myself. I stare at the king hatefully. The king misreads the disgust on Theo's face.

"Fear not, she was born clawless. I would not shackle you to a werewolf and have two monstrosities in my home." The king laughs, loud and obnoxious, unaware no one else in the room laughs with him. The girl flinches at the king's casual use of such a slur. He flicks his wrist at the guards, and they drop their grip on her. She sways, unsteady. "Olivia is clean, unspoiled, and willing."

"Willing?" Theo scoffs incredulously, breaking his silence. "Every single word of what you said was poison, but to describe this poor girl as *willing* crosses the line into a fucking delusion."

The king snaps his head towards Theo, mouth open. The young girl looks warily between them. My palms start to sweat and I will Theo to remember the plan.

"What did you say to me, child?" the king addresses the prince, his voice dangerously low.

Theo takes another step forward, looking down on his father from the raised platform of the throne.

"You heard exactly what I said," he replies. I am relieved to see his hands are no longer balled into fists, and his shoulders have relaxed. The king regards him for a moment before snapping his fingers again. The rest of his travelling guards pour into the room.

"The boy has gotten ahead of himself in my absence," he says to his guards, already turning away from Theo. "Put him in the dungeon for a few days until he is more grateful for what I have done for him."

But the guards do not move. They stand, motionless and open-mouthed.

Theo closes his eyes and his expression smooths as he clears his mind. Painlessly, peacefully, he draws on his faeth. A copper tang infests the air. His skin hardens into shiny scales, and his spine pushes out pointed spikes. He hunches over slightly before his limbs elongate, and his face spirals into a long snout. Even my mouth drops when I watch as large, leathery wings sprout from his back. He spreads them as though stretching a limb, and I realise his tattoos have shifted with them. They traverse the skin of his wings, inky black against gold. Theo grins with a row of terrifying teeth.

The king takes a shaky step back, eyes wide.

"No," Theo growls, his dragon voice reverberating through the room.

"Guards!" the king shouts before turning and sprinting towards his secret exit.

The guards jump into action, drawing their swords in a resounding clang of metal. Theo draws himself up to his full height, his head hovering inches beneath the high ceiling, and stands before them. He opens his mouth wide, and I expect a great roar to reverberate through the halls, but instead, the air around us shifts with static. Theo points his large snout near the guards, and lightning shoots forth from his throat. It is soundless but cracks the air in half, landing hard against the marble floor and shattering it with a flash of light. The guards shriek, falling backwards over each other to try and get away.

The king does not even notice, his back already to them while he flees. But when he reaches the secret door and tugs, he finds it has been locked. He blinks at it for a moment before pulling again, furiously yanking backwards.

"Fuck, fuck, fuck..." he angrily mutters. In his cowardly frenzy, he does not see me standing next to him.

"Hello," I say cheerfully, and the king yelps, startled. He raises his hands up in defence, but when I step out of the shadows, he sees who I am.

His face goes pale.

"You…you should be—" he stammers.

I cock my head at him, smiling sweetly. I want to say something cutting and witty, but instead, I leave him sputtering, brushing past him to rush to the young girl's side. She is frozen to the spot, shivering with her arms wrapped tightly around her. She looks at me with wide eyes before darting them back to Theo.

"It is alright," I whisper to her, wrapping my cloak around her shoulders. "Look."

I glance up at Theo, who allows himself to turn back, his scales sloughing off and his size shrinking to human level. The girl visibly relaxes as he does.

"L-Like a werewolf?" she asks me. I smile.

"Of sorts," I reply. "You are safe, but we need to leave the castle. Now. The rest of the staff are in the village. They will feed you and have you sent home."

"Home?" She swallows, and tears begin to fall. "I am allowed home?"

"You have my word."

She looks at me with round, watery eyes. She half-turns towards the castle doors but hesitation lines her body.

"But the king—" she starts.

"He is the king no longer." I turn to glare at him, and he stares daggers back at me. The young girl trembles, uncertain, so I place two fingers over my heart. "The wind at your back and fire in your chest."

With a trembling hand, she repeats the gesture.

"Soft snow underfoot and a safe home awaiting you," she whispers back, locking eyes with me.

"Run. Now."

The young girl seizes her opportunity and flees. As soon as she is clear of the doors, I turn to the king.

"Guards!" he calls again angrily, but they hesitate, looking between Theo and me.

"Long have you sat over this town and these people like a dark cloud," I say, taking a step towards him.

"Guards!" he makes another attempt, spittle flying from his lips as he takes a step back.

I raise my voice over his and keep walking forward.

"Long have you sat on a throne of malice and sadism."

"Stop! *Guards*!"

I draw on my au'mana, raising my hands and allowing the purple smoke to swirl around my fingers.

"Too many women have found themselves at your mercy," I hiss, and he stumbles back, falling with a cry. I stare down at him. "Too many *people*. Your wife. Your son. Your kingdom."

I take a long breath, the deep well of au'mana at my fingertips. My ophid hums, warm and full.

Something slams into my spine, sending a sharp pain ricocheting through my ophid. I shriek and fall to my knees. My legs go numb.

"Shivani!" I hear Theo cry from behind me.

"Run, Your Highness!" a guard calls.

I glance up at his voice. The guard tries to haul the king to his feet, something shiny and metal in his hand. The tip is tinged with blood. My blood?

I desperately reach behind me, twisting my arm to touch my back. My hand comes back wet and sticky. Panic floods my brain. Theo's hands scoop under my arms, trying to lift me up, but I cannot stand. His lips move, but the ringing in my ears drowns him out. I look behind him to see the king fleeing. He is going to get away.

No.

No.

My mind blanks. My ophid burns. My rage swells.

Au'mana, usually warm and sweet, courses through me like wildfire, sending every nerve alight. I send it to the great front doors of the castle and slam them shut before he can escape. Around me, the castle glows an angry, dark shade of purple. The colour of bruises and poison and wrath. The ground splinters and rises like tendrils, the walls snap and crack, writhing furiously. My heart thunders in my ears, and my skin burns. Theo steps back from me, his mouth open. When I turn to him, the muscles in my neck scream.

"Run," I whisper.

He hesitates, and I send a fraction of my magic to the ground at his feet. It rumbles and moves like a snake beneath him, dragging him out of the hall and safely outside.

"Shivani!" he cries before the door slams shut again for the final time.

I turn to the king.

He and the guards stare at me, terrified and trembling. There is some part of me, deep in the back of my mind, wondering if I should feel pity. But I do not. There is only resentment and anger there. Dark purple seeps into the corners of my vision like storm clouds. My ophid pulses painfully from where I had been stabbed, and my rage grows, fuelling my au'mana. The castle rumbles and groans as it collapses around us. A chunk of the ceiling breaks loose, falling and shattering against the marble floor.

"Please!" the king cries out, his voice breaking with desperation. "Mercy!"

I clench my teeth.

"Your death will be the mercy this town deserves," I spit.

I reach through the marble floor, splitting it with a crack. Broken pieces grab the king's leg, forcing him to the ground.

"Morraine," I whisper.

The marble swallows his other leg.

"Lucian."

His arm sinks into the ground, held fast.

"Honora."

The king cries out as his last free limb is pulled behind him, leaving him stuck and helpless.

"For all of us, you will know what it is to die alone."

I flick my wrists, and the ceiling crumbles above us.

The king and his guards scream like trapped animals, wild and hoarse. I close my eyes and let the castle fall, silencing them forever.

EPILOGUE

"My condolences, Your Highness." A man with a rough-hewn face bows in front of Theo, tipping his hat. Theo gives a soft smile in return.

The man is dressed in deep black for mourning, except for the colourful fabric flower pinned to the chest of his tunic. Most of Mossgarde is donned in similar attire as they come to give their sympathies to the freshly crowned king.

Theo stands patiently next to the casket, back straight and hands clasped behind him as he accepts the steady stream of villagers and citizens from nearby. It is a long and grand affair and he is struggling to rid himself of the tension in his shoulders.

I reach up and squeeze his hand. He squeezes it back.

The small portrait of Honora, smiling and content, sits next to the casket. We had no body to bury, so instead, the villagers chose to each put in a small fabric flower. It is soon overflowing.

"Love lives on," I whisper to Theo, kissing the back of his hand. His eyes are wet, but he smiles.

"*Svellenta*," he says quietly, putting a hand on the casket.

We are slightly outside of central Mossgarde, in a bare field with the wind at our backs. The ground is firm, and the trees are sparse, allowing a view of the open sky. A polished statue of the Idol, Honora's Saint, towers over us. We worked for weeks, carefully carving it from black rock—the colour of strength and perseverance. It glistens in the sun. Even though the Saints are not my gods, I now keep a small statue of Shivanya at my bedside to remind me of what justice truly means.

Nearby, encircling the Idol, lay eight fresh graves. It took several days, even with my aunt's magic, to clear the castle rubble and find the heads. It has been a week since the Never Queens were returned to their families, but fresh flowers stand at their graves each day. In the early mornings, if my back allows, I sit with them for a few quiet moments and give my apologies. Vanya assures me the guilt will feel less sharp over time.

We could not find Lucian's bones so we helped Inez build a small shrine in her new home instead. I painted a miniature portrait based on the description she gave me and I hope I have done him justice. I hope he knows I will look after Theo.

Through the trees and across the swamp lays the ruins of the old castle.

When it fell, it fell around me, though my ophid nearly snapped with the strain of protecting myself. My aunt says it will heal, eventually. In the meantime, I remind myself to turn my face up to the sky and drink in the sun or visit the town square, bereft of a chopping block.

When the condolences are over and the villagers return home, the area is left for close family and friends to grieve in private. I remain sitting in the only chair while my back heals as Theo, Inez, Vanya, and Aunt Meena find flat spots in the field to kneel on. Vanya has brought saffron cookies and tea for us and distributes them.

"A beautiful ceremony, Your Highness," Inez tells us with a sympathetic smile. Theo glances at the portrait of his mother.

"I fear it has come too late," he says, the corner of his mouth tugging downwards.

"Nonsense." Vanya waves a hand. "Not all those who knew Honora were caught. I know she would have been overjoyed to know the truth was brought to light. Her son and his wife are carrying on her legacy."

Inez nods eagerly.

"Just look at all the homes you have made

for us," she says.

"Sturdy homes," Aunt Meena adds.

"If they are anything like your library, I am quite certain they will hold fast," Vanya agrees, taking a sip of tea.

"Do not forget the new trade relations," I chime in, grinning at Theo. The hard wood of the chair presses into my tender bandaged ophid, but I ignore it—I am just grateful it is healing at all. My au'mana thrums happily.

Theo rubs the back of his neck bashfully.

"Swordstead were in a vulnerable position. It did not take much bargaining." He shrugs.

"You did not bargain," I say. "You were kind. And that is why Mossgarde will soon have a strong economy again."

"Kindness will only get you so far, if you do not mind me saying, Your Highness," Vanya tells Theo. He gives a lopsided smile and turns to me.

"Then I will have my queen to guide me," he says and plants a soft kiss on my temple.

"You would need to be made of tough stuff indeed to survive the castle falling." Inez nods.

"Well, not quite. I was able to control the castle enough, so it fell around me rather than on top of me."

Aunt Meena shakes her head, sitting back and crossing her wooden leg over.

"And only a year ago, you were happy to have stripped the rust off an old bucket." She grins, eyes shiny with pride. I am reminded of my life before the castle. I am reminded of my father.

I tried to find him after the castle fell, but he was gone. Fled as soon as the castle staff flooded the town square and informed the village what was happening—the king was being usurped. I wonder if, one day, I will see him again. I wonder if I will ever forgive him. I do not think so. If he should meet an unfortunate end, I would not lose sleep over it.

"And how are your studies going, child?" Aunt Meena continues. "Well, I take it?"

"She is truly brilliant," Theo gushes before I can answer.

"Oh?"

"The king exaggerates," I say, rolling my eyes with a smile as Theo looks affronted.

"I take exception to that. Shivani's tutors say she is flourishing, and I have had the honour of reading over some of her writing. Brilliant, indeed."

Warmth flushes my face. I reach over to brush a kiss against his cheek. It is not usual to have a student of the House of Learning live away from the city but, for a queen, they made an exception. Sparrows ferry my lessons back and forth along with my writing.

"Ah, and speaking of the queen and her writing." Vanya sits back and regards me. "She did not ever finish her story."

"What story?" Aunt Meena queries,

nibbling on a biscuit.

"The Siren and the Witch," I tell her and watch her face brighten.

"Ah! You used to love hearing me tell you that tale."

"Well, do not keep us in suspense!" Inez leans forward. "Go on."

"Very well." My cheeks ache from smiling but I smile nonetheless and begin the story. Theo clasps my hand as I look around at my family. Happy. Safe.

Free.

APPENDIX

The Siren and the Witch

A witch walks the golden sands of an isolated beach. The only footprints are her own. The sun shines and the air is clear, thick with salt. She comes across a small glass bottle, half-buried in the sand. Curious, she picks it up.

It is empty. But there is something distinct about it. A ringing in her ears, soft and sweet. And then she hears a voice from the sea.

It calls out to her. A greeting, the witch thinks, but she cannot quite hear. Slowly, curiously, she walks towards the water. There, amongst the gentle waves of the sea, a head bobs above the surface. Almost like a human, but not quite. Green-skinned and scaly.

The witch is at the edge of the land, the water lapping at her ankles. She holds the empty bottle in her hand, and she can still hear the ringing in her ears. So beautiful. So tempting. It calls to her. The person in the water smiles at her.

"Join me!" the mysterious figure calls, her head bobbing along with the waves. The witch is tempted, the beautiful melody still playing through her mind, but as soon as she drops the glass bottle, it disappears.

"I cannot," she calls back. "I will drown if I join you."

The strange figure contemplates this, but before the witch can say anything more, she disappears beneath the surface of the water. The witch searches the horizon but can see no sign of them. She begins to wonder if they had been there at all—the waves are hypnotic and constantly shifting. It is difficult to see anything.

And then, just as suddenly as she had left, the figure reappears. She is closer now, close enough for the witch to see the glistening green scales running along her skin. Her hair is dark as emerald, hanging down her back and over her shoulders like seaweed. The witch has never seen anything like her.

"Here, come a bit closer," she says to the witch, beckoning her. The witch hesitates, water swirling around her ankles.

"I should not trust you," the witch replies, to which the figure cocks her head.

"Why not?"

"Because I do not know you."

The figure grins.

"Then how do you know not to trust me?"

The witch stands still, uncertain, but she is dazzled by the way the sun catches the scales of the figure's skin, causing a hazy glow around her.

"Look." The figure throws something at the witch, and instinctively, she catches it. It is another glass bottle, like the one she found before, but filled this time with a strange, iridescent liquid. The witch tips it sideways, watching it swirl, and the melodic ringing reappears. She can *hear* the liquid.

"What is it?" the witch asks.

"I do not believe land folk have a word for it," the figure replies. "But we call it bahk. It is our magic."

The witch is, of course, familiar with magic. But her kind does not come in bottles. She regards it warily.

"What does it do?"

"It will let you breathe underwater."

The witch's eyes snap up.

"Why?"

"You said you do not trust me because you do not know me. I cannot come onto the land with you, but for a while, you will be able to come into the sea with me."

"Why can you not come onto the land?"

"I will turn to marble if I leave the water."

The witch thinks for a moment, listening to the liquid as it sings to her softly and watching the figure as she waits patiently.

With one swift movement, she uncorks the bottle and drinks it.

At once, it is hard to breathe. The witch gasps, but it feels like there was no air left around her. She clutches at her neck and finds the sides of her throat are soft and wet as gills form along her skin.

"Quickly! Come into the sea!" the figure calls.

The witch stumbles forward, desperately wading deeper until she tumbles into the water. As soon as the sea hits her new gills, she can breathe again.

Relief floods through her as she takes another deep breath and then another until her heart begins to calm again. The water is warm and soft around her. In the gloom of the sea, she feels a hand grasp her own.

"What are you?" the witch asks, her voice somehow penetrating the water and sending bubbles to the surface.

"I am a siren." Her voice is different underwater. She sounds like waves whispering against sand. "What are you?"

"A witch."

The siren smiles widely, showing her sharp, serrated teeth. The witch blinks at her before smiling back, watching the siren's hair as it floats around her. She wants to reach out to touch it, to see if it feels like fingers running through seaweed, but she holds back.

The bahk potion does not last indefinitely, but the siren and the witch spend many hours swimming together. When it comes time for the witch to return home, she finds she does not want to.

Nevertheless, the potion wears off, and the witch drags herself to the shore. Her body is tired, and her clothes heavy and laden with seawater. The smell of salt clings to her. She inhales it deeply and thinks of the siren.

The witch returns the next day, and the next, and the next. Each time, she drinks the bahk, listening to it sing, and swims next to the siren as she gracefully cuts through the water. And each time she returns to land, both their hearts are be heavy with longing.

Fifteen years pass. A few more crinkles appear in the corners of the witch's eyes when she laughs, and a few scales become discoloured on the siren's long, emerald-green tail. The witch's joints become sore, and the siren's fins become ragged.

Regardless, they clasp hands and swim and talk and press their foreheads together at the end of each day when they must part. The witch keeps the smell of salt close to her heart.

And then, one day, the witch does not appear.

The siren waits for her at their spot by the shore, bobbing with the waves as she did that first day.

She waits.

The sun dips below the horizon and rises again.

She waits.

Her chest begins to ache, as heavy as lead.

She waits.

But her witch does not come.

A siren cannot cry tears but she feels the weight of them regardless, pressing behind her eyes. Slowly, she swims to the shore.

She knows what will happen. But she thinks of the witch, and she does it regardless.

The siren pulls herself from the sea, the safety of the water slipping away from her. She tries to breathe, but the air is oppressive and pushes in around her. She grits her teeth and reaches forward, digging her hand into the hard, wet sand and dragging herself forward.

She feels it start to happen. First, her ragged fins harden, turning stiff and heavy. Nevertheless, she persists, eyes forward and mind determined.

The rest of her tail becomes rigid and unfeeling, and she cries out. For her witch. For her love. She punches a hold in the sand and hauls herself forward, the muscles in her arms burning.

The marble crawls up her waist, and she knows it will reach her heart soon. But it does not matter—it belongs to the witch, and no stone can claim it.

The siren is almost at the edge of the beach, arm outstretched and a deep trail in the sand behind her when she is finally stopped. Her statue lays there, unmoving. A small marble tear rests on her cheek.

Above her, the Saints watch, intrigued. The Idol, charged with strength and endurance, looks fondly at the siren. They reach down with a golden finger and gently tap the marble.

At once, the rock turns back to flesh. The siren gasps, the air rushing back to her lungs, and she feels her tail split into two legs. Without another thought, she stumbles onto her new feet and rushes to find her witch.

It takes her a full day and night, and when she does, the witch is lying in her bed, tired and sick. The siren sinks to her knees.

"My love," she whispers, grasping her hand. The witch is feverous and she cannot see but she knows who has come. She can smell the salt of the sea.

"My love," the witch whispers back. When the siren presses their foreheads together, her heart is full again.

ACKNOWLEDGEMENTS

This book wouldn't have been possible by myself. I had the support and guidance of so many incredible people, who turned Wrath of the Never Queen from an idea in my notes app to a fully-fledged novel.

To my amazing beta readers. Thank you for your honest feedback, thoughtful suggestions, and for pushing me to make the best story it could be. Without you, I would have been stuck at draft five with no prologue and more plot holes than plot.

To my editor. Thank you for your expertise and keen eye. Wrath of the Never Queen is only as polished as it is because of you. You truly elevated this book.

To my ARC readers. Thank you for sharing your early reviews and your infectious enthusiasm. It's been a dream to see people get excited about something I wrote and your reviews are the life blood for debut indie authors like me.

To the folks on r/PubTips. Thank you for absolutely shredding my blurb (in a good way). Without you, I wouldn't have figured out how to strengthen my story and make it a book worth reading.

To my friends and family. You've been my constant cheerleaders and I can't thank you enough. A special thank you to Grant for reading every single iteration of this book, from its first draft at a mere 30k words and - let's be honest - a total dumpster fire, to the final polished product. Thank you for your unwavering support and patience.

This book is as much yours as it is mine. Thank you, thank you, thank you.

ABOUT THE AUTHOR

Storm Lomax

Storm Lomax spends most of her day working in cybersecurity (true), protecting national secrets from international threats (not true). Outside of work, Storm writes stories which range from fantasy to romance to horror, sometimes all at once. Her work has been published in The Chamber Magazine and Metaworker Literary Magazine. She lives with her incredibly supportive partner, who endures several book-based ramblings a day, and her dog, whose snores serve as the essential white noise she needs for peak concentration.